Leaving Whiskey Bend

BOOKS BY DOROTHY GARLOCK

DOROTHY GARLOCK

Leaving Whiskey Bend

GCP

GRAND CENTRAL
PUBLISHING

NEW YORK   BOSTON

This book is a work of historical fiction. In order to give a sense of the times, some names or real people or places have been included in the book. However, the events depicted in this book are imaginary, and the names of nonhistorical persons or events are the product of the author's imagination or are used fictitiously. Any resemblance of such nonhistorical persons or events to actual ones is purely coincidental.

Grand Central Publishing
Hachette Book Group
237 Park Avenue
New York, NY 10017

Printed in the United States of America

Grand Central Publishing is a division of Hachette Book Group USA, Inc. The Grand Central Publishing name and logo is a trademark of Hachette Book Group, Inc.

ISBN-13: 978-1-60751-443-5

This book is dedicated to my good friend
Denise Hathaway Easley

Leaving Whiskey Bend

RESCUE

I glimpsed you first in the lightning's flare.
I heard you call above the thunder's roar.
I stood alone, wet with tears and rain.
And you were there for me.

Now you stand alone beneath the cruel sun.
In mortal danger amid the graveyard's stones.
Share with me your fear, regret, and sorrow.
I am here for you. . . .

F.S.I.

Prologue

Wɪᴛʜ ᴀ ɴᴇᴀʀʟʏ empty whiskey bottle swinging precariously from his limp hand, Caleb Morgan struggled to put one foot in front of the other as he stumbled down Bison City's main thoroughfare. Every step, shuffle, or stumble was more wobbly than the last. A buzzing filled his head and his eyes swam in their sockets, but he somehow managed to stay upright.

Even though it was well after midnight, people milled about all around him as they continued to celebrate the Fourth of July holiday. Along the storefronts that lined the street, shouts, whistles, and laughter filled the air. Above him, fireworks exploded into a bright kaleidoscope of colors; reds, whites, greens, and blues lit up the night. Occasional gunshots further punctuated the festivities, rifles and pistols firing into the air.

"Evenin' Caleb!" someone shouted.

"Evenin' yourself!" he responded, his voice deeply slurred. He hadn't even seen who had spoken to him and, to be honest, wasn't even certain from the sound if it was a man or woman.

What the hell difference does it make anyhow?

Stopping in the middle of the street, Caleb threw his head back and stared up at the sky. In the inky blackness of the Colorado night, he knew that thousands of stars shone down on him, even though he couldn't quite make them out. The moon, nearly a quarter full, shone in the west. A gentle breeze, a welcome respite from the sweltering summer day, rustled lightly against his face.

Doing his best to balance himself, he took a long pull of whiskey. The liquor burned a path down his throat and into his belly. What missed his mouth ran down his chin and added to the stains that littered his shirt.

Caleb could feel the effects of the alcohol pounding in his head. Doubtless he would be sick as a dog in the morning. He'd been drinking for hours—since well before the sun had set—and should have stopped much earlier if he were the least bit concerned about his own well-being. *Who knows how many bottles I've already had a hand in finishing?* Instead, he kept on, consequences be damned. After all, he'd found long ago that drink was the key that opened the lock to his prison.

And the ranch, as well as my father's booted foot, is undeniably my prison.

At nineteen years of age, Caleb Morgan struggled

mightily against the yoke that was his life. His father, Milburn Morgan, had come to Bison City decades earlier with but two things in mind: to raise a family touched by the grace of God and Country, and then to use the same determination to raise cattle. In that endeavor, he'd had mixed results. Nearly three hundred head grazed the grasslands from the family ranch to the south of town all the way to the Cummings River.

His family was another matter.

As the youngest of three brothers, Caleb hadn't expected to have to shoulder the burden of carrying on his father's legacy. His eldest sibling, Abraham, should have been the one, but he was . . . well, Abe was Abe, and there wasn't anything that could be done about it.

Eli, only two years older than Caleb, had proven himself to be the Morgan boy blessed with true smarts. Good-looking, apparently wise beyond his years, and possessed of a strong work ethic, Eli seemed perfectly positioned to take over the family business from Milburn. The problem was that Eli wanted more out of life than Bison City could ever hope to offer him. To that end, he'd bided his time, doing all that he could to play the dutiful son. But it had all been an act. When he was ready, he'd opted for the first road that led out of town. In two days' time, Eli was set to ship out on a troop train for destinations unknown, surely somewhere exotic, as a new recruit in the United States army.

"Lucky bastard," Caleb muttered as he took another drink.

When he'd begun drinking, Caleb had told himself that he was toasting his brother's departure, but in truth he knew himself to be green with envy. It wasn't just that Eli was leaving, but that he'd had the *strength* to defy their father. Even in the face of Milburn's rage, Eli had held his ground, refusing to give up his own dreams and wants, even if it cost him his father's love. Deep down in Caleb's stomach, drowning in the booze he'd consumed, he knew that if he had been standing in his brother's shoes, he would have surrendered to his father's will. The very thought of his weakness made him want to puke.

All that he could do was to strive to be more like Eli. Maybe, in a year or two, he could follow his brother into the army. Maybe he could find a way to get out from under his father's thumb. Maybe he could escape.

"My day will come," he promised himself.

Until then, he'd continue to do what he had always done to escape his prison; he'd drink himself into a stupor.

So far, the night had been a success. There had been as much laughter as there had been drink. *The only downer had been running into that son of a bitch Seth McCarty!* Caleb had been stumbling down the steps of the saloon when he'd bumped shoulders with the man. There had been the exchange of tense glares, a hint of violence in the air, but, thankfully, the encounter had ended peacefully.

The crack of a gunshot interrupted Caleb's thoughts. He turned to the noise and peered through the gloom and haze of alcohol to see a heavily bearded man raise his rifle to the sky and fire off three more quick shots. Lowering his weapon, the man grinned through a mouth haphazardly filled with chipped teeth. "And God bless America!" he shouted.

"Amen, brother!" Caleb added enthusiastically.

Stumbling on down the street, Caleb was filled with the sudden urge to empty his bladder. Weaving between gaggles of revelers, he managed to make his way to the darkened space between the mercantile and the hardware store. Steadying himself with one hand planted firmly against the wall, he sent a stream of warm urine spattering against the wall and down onto his boots.

"Damn!" he cursed, trying to move his feet without pitching over onto his face. Even as drunk as he was, he was clearheaded enough to know that he'd be mighty angry at the rank smell of piss on his boots come morning. *If I could . . . just move . . . a bit . . .*

"Stay away from me, you brute!"

"Come on now, darlin'!"

Looking over his left shoulder and back out into the street, Caleb watched as a young woman squealed with delight, her hands lifting the hem of her dress, as a man chased her. With every step, his hands snatched hungrily for her bottom, hoping for a piece of flesh. While the woman's words were fearful, the look on her face was one of pleasure. It was a ritual of courtship, such as it was in Bison City, on display for all to see.

"Well, I declare," Caleb said softly. "What an idea!"

In that moment, Caleb knew that that was just what the festivities still needed: a warm body to lie against through the night. While he wasn't quite the looker that Eli was—his brother more resembled their mother than father—he certainly wasn't without charms of his own. Besides, at this point in the celebration, he wouldn't expect any of the women he'd encounter to be very choosy. After all, he still had whiskey, so . . .

"Caleb!" a voice whispered from behind him.

Turning quickly at the sound, Caleb's head swam with dizziness and he nearly toppled over. Once he'd steadied himself, he peered intently into the depths of the alley but could see nothing but blackness. He'd just about convinced himself that he had imagined the voice when it came again, louder and more insistent.

"Caleb! Come here!"

"Who's there?" Caleb asked hesitantly as he managed to push his pecker back into his pants. Rubbing his fingers over his blurry eyes and his stubbly cheek, he stared at where the voice had come from, but he was still as unseeing as a blind man. Behind him, another volley of gunfire rose into the sky, but he paid it no mind, his attention fixed before him. "Who's calling me?"

"I need your help!" the voice said in answer.

In his drunken haze, Caleb was dimly aware of something tugging at his thoughts, although he wasn't sure what it was trying to say. Behind him, laughter and shouts called to him. Before him, something unknown and unseen waited. He didn't know which way to turn.

As he stood in the alley, racked with indecision, a moment of clarity passed through his alcohol-clouded head. *This situation is much like my life!* Unlike Eli, he was always willing to run to what he knew, what was safe. His brother embraced adventure and even conflict and, because of these virtues, he'd managed to obtain his freedom. Maybe this was a test. Maybe he was destined to be right here, right now.

Maybe . . .

"Hurry, Caleb! Hurry!"

"I'm coming!" he managed with as much conviction as he could muster.

Dropping the whiskey bottle at his feet with a clatter, Caleb stumbled forward into the darkness, his eyes searching for something, anything that would explain what was happening. Suddenly, a shape appeared before him; he couldn't even tell if it were large or small, man or woman. Before he could say even a word, another gunshot lit up the night.

With surprise, Caleb realized that the gunshot had come from in front of him rather than behind. With the realization came sharp pain that washed over him like a summer storm, violent and without warning. His hands moved to his chest where they found a wetness that startled him. Concern knit his brow and his heart began to hammer in his chest. His legs wobbled, then buckled, and he crashed onto his rump in the dust.

"Wh-why?" was all he could manage to say as he sucked wet gasps of air through clenched teeth. Desperation, fear, and then sadness coursed through his mind. He was dimly aware of a single tear sliding hotly down his cheek.

From the darkness came an answer that was both soft and bereft of emotion. "I didn't have a choice."

Unable to control himself, Caleb Morgan slid onto his side and then to his back. He could no more move his arms or his legs than he could move the heavens. As he stared up at the moon and stars, he realized that the pain that moments before had threatened to overwhelm him was going away; in its place came an overwhelming coldness.

Freezing in July was the last thought that passed through Caleb's head before the darkness overtook him.

Chapter One

Whiskey Bend, Colorado, 1890

CHESTER REMNICK FLINCHED as the bullet whizzed past his face and slammed into the side of the house. Splinters flew like frenzied insects. The thunderous clap of impact echoed in his already dazed head. It took all his self-control not to soil his britches.

"You stupid, lazy, no-good son of a bitch! I warned you that if you took so much as one damn step I wouldn't hesitate to shoot. Are you as deaf as you are ugly?"

Pearl Parsons cocked the rifle quickly, adjusted her grip on the weapon, and sneered down the length of its barrel. She was in her early forties, strong limbed and tough, with deep lines etched into the rough skin of her face. Her dark hair, streaked with strands of gray, was pulled to the back of her head and pinned in a loose knot. Built close to the ground, she had broad shoulders, sturdy arms and legs that could work alongside any man in town—and she wasn't a stranger to using a weapon.

Even as she ignored the urge to wipe a bead of sweat from her brow with the crimson scarf that lay across her shoulders, her eyes never left her target. If Chester was to underestimate her resolve, he would be making a mistake—the last mistake of his life.

"What—what the hell are ya doin' here?" Chester yelled.

"Shut your mouth!"

"You can't come in my house and order me about," the man continued, his nasal voice rising with indignation. Color began to return to his face with every word. "You roust me outta my sleep, then you take a shot at me! You got balls, bitch! You got balls that'd put a bull to shame!"

Early morning summer light bathed them in an orange glow. Having barely crested the horizon, the sun hung low and large in the eastern sky, a buttery orb readying to spread its warmth. The day would undoubtedly be hot, but for now the coolness of night clung to the air. Where birds had chirped loudly only moments before, they now fell silent in the wake of the gunshot. No breeze stirred the air. It was as if all nature were paying witness, holding their breaths for the next outburst.

"You're gonna pay for this, bitch!" Chester threatened.

"You call me that again, chicken shit, and I'll make a hen outta you." Clutching the rifle, Pearl pointed it at his crotch, a sign of her resolution to use it.

She wondered if Chester Remnick was smart enough to even understand how desperate she was. He reminded her of a rodent. In his midtwenties, he was skinny and scraggly of body, with dirty brown hair that hung limply over his sharp features, and his face was defined by a hook of a nose and a receding chin. His beady black eyes, small teeth, and the ever-present stubble on his cheeks completed the picture. Like the rat that he resembled, he made Pearl feel the need to be alert when near him. She was glad that she wasn't facing him unarmed. Glancing over her shoulder, she called to her companion, who stood stock-still in the grass twenty feet away.

"Hallie, are you all right?"

From somewhere in a deep fog, Hallie Wolcott finally managed to nod her head in response. The gunshot had frozen her almost as effectively as it had Pearl's intended target. Her hand trembled as she pushed a strand of auburn hair from her smooth face. In all her twenty-two years, nothing had prepared her for what had taken place before her green eyes, and the shock had almost overwhelmed her.

"I'm all right."

"Go see about Mary. This horse's ass shoved her down," Pearl said in a calm and firm voice.

With the mention that Mary needed her attention, the fear that had gripped Hallie suddenly released her.

Mary Sinclair lay in a crumpled heap several feet away, as if she were a doll that had been haphazardly thrown aside. Lifting her dark skirt, Hallie rushed to Mary and fell to the ground beside her. Deep sobs racked Mary's body and shook her tiny frame. Her simple green dress rose and fell as each wave of emotion washed over her. She lay with her face pressed to the earth, her stringy hair swirling about her shoulders as if it had been tossed by a strong wind. Mewling, wet sounds escaped from her mouth.

"Is she all right?" Pearl asked anxiously.

"I—I can't be certain," Hallie admitted.

Gently she pushed the wayward strands of hair from Mary's pale brow and turned her friend's face toward her own. The woman's eyes, bloodshot and red rimmed from crying, searched her own frantically, as if looking for shelter in a storm. Mucus and spittle were smeared across her nose and mouth. While these sights unsettled Hallie, what truly made her stomach churn were the cut and swollen lips and the bruises that covered Mary's face; it was like a bizarre rainbow of colors, with greens, browns, purples, and all shades in between.

"Get yer goddamn hands offa her!" Chester bellowed. "She's my woman."

Pearl gave a derisive snort. "She's not your woman,

you son of a bitch! Just 'cause your pa married her ma
don't mean you have any claim to her."

"Pa gave her to me!"

"Don't say another word!"

"Ya stupid bitches don't have no idea what yer getting
into!" he continued, undeterred. "Ya ain't got no right to
butt in. What happens between a man and his woman
ain't none a yer business!"

"One more word out of you and you're goin' to be
missin' some parts and walkin' spraddle legged—if'n you
can walk at all!" Pearl shouted back.

Hallie cradled Mary's head in her arms and stared
coldly at Chester Remnick. If hatred were an emotion she
could translate into action, she was certain that in that
moment she would have killed the man. With that realization, she was glad that it was Pearl who held the rifle.
Still, Chester wasn't her real concern; *Mary was*.

"We're taking you out of here, Mary," Hallie soothed.

Putting all thought of Chester behind her, Hallie
turned her attention back to her devastated friend. Placing a hand tenderly upon the woman's shoulder, she
softly asked, "Can you hear me, Mary?"

The only answer she received was a racking sob.

"She'll be fine as soon as we're gone from here," Pearl
offered.

"We're leaving, Mary. We're leaving Whiskey Bend,"
Hallie said.

And you're coming with us.

* * *

Hallie found it hard to believe that it had only been a few short hours since she had witnessed Chester viciously slapping Mary's face in the center of Whiskey Bend. She and Pearl had happened upon the scene on their way home, and what they witnessed horrified them. Mary had stopped to speak with a young man, a clerk in one of the stores. Chester took her act as an affront and slapped her viciously. He punctuated each blow with a curse or slur, further demeaning the girl whose only crime was stopping to talk with an acquaintance.

Hallie flinched at every blow, as if she were the one being struck. Tears clouded her vision.

"Stop it, you brute! Stop hitting her!" she shouted.

"Tend to yer own business, slut," Chester barked in answer.

Pearl's hand grabbed her arm, refusing to allow her to become involved, when not a man along the street offered to interfere between a man and his woman.

"Now isn't the time," Pearl said.

"But he's going to kill her!" Hallie argued.

"I'm not disagreein' with your concern," the older woman explained, her jaw set as firmly as if it were made of stone, "only with your timing. Not here and not now . . . but we will do something."

In that moment, unspoken between the two of them, was the realization that it was time to leave Whiskey Bend. It was inevitable that, if they didn't take Mary with them, Chester would surely kill her. Maybe not that night, or the one that followed . . . *but it was going to happen*! In order to save the life of Mary Sinclair, a girl they had befriended, they had to act fast. They needed to get themselves and Mary as far away from him, and Whiskey Bend, as possible.

Their plan had not yet been solid, but they had to act quickly. Hallie and Pearl each had her own reasons for leaving Whiskey Bend, and the sight they had witnessed was simply the final straw. They were leaving and they would take Mary with them.

After procuring horses and a wagon, the two women loaded it with their own meager belongings. Hallie held her tongue when Pearl placed the rifle in the wagon beneath the seat. It had still been pitch-black when they headed for the ramshackle cabin that Chester and Mary inhabited on the far outskirts of the township. Conveniently, the closest neighbor lived over a mile away; if things became messy, there'd be no one to interfere.

Regardless, they stopped the wagon a safe distance from the cabin and went the rest of the way on foot. They walked in silence, each keeping her thoughts to herself. As the sun just began to brush the horizon pink, the cabin came into view.

The place Chester and Mary lived was pitiful. Boards of many different shapes and sizes were nailed haphazardly together creating a small frame. Most of the windows contained broken glass and some no glass at all.

The front door had been hung crookedly; it looked as if it were leaned shut. Hallie's heart sank at the thought of her friend spending her days and nights in such squalor.

When they were no more than a stone's throw from the cabin, Pearl spoke. Her words chilled Hallie all the way to the bone. "I'll kill him if I have to," Pearl promised, tightening her grip on the rifle.

"You can't, Pearl," Hallie replied. "You just can't."

"Don't worry, Hallie," the older woman said, a smile cracking her face. "I won't if I don't have to. It ain't somethin' I want to do, but I've gotta be ready for that snake if he strikes!"

Hallie wasn't able to offer any further argument. Even though she couldn't bring herself to admit it, the gun in Pearl's hands made her feel safer. Chester Remnick *was* as sneaky as any serpent. There was no telling what he would do. He wouldn't let them walk in and simply take Mary; Hallie was sure of that.

Slowly and quietly they made their way to the tiny cabin. Saying a silent prayer, they eased their way inside the crooked door. On the other side, in the room that made up most of the ramshackle home, they had found Chester sprawled on a filthy bed. He was dressed only in his pants and was snoring loudly. The room smelled strongly of the whiskey that had spilled from the bottle at his side.

"Quickly," Pearl whispered, leading Hallie farther into the cabin.

In a lean-to attached to the back of the house, they found Mary asleep on a stained, sagging cot. She looked terribly young as she lay there, temporarily safe. Hallie felt a sudden urge not to wake her, not to bring her back. Pearl did not share the same sentiment and attempted to wake their friend. What happened next was the true nightmare.

"Mary," Pearl cooed. "Mary, wake up."

As the sleeping woman's eyes had fluttered once, twice, then opened, the look that filled them wasn't one of joy at seeing her friends, or even surprise as to why they happened to be standing in her bedroom. Instead, they reflected terror, sheer terror.

"No, no, get away! Get away from me!" Mary screamed.

Too stunned to think, both Hallie and Pearl remained frozen in place as Mary sprang up from the bed and made a dash for the door, desperate to escape. Pearl was the first to move and, after what had seemed like forever, Hallie followed.

"Mary! Stop, Mary! It's Pearl and Hallie!"

"Get—get away from me!"

They passed Chester, still groggy yet quickly awakening from his drunken stupor, and burst back out into the growing daylight, when Mary simply collapsed onto the ground and began to wail. Hallie was about to run to Mary, to offer some comfort, when Chester's liquor-addled voice burst into the morning.

"Stay away from her, ya stupid bitches," he growled.

*   *   *

From the time that Chester had first spoken to this moment seemed no more than a blink of the eyes to Hallie, punctuated by a gunshot. As she looked down at Mary's shaking form, she couldn't help but wonder if Chester's first question had a logical answer. *What* are *we doing here?* Hallie assumed that Mary would be thrilled at the thought of leaving her squalid life, but she was terrified instead. Now, with Chester alert and threatening, Hallie knew that their chances of leaving without violence were slim.

"Just stay where you are, you miserable son of a bitch," Pearl snapped. "She didn't know who we were, Hallie. She thought we were some of this buzzard's drunken friends," she said without turning around.

"Ya stupid whore." Chester spat. Anger coursed through him now, the corners of his mouth rising in a sadistic sneer. "Ya think yer just gonna take her? She's mine, I tell ya!"

"She's no more yours than I am!"

Chester glared at the woman defying him. "There ain't nowhere ya can go that I ain't gonna be able to find ya . . . and when I do, I'm gonna kill ya! Both of ya!"

Hallie understood that Chester believed his own words. Even if they managed to get Mary away, she knew that he would never stop looking, never stop hunting until he had exacted his revenge and retrieved what he felt belonged to him.

Pearl, however, didn't seem to share her concerns. "If you ain't too stupid to know what's good for you," she said as calmly as a smooth spring breeze, "the only thing you'll do is keep your mouth shut and not move an inch. If you want to test me, go ahead. I swear that I'll shoot you like the dog you are."

"Go to hell!"

"Hallie," Pearl said, ignoring Chester's curse, "get Mary back on her feet and start for the wagon. I'll be right behind you."

"Ya sure as hell better worry about me, damn ya!" Chester shouted, any fear for his own safety giving way to anger. His hands clenched tightly, he suddenly sprang toward them, the look in his eyes one of madness. But before Hallie could so much as scream, Pearl steadied the rifle and fired.

The bullet tore into the soft flesh of Chester's left thigh, and the man howled in pain. He crashed to the ground, his hands leaping to the wound, crimson blood pouring out from between his fingers and staining his pants. The agony that filled his face was mixed with surprise at the fact that Pearl had the guts to shoot him.

"I told ya, you stupid son of a bitch," she said coldly.

Chester's only answer was an unintelligible cry.

Hallie was dimly aware of Pearl's hand on her shoulder; once again she had been struck dumb by the sound of gunfire. Blinking quickly, she looked into her friend's eyes through a haze of tears. She helped Mary off the ground and they followed Pearl, putting one foot in front of the other, each step taking them farther and farther away from the cabin and Chester's cries of pain.

"What are we going to do now?" Hallie finally managed to ask.

For a long while, Pearl was silent. It wasn't until the last of Chester's shouts had faded into the air like morning mist that she said, "We'll do what we came here to do—take Mary and leave Whiskey Bend forever."

Chapter Two

ELI MORGAN WAS nervous.

Shifting uncomfortably on his wicker train seat, he peered out the window as the Colorado countryside sped by. In the bright summer afternoon, wildflowers dotted the wide plains with bright yellows, whites, oranges, and reds. Along the many burbling rivers and creeks, tall elms, oaks, and pine trees spread their broad branches, soaring high into the crisp blue, cloudless sky. In the distance, mountains rose into the heavens, their crowns capped with snow although the summer was in full sway. He spotted a wild stallion as it lifted its head in curiosity at the noisy locomotive before returning to its grassy meal. These were the familiar sights of home, a home that he had not seen for four long years.

"Four years," he muttered to himself.

The fact that he was now able to take a train to Bison

City was a testament to just *how much* things had changed since he'd left. Even though the train constantly tossed him from side to side and the passenger car held heat like an oven, it was a remarkably quick way to travel. The new route, a direct line running from Denver to Cheyenne, had only recently been completed. Hundreds of miles of track—iron rails and thick wooden ties—cut through the countryside. Among the many familiar town names there were even a couple of new places that had sprung up alongside the tracks.

Eli was also well aware that he himself had undergone a great change. While his thick, coal-black hair, piercing green eyes, and sturdy chin were the same as when he had left, much else about him was different. His tall, lanky frame had filled out dramatically; underneath his white shirt, taut muscles spread across his broadened shoulders. As he placed his black suit coat on the empty seat next to him, he was aware that his way of thinking had been transformed by his time as a member of the United States army. However, he had always been scrappy and hardworking, determined to make the most of what life had to offer. Such effort and devotion had paid dividends. Four years earlier, he had left Bison City little more than a boy. Now he returned as a man.

Still, concern lined his face. Pulling a thin, worn slip of paper from the inside pocket of his coat, he smoothed out the telegram that had brought him home. Even though it was now heavily sweat stained, he had no trouble making out the words. No matter how many times he reread it, memorizing every syllable, he felt no closer to discerning the message's true meaning.

YOU ARE NEEDED AT HOME STOP

COME AS SOON AS YOU ARE ABLE STOP

HANK

In the four years that he'd been away, Eli hadn't received a single letter, telegram, or correspondence of any kind from a single member of the family except from his uncle Hank. Eli had sent cards now and then to let the family know when he had returned to the States and had been discharged from the army. The silence from his parents had been hurtful. They had been dead set against his leaving the ranch and joining the army, and they had refused to write. It had taken him some time to get used to the break between them, but he'd managed to adjust.

But still . . .

The telegram from his uncle Hank had given him reason for concern. That it had been so short, so empty of clear meaning, had only caused him further worry. He wanted to send a telegram in return, to try to find out what had happened, but he resisted the urge. Instead, he packed his trunk and returned like a dutiful son, the kind of son he had always been, except for the one time when he had gone against his parents' wishes and joined the army. In the end, the message that he'd sent in reply had contained only the date and time of his arrival.

Even now, as Eli bounced about in his train seat, he wondered *why* he had decided to come back. There was certainly a part of him that had wanted to stay away forever. He had begun a new life, far from the one that he had known. He'd looked forward to setting down in Galveston, Texas. He'd thought about opening a business, maybe even with a new bride and a bundle of joy or two, if he could find the right woman for the job. Even though it had pained him, he had put aside his future plans and was returning to the ranch.

When he thought of his former life in Bison City, in the midst of the Morgan family, he remembered vicious arguments with his father, his mother's intolerance and complaints, but more hurtful than all others, the murder of his brother Caleb.

"Caleb," Eli whispered aloud.

Every time during the last four years when he allowed the memory of Caleb's death to enter his thoughts, it was as if someone were plunging a hot knife into his belly, then twisting it cruelly. The anger at not knowing who was responsible for the crime gnawed at him, his rage a tangible thing. Even now, four years later, the pain of loss was no less real. *My younger brother is gone . . . forever.* That it had happened two days before he was to leave for the army had only made matters worse. He agonized over what to do but, in the end, decided to stay true to his intentions and go. Somehow, he felt in his heart that Caleb would have understood; he'd had the same spirit of adventure that coursed through Eli's own veins. Unfortunately, his parents did not understand. When he left by wagon the day of his brother's funeral, no member of the Morgan family saw him off.

Folding the telegram, Eli placed it back in his suit coat. Regardless of *why* he was summoned to Bison City, he would soon arrive. All his questions would then be answered. His willingness to face the unknown was what led him to leave in the first place. That trait would undoubtedly serve him well on his return.

Eli couldn't be certain when he became aware of the familiarity of his surroundings, but a sight here and there began to spark his memory. First there was a towering, gnarled mess of an elm tree. Then he spied the meandering stream where he and Abe used to fish for trout. Finally, when Elmer Watt's sagging barn came into view, the very spot where he stole his first kiss from the man's daughter, he knew he was home.

"There's Bison City," the woman in the seat in front of him said to her son, her arm pointing out the open window.

And there it was. Eli couldn't suppress the smile that crossed his face at the sight. Many of the buildings looked the same as when he had last seen them, albeit a bit more weathered, but new buildings had sprung up as if they were spring crops. The town had certainly spread out;

even now, as the train slowed into the depot, he could see men sawing and hammering wood for new buildings. Everywhere he looked, people bustled about. While he was used to the multitudes of Galveston, there were certainly more faces here than he remembered. Change, it seemed, had come even to Bison City.

When the train finally came to a full stop, its shrill whistle piercing the noon sky, Eli rose from his seat, gathered up his coat, and headed for the door. Few of the other passengers stirred; most were destined for bigger things in Cheyenne. Stepping out onto the platform, Eli wiped the sweat from his brow with the back of his hand and began to scan the crowd. All around him, happy reunions were taking place; an elderly woman held tightly to a young girl, smothering her with kisses, and two young lovers stared into each other's eyes with passion. Eli couldn't spot a familiar face. He checked his watch, saw that the train was on time, and shrugged his broad shoulders.

Lending a hand to the depot's porters, Eli hauled trunks, satchels, and other packages from the train's cramped baggage car. It was heavy work but not unfamiliar; growing up on his father's ranch, as well as his time in the army, had made him no stranger to lifting things. He'd just retrieved his own large black trunk, its brass clasps and hinges shining in the summer sun, and dropped it to the platform with a heavy thud, when a familiar voice sounded from behind him.

"Sure looks like I picked a mighty fine time to be late."

Eli turned to find Hank Gallows standing before him with a wide grin on his tanned face. Uncle Hank, his mother's youngest brother, had been a fixture in Eli's life, and on the family ranch, for as long as he could remember. A lifelong bachelor and lover of the outdoors, Hank's disposition was as bright and sunny as a June day. Even now, as he stood on the train platform, his blond hair, ruddy cheeks, and warm blue eyes had been only slightly touched by age since Eli had seen him last. With his worn hat in his hand, wearing a faded blue shirt and pants, Hank hadn't really changed a lot.

"Figures that a polecat like you would make sure he was far away from any good, honest work that needed to be done," Eli said as sternly as he could manage, a smile threatening the corners of his mouth. "But isn't that the way you Gallows have always been?"

"That's *old* polecat to you, youngster. Show me some respect."

At that, both men burst into laughter and shook hands warmly. Hank had been one of Eli's favorites, a man who always seemed to look on the bright side of life. The path that Hank had chosen for himself was undoubtedly a hard one; ranchers' days were filled with riding, roping, branding, helping to birth new calves, mending fences, and many other tasks that were equally rough on a man.

Still, regardless of whether he was under sun, wind, rain, or snow, Hank Gallows was ready to smile.

"I almost didn't recognize you standing there," Hank said as he stepped back to get a better look at his nephew. "You ain't quite the same kid as when you left. I swear your shoulders are wide enough to give some of the bulls back on the ranch a run for their money."

"I haven't changed that much," Eli said with a chuckle.

Hank beamed, his hand rubbing at his whiskered chin. "Son, if there's one thing this old cowboy has learned in all his years, it's that everything changes whether we like it or not."

"Kind of like this," Eli said, thumbing up at the train.

"What kind of ride did you have in that contraption?"

"Not too bad if you like having your insides turned into oatmeal," Eli said with a chuckle. "Sure as heck beats being out to sea, though. When I was down in Texas, the army needed to move our unit up the coast for maneuvers. Some big shot figured it'd be easiest if they shipped us there by boat. I spent the whole time with my head hanging over the rail!"

"I'd have been right there next to you. Give me a horse any old day."

Still laughing, the two men each took an end of Eli's army trunk and hauled it out of the depot. The day had turned into a scorcher. As the sun blazed down on them mercilessly, they were quickly covered with beads of sweat. Weaving among the other passengers, they made their way to the wagon and team that Hank had driven into town. With a grunt, they heaved the heavy trunk into the wagon's bed.

Once again wiping his brow, Eli remarked, "I kind of thought Pa might have come along with you to get me. I know things weren't the best between us when I left, but I'd hoped time would have healed some old wounds. He isn't still mad, is he?"

For a brief moment, a cloud passed over Hank's face, pushing down his smile. But then in an instant, the look was gone. "Let's get ourselves back to the ranch. You'll have all your answers when we get there."

Unable to help himself, Eli suddenly thought of Caleb, of his murder in the very town in which he stood, and his heart rolled over with anguish. Dread filled his heart. "What's the matter, Hank?"

"You'll find out in due time, my boy," he answered, putting his worn hand lightly on his nephew's shoulder. There was something in Hank's eyes that Eli couldn't quite make out; was it *pity*? "All in due time."

After they climbed up onto the wagon's seat, Hank grabbed the reins and began to coax the horses on their way. As they left, the train chugged its way slowly to the north, its whistle announcing its departure. The passengers on the train still had miles to travel.

But he was *home*.

*   *   *

As the last of Bison City's outlying houses fell into the distance behind them, Eli drank in the sights that still warmed his heart. The town sat in a wide valley in the northern part of Colorado, only a couple of dozen miles from the Wyoming border. To the west, tall crags of stone, the farthest reaches of the Rocky Mountains, rose high into the sky until one had to squint to see their summits. To the east, grasslands and rolling hills stretched as far as the eye could see. Wild game of all shapes and sizes roamed amid the tall trees that covered the landscape; deer, rabbits, wild turkeys, and even bear called this land home.

"I noticed a lot of new houses back in town," Eli said as Hank drove the team of horses down the familiar road to the family ranch. "If I hadn't known better, I'd have sworn the train had stopped in the wrong place."

Hank nodded. "Things are different. With the coming of the train, everything in these parts has changed. Seems that everywhere one of those things goes, there'll be folks flockin' to make a quick dollar."

"What do you mean?"

"When I was a lad—hell, when *you* were knee-high, all the folks back in town made their livin' off of ranchin', pure and simple. Now with the railroad, just about anybody can set up shop. There're so many new faces that I can walk on down the street and not see a soul I know! It's gettin' so that I just as soon keep myself on the ranch."

"Probably best to keep that face of yours hidden," Eli said with a grin.

"Nice to see your humor ain't changed none."

Even though they laughed about the matter, Eli knew that Hank was right about one thing: Things *had* changed. While he was gone, Bison City and all the people who lived there had undergone transformations of their own, right along with him. He couldn't help but wonder just what else was different.

Hank guided the wagon down the dusty road, between tall trees that shaded them from the blistering heat, and across a bridge that spanned a gurgling stream. Eli couldn't stop taking it all in; with all the talk of change, he was happy to find that some things were the same.

As they rounded a turn in the road, they came across a couple of men mending a broken fence. One of them, a younger man with his shirtsleeves rolled up to expose bulging muscles, hefted a large wooden post as easily as most men would pick up a stick. The older man doffed his hat, wiped his brow, and greeted them.

"Afternoon," he said.

"Afternoon, Silas," Hank had time to say before they were past them.

It took Eli a moment longer to realize who they had just met and surprise made him turn around in his seat for another look. "Silas?" he wondered aloud. "That was Silas Givens?"

"Yes, it was."

"Then the fella with him would have to be his oldest boy, William," he said incredulously. "But the last time I saw William he wasn't much more than a cornstalk in baggy clothes. That man back there was as fit as an ox and nearly half as big!"

Hank laughed. "It's like I told you. Things change!"

The miles passed by with more talk and laughter, but Eli felt that there was something gnawing at Hank. Eli had known the older man nearly all his life, and he knew Hank would tell him when he was ready. Soon, they neared the homestead. They passed over a short rise in the land, and the ranch buildings came into view.

"Home," he muttered.

The Morgan ranch lay on a stretch of flat land at the end of a large grove of elm and pine. The main building, a squat, single-story house hewn from the neighboring trees, sat at the ranch's center. All around it, smaller buildings, tall barns, and corrals for cattle spread out over the land. As they rode on, Eli could see a ranch hand driving cattle into a pen. The familiar sounds and smells washed over him, and he was suddenly filled with the sensation that he had never left. This life was as much a part of him as the blood that coursed through his veins.

"Before we arrive, there's something I think you ought to be made aware of." Hank fidgeted beside him. "It's a mite strange and a bit hard to get used to, but there ain't nothin' any of us can do to change it."

As Eli stared at his uncle, he was filled with dread. He

was certain that he was about to be told the reason that the telegram had been sent, the reason that he'd been called home. His hands clenched into tight fists as he said, "What are you talking about?"

"Well . . . it's just that . . ." but before he could say more, his eyes fixed on something in the distance. His shoulders relaxed and he sighed. Pointing on ahead, he said, "I guess you can just see for yourself."

Eli followed Hank's arm. They had just passed by two of the holding corrals and were nearing the main house. The sight that greeted Eli's gaze was enough to strike him mute. He blinked once, twice, and even a third time in the hope that he wasn't seeing a mirage. His mouth opened and closed but no sound would dare to come out.

There, on the front porch, stood Abraham Lincoln.

Chapter Three

Eli could scarcely believe the sight that greeted his eyes. As he looked at the man who was even now making his way from the porch toward their wagon, his mind raced to take in all the details. The man's frame was long and thin, his arms and legs gangly under the coal-black suit that hung loosely off his body. A tall hat the same color as his suit was perched atop his head. Scraggly black hair lined his jaw below his bare upper lip.

"Ho—how in the hell?" Eli sputtered.

He would have readily admitted that he hadn't been the best student in school, but he wasn't an ignorant fool either. As a boy, he'd seen photographs of the man from Illinois who had gone on to become the sixteenth president of the United States. The figure walking toward him was the spitting image. Eli blinked quickly, hoping that the trick that assailed his vision would go away. What he saw couldn't possibly be true. After all, Abraham Lincoln had been dead for nearly thirty years!

Somehow, Eli managed to get himself out of the wagon, although he landed on wobbly legs. His jaw hung limply as the man reached him and took his hand in his own, pumping it vigorously.

"Splendid! Just splendid!" the former president enthused. "I must say that I've been awaiting your report from the front line with such anticipation that I haven't been able to so much as sit! Tell me, sir, what word have you?"

Even though he had been asked a question, Eli found himself completely and utterly incapable of answering; he had been struck mute. Instead, all he could do was stare. *Surely I must be dreaming!* He felt taunted, even teased by the truth. Slowly, as if he were trying to put together a puzzle solely by touching the pieces instead of looking at them, he could feel the answer to this mystery falling into place, but it was still temporarily out of reach.

"Pardon my manners, good sir," the bearded man said with a smile. Even in his black, heavy clothing, he didn't seem the least bit uncomfortable under the blazing summer sun. "I should have realized your predicament. I can imagine that after such a long and arduous journey your throat must certainly be parched. I'll send a porter for refreshment."

Suddenly, Eli knew who stood before him. It was all in the details; the mole to the right of his nose, the way that his dark green eyes danced about mischievously, the slight downturn of his mouth when he spoke. He couldn't understand why his older brother, Abraham Morgan, was dressed like the former president of the United States.

"Abe, it's me, Eli," he finally managed.

A frown crossed the other man's face. "I understand that you have been on a long trek, sir, but I do believe that the use of a first name is inappropriate for your commanding officer. 'President Lincoln' or 'sir' should suffice. I do believe that I have earned such courtesies."

Hank moved from his perch on the wagon to stand beside the two men. Eli expected his uncle to let him in on the joke, to break the charade that they'd created to trick him, but instead his tone was one of dead seriousness. "I'm terribly sorry, Mr. President, sir, but you've got to understand that General Morgan has just returned from a particularly dangerous mission and ain't quite used to being back among us more civilized folk." Turning to Eli, his eyes imploring his nephew to go along, he added, "Ain't that right, General Morgan?"

What in the hell is going on? Eli thought even as he managed to say, "Yes—yes, that's right." His mind was reeling. He felt as if he were trying to catch up to a runaway horse, yet always remaining a step behind.

"He'll have a report for you shortly," Hank promised further.

"Yes . . . I'll think of something," Eli agreed.

"Splendid! Just splendid!" Abe crowed. Shooting his

cuffs, he grinned from ear to ear. "In the meanwhile, I am going to walk the White House grounds and ruminate upon my upcoming speech before Congress. As I'm sure you're aware, a president's work is never done." With that, he headed off toward the outlying barn, his hands clasped firmly behind his back, his face turned up to the hot summer sun.

For a moment longer, Eli was as mute as he had been before the transformed face of his older brother. Hundreds of questions filled his mind, so many that he couldn't decide which one to ask first. Finally, when the words came, they arrived laced with shock and surprise. "What in the hell happened, Hank? Abe doesn't think he's Abraham Lincoln, does he?"

"I'm sorry that I didn't give you fair warning about your brother." Hank sighed, wiping the sweat from his brow. "But some things are easier seen than explained."

"What could possibly be the explanation of that?"

"I don't know if there is one," his uncle admitted with a nod.

Eli's thoughts raged like a tornado. Abraham was one of the things in Eli's life that had remained constant. Tall, strong, and confident, Abe had been there for him, teaching him to swim and fish, sharing a laugh, and keeping him from getting too big for his britches. Even when Caleb had come along, Abe had simply taken him under his wing and carried on.

Abraham had always been a bit peculiar, prone to

burst out into song or to laugh at the wrong time, but no one had ever paid it any mind; it was just Abe being Abe. As he'd gotten older, things seemed to worsen. Out of the clear blue, he'd fly off the handle, curse their father, and then ride off for days at a time. Their father—as had everyone else in town—realized that Abe would never be able to take over the ranch.

Eli had always assumed that his brother had grown tired of chafing under their father's yoke, just as he himself had, but maybe it had been something more. To find him like this, to see him dressed and acting as the dead president of the United States, was nearly too much to bear.

"How—how did this . . . ," was all that Eli could manage to ask.

"It happened shortly after you'd left for the army," Hank began evenly, his eyes locked on Abe's back as he made his way across the ranch. "He hadn't been feelin' all that well, complainin' about his head for a couple of days, when he up and fell like a sack of potatoes after dinner. Try as we could, wasn't nothin' that could get him to wake up. In the end, all we could do was put him in his bed and hope for the best."

"What about Doc Holland?" Eli asked, referring to the elderly physician who ministered to the town of Bison City and all the ranchers who lived nearby. "Wasn't there anything he could do?"

"We fetched him right away the next mornin'—rode

right through a bear of a summer squall, I did," Hank explained, "but he wasn't able to do anythin' to help. Whatever it was that got ahold of Abe, it was more than the doc was capable of fixin'. He reckoned that it wouldn't be but a couple of days before he'd give up and pass on. The only thing we could do for him was to keep him comfortable and give him some water from time to time. Your mother sat by his bed for weeks, never leavin' no matter how exhausted she was."

"For *weeks* . . . ," Eli echoed.

"Your mother spent all her time beside her remaining son. I ain't much of a religious fella, but I'd swear on a stack of Bibles that it was her will that kept that boy alive. He didn't die because she wouldn't let him!"

Eli felt the sting of his uncle's words, even though he was certain that Hank meant no malice. After Caleb's murder, Eli had left for the army, secure in the knowledge that Abraham remained behind to help their father with the ranch work. As much anger as there had been between him and his father and mother, he certainly hadn't wanted any hardship to befall them. What his brother had gone through made him sick to his stomach.

"But he didn't die," Eli said.

"No, he didn't." Hank nodded. "One day he just up and opened his eyes, like he'd been sleepin' or some such. At first, we were all about as happy as pigs in slop, but then we begun to understand that somethin' wasn't quite right."

"What was the matter? He didn't know who he was?"

"Oh, he knew who he was all right—it just wasn't the same as who *we* thought he was," Hank went on. "He'd answer to his name. But after a touch, he started callin' all of us by different names and carryin' on about the White House, the war, and his boyhood. At that point, it sure as hell wouldn't take no doctor to know things weren't the way they was supposed to be."

"But why go along with it? Why does he still think he's Lincoln?"

"Because try as we might, we couldn't convince him he wasn't." Eli's uncle shrugged. "Sure, we tried tellin' him he was *our* Abraham, but he wouldn't have any of it. The more we kept on, the madder he got. Your mother finally put a stop to it because she was afraid he'd go and have himself another episode. The weeks turned into months and, before you know it, he's dressin' like Lincoln, talkin' like him, even growin' his beard to look like him."

Even as Hank explained what had happened, Eli could feel himself rebelling against his uncle's words. This was an unnatural thing, wrong in every way, and needed to be stopped. "We have to get him to a doctor—a hospital where they deal with this sort of thing. Surely, there's somewhere in Denver they can make this right!"

"You wouldn't be doin' your brother no good," Hank said matter-of-factly.

"What are you talking about? He needs help!"

"If you take him to some fancy hospital, they ain't

never gonna let him back out. Some doctor would take one look at him and he'd say the boy was crazy. They'd throw the key away!"

In his heart, Eli realized that what his uncle was telling him was the truth; he'd seen much the same while in the army. Soldiers who had been tired, had seen too much action, or were simply afraid were locked in a room and classified as insane. When one acquaintance had gone into the hospital, Eli never saw him again. To imagine Abe in the same predicament was a nightmare.

"I suppose you're right," Eli admitted.

"Darn straight I am," Hank said, nodding solemnly. "What's best for Abraham is for him to stay here on the ranch among people who care for him. We can best keep a watch over him and make sure that things don't get any worse. After all, that's what family is for."

Eli looked across the ranch to where Abraham stood near a cattle pen. He couldn't be certain, but it appeared that his brother was regaling a large heifer with some tale or other. For reasons that couldn't possibly be explained, his brother believed himself to be the former president of the United States. The gentle young man, who had been such a large part of his life while he was growing up, was gone.

"What about Father?" Eli asked his uncle. "How is he dealing with this?"

The same look that had crossed Hank's face back at the depot returned, but this time, it didn't quickly disappear. Eli found it difficult to read; it held unease and even a touch of sadness. Hank gave no answer.

"What is it?" Eli prodded. "Why won't you answer me?"

With a sigh, Hank placed his hand on his nephew's shoulder. "I think it's time," he said slowly, his eyes never leaving Eli's face, "for you to have a talk with your mother."

Eli rounded the corner of the house to find his mother toiling away in her garden. It wasn't much—a small plot set just off the back porch that ran the length of the building—but it was an important part of his mother's life. Every summer without fail this was where she could be found, engaged in a labor of love to which she devoted as much time as she could spare.

Even now, Eli could see the fruits of her work: bean plants bunching against cucumber and squash, potato vines lining one end of the garden, and even tomatoes, small and as green as the vines to which they clung. She fought against weeds, rabbits, and any other threat to her charges, and she coaxed the plants along until they were ready. As the weeks passed, her garden flourished until those same tomatoes were large, juicy, and red.

Much like her beloved fruits and vegetables, Adele Morgan was much more robust than her outward appearance might lead a stranger to believe. Bent over among the plants, her gray work dress stained with sweat and dirt, she looked no bigger than a child. Though her frame was small, her face showed her true age; an oval with a small nose, thin lips, and chestnut eyes, it was crisscrossed with deep lines. Her salt-and-pepper hair was pulled back in a tight bun that hardly moved as she worked.

For a moment, Eli simply watched his mother weed. The last time that they had spoken to each other, voices had been raised and feelings hurt. She had been adamantly opposed to his leaving for the army and hadn't been shy about making her feelings known. Still, she was his mother and no amount of time away would change that.

"Mother," Eli called to her.

She looked up quickly at the sound of his voice and turned her head to face him. There was a moment of recognition mixed with surprise, but it vanished beneath a tight-lipped look of scorn.

"What are you doing here?" she said without rising.

Momentarily taken aback by her brusqueness, Eli stared hard at her. It seemed that little, if anything, had changed between them. "Hank sent me a telegram asking me to come back. He said I should return immediately. After seeing Abe I—"

"He shouldn't have done that," she cut him off. "Hank's always putting his nose into other folk's business. He's been like that since he was a boy. What happens here ain't no concern of yours."

"But now that I'm—"

"You just go back to where you come from," she said,

refusing to let him speak. Turning back to her garden, she added, her voice dripping with scorn, "You needn't act like you give a damn about what goes on around here."

Eli was nearly beside himself with anger. From his mother's short, harsh words, he knew that she regarded him with the same disdain she regarded the rabbits and weeds that attacked her garden; he was just another threat to her way of life. What she failed to understand was that for all his days he had wanted to see what was beyond the ranch, beyond Bison City.

"Where's Father?" he demanded.

Mrs. Morgan didn't even bother to lift her head as she tossed a weed over her shoulder in answer to her son's question. She acted as if he had already followed her command and left.

"Don't ignore me!" Eli barked. His hands were clenched tightly into fists and he knew his face must be a bright crimson. "I asked you where Father was, and I deserve an answer!"

Slowly, as if time had indeed withered her old bones, his mother rose to her feet and stared at her son. In her eyes there was not the slightest trace of motherly love or concern; there was only venom and disgust. She held the moment, letting her gaze speak more than any words she could give voice to. When she finally spoke, her words drove a dagger through Eli's heart.

"Your father is dead," she spat coldly, "and you're the one who killed him."

Chapter Four

YOUR FATHER IS *dead . . . and you're the one who killed him.* Adele Morgan's words flew at her son's head as if they were crows looking for a place to roost. Eli kept shooing them away, refusing to allow them to alight, even as more and more of their number darkened the sky. His heart pounded furiously, and the hot breath of the summer day was momentarily trapped in his chest. He felt as if he were back at sea, his legs wobbly and unsure beneath him, ready to betray him at any moment.

"Father is dead? What—what in the hell are you talking about?" he managed.

"Don't you use that kind of language with me," Mrs. Morgan scolded. "I'll—"

"Answer me, damn it! Why wasn't I told?"

The harsh coldness of his mother's gaze hadn't thawed; if anything, it had grown icier as she stared unblinkingly at her middle child. As he roiled in the confusion and concern that raged in his breast, Eli searched his mother's face in vain for some sign that he had misheard her.

"There ain't no father under God's watchful eye that can take all of his sons leaving. One, maybe two, but not all. It's more than a man's heart is meant to bear," she declared. Scowling, she folded her dirty arms across her narrow chest, and added, "But then, I can understand why you wouldn't know what your father went through. You've never cared for anyone but yourself. You left us to sink or swim. You didn't care that we could have lost the ranch."

"I didn't leave you alone—Abe is here."

"You're selfish, always have been."

"I left because—"

"He'd just lost one son. It broke his heart."

Eli felt as if he were trapped within a dream from which he could not wake. Even though he wanted to argue with his mother, to refute her hateful words as lies, he could do nothing but stand silent and listen; the anger that raged through him had momentarily struck him as mute as a post. Even his fists, still clenched tightly at his sides, were worthless to protect him. His mother's words struck him as if they were blows, battering him mercilessly from all sides without end. With great effort, his voice cracking, he asked, "What happened?"

Much as she had when he was a child, his mother refused to give him the easy answer to his question. "From the day you packed your bags and ran away from the only people who ever cared about you, from the place where you were born and raised, your father waited for you to come to your senses." Sighing deeply, she continued: "Every morning and every night he'd look out at the horizon, always expecting to see you there, but always turning away with his heart broken all over again. He was a fool."

"Don't speak of him that way!" Eli spat, but his mother kept on.

"I figured that eventually he'd get tired of looking, that he'd realize how little you cared, but he never stopped. No matter how often I pleaded with him, he refused to give up hope you'd be back. Years passed and still, there he was, looking and waiting for his boy to come home. He never quit believing in you, no matter how much pain and suffering that belief caused him. When the time came, he died with the broken heart you gave him."

"Stop saying that!" Eli barked, another flash of anger rising.

"Even though I loved him with all of my heart, it wasn't enough," she said with a frown. "The way he kept holding out hope for you, only to have you let him down again and again. He should have just written you off as dead."

"I wasn't dead."

"You might as well have been."

His mother's words cut him to the quick, and he looked

out over the ranch to keep from being overwhelmed. As he took in the buildings, cattle pens, and the land on which they stood, a vision of his father leaped to his eyes. As plain as the brilliant sun in the sky, there he was: leaning on the fence, his broad shoulders framing his wind-worn face, lined yet strong. He was sharing a joke with Hank, his laughter warmer than the summer day. If what Eli's mother was saying was true, it was a sight he would never see again.

He can't be gone . . . he just can't be!

Though they had often fought and argued, cussing and yelling, Eli held nothing but love in his heart for his father. All that he was and much of what he would be, he had learned from that gruff man. To think that his leaving the ranch and striking out on his own, as necessary as it had been, had caused his father such worry and anguish was painful.

"Tell me what happened to him," Eli demanded.

His mother sighed deeply. "It all became more than his broken heart could take. One morning while he was out in the barn, it finally gave out on him. Hank was the first to find him. By the time I reached his side, there wasn't a thing that could be done. He was already gone." She paused; Eli could see the sadness in her eyes, but it soon was lost behind the mask of anger and stubbornness. "Even though losing him nearly killed me, I was glad he was done worrying about you."

Eli's heart was as raw as a hammered thumb. He felt

as if a knife had been stuck deep into his belly, the blade hot and twisting. *How could this possibly be true?* But it was more than the loss of his father that wounded him; it was the way in which his mother wielded that loss like a weapon.

"When did he pass?" he asked.

She stood silently, offering no answer.

"How long ago?" he demanded, his voice rising in anger.

As he stared at the rigid face of his mother, her eyes regarding him as warily as she would have a wolf or other predator, Eli wondered if she would ever bring herself to tell him what he wished to know. She was famously stubborn, refusing to yield an inch when she held the belief that she was right. He was about to shout at her again, when she finally spoke, her voice was flat and emotionless.

"Six weeks," she said. "He died and we buried him six weeks ago."

"Why in the hell didn't you tell me?" Eli shouted incredulously, all the words exploding out of his mouth with a will he could not have stopped even if he had wanted to. "Why, Mother? Why didn't you at least send me a letter so that I would have known that Father was gone? Tell me why!"

"I reckon that's why Hank wrote you."

"Why didn't *you* write?"

"Because you're dead to me."

His mother's words were the last straw. As if he were the vicious animal his mother thought him to be, Eli shot across the rows of his mother's garden, his boots pounding the tender plants into the ground, and grabbed the woman by the shoulders. His grip held her locked in place, his face turned down to hers, his eyes burning with fury. Through it all, she didn't flinch.

"I am *not* dead, Mother!" Eli insisted. "I'm right here!"

"But I don't want you to be," she retorted. Her small body seemed to grow larger with every angry word. "When you left this place, you left for good. You were more than willing to leave your father behind, no matter how much he begged you to stay. If he didn't matter to you when he was alive, why should it matter to you that he is dead?"

"You've never understood—" he began, but his mother was no longer listening.

"It's not just your father, either. Where were you when poor Abraham was sick?" she asked accusingly. "It was for your father and me to bear, watching him lie in that bed, unable to say a single word and then, when he woke, to no longer even remember that he was our son. You were nowhere to be seen."

"If I had known that Abe was sick, I would have done all I could to see that he was cared for," Eli argued. "When I left, you knew damn well I had no intention of turning my back on you, Father, Abe, or any of this forever. That was never what I wanted."

"But it's what you chose."

Eli was at his wit's end. Try as he might, he couldn't think of what he could possibly say to make his mother understand why he had chosen the path he had taken. So much had changed for him after he left Bison City and the family ranch, but so much there remained exactly the same. He was about to try again, to attempt to find another argument, when his mother mentioned the one name that always managed to stop him cold.

"Then, of course, there was Caleb."

"What about him?"

"It's still so hard for me to believe that my boy has left me," she said, her gaze turning away from Eli for a moment, as if facing the son who had returned was more painful than speaking of the one who was forever gone.

"What happened to Caleb was not my doing, Mother," Eli explained, his ire rising at her suggestion. "You can hate me for many things, but I won't allow my brother's death to be one of them."

"It's more than that," she shot back, shaking her bony shoulders free from his grip; he let her go without comment. "That you, Caleb's own brother, could bring himself to up and leave town just as soon as we put his body in the ground . . . well, it's more than I could stand."

"I left because it was what Caleb would have wanted. I left—"

"Don't you even pretend to speak for him," Mrs. Morgan barked, her wrinkled face growing crimson with rage. "You don't know the first thing about the matter! What he would have wanted was for you to find the bastard responsible for killing him!"

Eli's jaw hung as if on broken hinges. "Wh-what are you saying? They never caught Caleb's killer? In all this time, in all the years I've been gone, they never found the son of a bitch that did it?"

"Oh, they thought they had, at least at first," she explained. "'Bout the same time you became settled in your new life, the sheriff saw fit to arrest Will Jenkins for the crime."

Will Jenkins was a fixture in Bison City. Whenever there was a bar fight, a drunken episode, or any other occasion that required the sheriff's attention, Will was almost certain to be there. To hear his name now was of no surprise to Eli.

"What happened?" he asked, a lump in his throat.

"A couple of days after Caleb's murder, there was Will, stumbling into one of the saloons wearing Caleb's hat. To make things worse, when the sheriff questioned him, he couldn't remember what he'd been doing the night Caleb was shot. Your father and I, we both thought that justice had been done and that Will would hang for the crime."

"Why didn't he?"

"It wasn't him," his mother said matter-of-factly.

"What?"

"A gal in the rooming house said that he was with her the whole evening," Mrs. Morgan explained. "When he was spotted coming out of the alley, he'd been leaving her room. He said that he found the hat just laying there, slipped it on, and that was that. There wasn't anything for the sheriff to do but to let him go on his way."

"Then who did it?"

"If you hadn't walked away from us, if you hadn't left your father and me here alone, then maybe you could have looked into it, asked around—but there was no one to do it. Not your father, with his heart broken and all, and then Abe had his spell soon after. You were Caleb's only hope, but you let him down just like you did the rest of us!"

Eli had no answer to give his mother. Everything that he thought he knew about life in Colorado was dumped on its ear! His father's death, Abe's bizarre slide into a kind of madness, and Caleb's unsolved murder shook his very being.

"Things have changed, Elijah," she said coldly, "with or without you."

When his mother turned on her heel and made her way back toward the house, the cold scowl still etched across her rigid face, there was nothing for Eli to do but watch her go.

Eli leaned against the large barn door and watched the fading summer sun streak the horizon in deep crimson and purple hues. A pair of eagles turned in lazy circles, their sharp eyes still looking for unwary prey. Sweat trickled down the sides of Eli's face as he watched the birds hunt; the hot summer day had begun to slowly slide into night, but there still wasn't much of a breeze and the early evening was humid.

Ever since he was a small boy, Eli had felt at ease among the ranching tools that lined the barn walls. Leather straps, cattle brands, hammers, and saws filled the large space. In one corner lay a fire pit and anvil that was used to repair broken clasps and hooks, as well as to shoe horses. Drawing in the rich and musky smells, Eli could still see his father bent over his labors, beads of sweat and streaks of grime lining his face.

And now all of that is gone . . .

With his father's passing, Eli realized that life would never be the same. As much as it pained him, there would be no going back to those simpler times before the fighting, before the harsh words that he'd give anything to take back. First Caleb; then his father; and then, in a sense, he'd also lost Abe. *What more do I have to give?*

"I reckon you'd like to slug me one." Hank had come up behind him.

Eli turned to look at his uncle. Hank ducked his head sheepishly, his hat in his hand like a man who'd stepped inside a church. In many ways, Eli knew that that was exactly what the barn was to the old cowhand; ranching was in Hank's blood as deeply as a tick's grasp on a mangy dog.

"The thought had crossed my mind," Eli admitted.

"If it'll ease your head a bit, I won't stop you."

Ever since he'd spoken with his mother, Eli had

mulled over every word, every curse, and every look that they had exchanged. He'd spent the rest of the day alone, uncertain what he should do next. Try as he might, his thoughts kept returning to Hank and the one question for which he had absolutely no answer.

"Why, Hank?" he asked, finally giving the question voice. "Why didn't you tell me about my father?"

"Because even though your mother is a hard-nosed, thickheaded, iron horse of a woman, she's still my sister and the only family I've got left." Running a hand through his salt-and-pepper hair, Hank leaned against the large barn door opposite his nephew. "When your father died, I tried to get her to write you, to tell you what had happened, but she wouldn't hear of it. She made me promise that I'd hold my tongue and, like the good brother I've always tried to be to her, I gave her my word."

"Then why'd you send me that telegram?" Eli asked. "Why get me all the way back here to Bison City, to the ranch, when she's made it clear she doesn't want me?"

"Well, then . . . maybe my word ain't as good as I thought it was," Hank said.

Eli looked at the ragged, dust-worn crags of his uncle's face and could see that he was telling the truth; Hank Gallows had been unable to resist the force of his sister's anger. He'd simply looked after both her and his nephew; and that was certainly something that Eli could respect.

"You gonna forgive me?" Hank asked.

"How could I not?"

"Good." The older man nodded. "Now, what happened with your mother?"

"Nothing good," Eli said with a shrug. "I just couldn't believe some of the things she said. She blamed me for what happened to Pa and for Caleb and Abe. It made me mad as hell!"

"Your mother's had it rough. I ain't gonna make no excuses for her, but she's been through enough to put most folks into the grave. Her bite can be as sharp as a snake's, but that don't mean her heart's bad. I suppose that ain't gonna make it no easier to bear, huh?"

For a while, both men were silent, content to stare out into what little of the day remained. A sliver of sun clung tenaciously to the horizon; the moon had already risen in the east, accompanied by the hundreds of stars already visible in the sky.

"I'm thinking about leaving," Eli finally said. He'd been rolling the thought around in his head from the moment his mother had walked away and, try as he might, he hadn't thought of a reason to stay.

"I was afraid you might be."

"It's just like you said, Hank. Things change whether we want them to or not. Hell, I've changed, too. I've got a life waiting for me back in Galveston and I can't think why I shouldn't get back to it."

Hank crossed the short distance between them and placed his worn hand on his nephew's shoulder. "Give it time," he said solemnly. "Spend some time helpin' me out with the work around here, maybe do a little ridin', and then make up your mind. Leavin' now ain't gonna do nothin' 'cept make the break wider and deeper."

"It's just that—"

"Stay for this here old cowboy," Hank said, silencing him. "Just give it a couple of days' time before you make up your mind. You still feel the same way then, I'll help you pack up and go."

Looking into Hank's eyes, Eli knew that he couldn't refuse him. With a deep sigh, he nodded. "All right. I'll stay for a while and help out with the cattle. Maybe with time, Ma will be able to stand the sight of me."

"I hate to tell you, Eli, my boy," Hank said with a chuckle, "but that face of yours ain't one that gets easier on the eyes!"

"Watch yourself, old man," Eli said as he punched his uncle's shoulder.

As they made their way back to the house, Eli knew that, as hard as it was, staying for a couple of days was the only choice he had. As bad as things were between him and his mother, as pitiful as Abe's condition was, there was one other matter that he simply couldn't ignore.

I have to find the answer to the mystery of Caleb's murder!

Chapter Five

"I SHOULD HAVE just shot that bastard where his brains are—between his legs!"

Hallie turned in the wagon seat to look at Pearl. The older woman's face was drawn into a tight mask of anger and regret. She looked tired. They had been on the rough road for the last two days, bumping and jostling their way to the north and west. All around them stands of elm and oak trees dotted a hilly landscape overgrown with tall grass. *Every mile seems to be as trying as pulling teeth,* she thought. They'd planned to travel only at night in order to avoid the orange sun that blazed above them, but the fear of being followed gnawed at their nerves, and they had kept moving.

"You did what you had to do," Hallie said simply.

"I know, I know." Pearl nodded, her hair loosened and flowing in the scant breeze afforded to them. "I swear I didn't go there with the intention of shootin' him, but that worthless son of a bitch wasn't gonna just let us walk out of there with Mary without a fight. No sir, he wouldn't have! He woulda killed us both."

"Do you think he's dead? Do you think you killed him?"

Pearl was silent for a moment. The only sound came from the clopping of the horse's hooves against the dirt road. Hallie could tell that her friend had given the matter a great deal of thought.

"I can't say for certain," she finally said. "I only shot him in the leg, but he was all alone out there. He might not have been able to make it to town and a doctor in time to stop all the bleedin'. Whether he was dead or not, we didn't have a choice but to leave Whiskey Bend."

"I suppose not."

In many ways, leaving Whiskey Bend was something that Hallie had been prepared to do for quite some time. It hadn't begun that way. She'd arrived in town two years earlier after a long journey from Ohio. Deciding to travel alone, she'd incurred the wrath of her overprotective parents, a minister and his wife, but she had been determined to escape the stifling atmosphere in which she had been raised. She was trained as a teacher, and she'd headed west full of excitement, confidence, and hope in her quest to find a better life.

At first, her initial months in Whiskey Bend had been all that she hoped: she settled into a healthy work life at the one-room schoolhouse, had become involved in the community and church, and had no shortage of new friends. But the fact that she had been both unmarried and attractive had brought unwanted attention. It wasn't that she wasn't interested in finding a husband; on the contrary, it was something that she deeply desired. The problem was that she had yet to find the right man. Thankfully, most of the men whose advances she had politely turned down had taken her at her word, tipped their hats, and moved on.

But not Zachary Wall.

Even when she rejected him, telling him as firmly as she could that she was *not* interested, Zachary pursued her relentlessly. It hadn't mattered to him that he was already married or that two of his children were Hallie's students. His interest only seemed to grow with every no. Every time she came into contact with him, whether it was in the mercantile or even in church, she cringed, waiting for an inappropriate look or word. In the end, when he seemed to realize that she would *never* take him to her bed, he turned vicious, spreading rumors around town that accused her of drinking, immoral sexual conduct, and being generally unfit to have charge of the townspeople's children. Slowly Hallie began to hear whispers when she entered a room.

Finally, it all came to a head. One night, he came to her boardinghouse room, drunkenly pounding on her door and demanding entry. Against her better judgment, she relented and let him inside, thinking to quiet him and then . . . The details of what occurred that night haunted her, filling her with disgust and dread. Since the passing of those horrible hours, she'd confided what happened to only one other person, Pearl, and Hallie knew that she'd never again give them voice.

In the end, leaving Whiskey Bend had been an easy decision.

"Do you have any regrets?" Hallie asked her friend.

"About leaving Whiskey Bend?" Pearl laughed. "If there's one thing I'll *never* regret, it'll be leavin' that flea-bag town. Like my momma always used to say, 'Ain't no point in stayin' where you ain't wanted.'"

"I suppose you're right."

"Damn right, I am."

Hallie knew that Pearl also had more than her share of reasons to leave Whiskey Bend, although the matter had roots that had been formed many years earlier.

In the heady years after the completion of the trans-continental railroad, Pearl and her husband had done as thousands of others had and headed west. They'd settled in the aptly named town of Simple, wedged next to a river just across the Colorado state line from Nebraska. There, they'd built a tavern with the idea of establishing something they could be proud of and that would grow right along with the town. In the back of their minds there was even the idea of a child or two or three. It had all seemed ideal and attainable, but something had gone wrong.

Pearl's husband always had a taste for whiskey, but now, with unfettered access to the tavern's stock, he imbibed as never before. Soon, a slap here and there turned into a closed fist. One night, deep in the blistering cold January of their second year in Simple, he came to their bed not in the mood for love but for blood and beat her nearly half to death. The next morning, her meager belongings hastily packed into a rickety wagon, she left without regret and without ever once looking back. Six months later, Pearl received word that her husband had gotten drunk and burned the tavern to the ground, killing himself in the process.

For the next ten years, she drifted from one town to another, tending bars and doing other odd jobs before yet another ruined relationship forced her to once again move on. Finally, she came to Whiskey Bend determined to do things differently.

The biggest change in her life was to refuse to take another lover; after all her failed attempts, she'd come to realize that she just didn't know how to pick them. But there was one thing about herself that she was unable to change: all the years behind alcohol-soaked bars had given her both a salty vocabulary and a wit quick enough to sharpen her tongue.

Then, one morning, while walking down the town boardwalk, after a long night working at the saloon, she was bumped into by an older man. Before he could even offer a word of apology, she'd shouted, "Goddamn stupid bastard! Why don't you watch where in hell you're goin'!" A moment later, she realized that she'd insulted the eighty-year-old pastor of the only church in town.

Soon after, Pearl Parsons had found herself the talk of the town. Wives told their husbands not to frequent the bar in which she worked in order to avoid any further scandal. She knew that it was only a matter of time before the bar's owner asked her to leave.

Like Hallie, she had become a pariah, although of a different type.

Hallie stole another quick glance at her friend and couldn't help but smile. In all the time they had known each other, she had seen nothing in Pearl that resembled what caused the whispers and stares back in Whiskey Bend. To Hallie, she was a warm, passionate woman who put her friendships before all else. She was outgoing, vivacious, colorful, and loyal to a fault—although, Hallie had to admit, she could swear as colorfully as any man.

Now whatever we face, we will face it together.

"How's Mary doing?" Pearl asked.

Hallie looked into the back of the rocking wagon. There, nestled among the meager belongings they managed to throw together, Mary Sinclair slept fitfully. In the two days since they'd left the decrepit cabin she shared with Chester, Mary had done little *but* sleep and sob. Whenever they stopped, mostly to rest the horses and to get whatever respite they could manage, Hallie nearly had to force Mary to drink. Even now, her pale cheeks were stained with tears. Hallie and Pearl began to fear that she would waste away before their very eyes.

"I don't know if she's ever going to get better," Hallie said and sighed.

"She will once she's spent some time away from Chester," Pearl assured her.

In Hallie's mind, the image of Pearl shooting the man, the bullet exploding into his leg and his yelps of pain and threats following them until they were out of earshot, suddenly flashed. She'd known a few mean men in her life, but Chester Remnick might very well be the worst.

"Do you reckon that he intended Mary to be his wife?"

"Men like Chester are a dime a dozen," Pearl spat. "They don't give a good goddamn where they put their pecker! It wouldn't have made any difference to him if she was his stepsister or his half sister. It wouldn't have mattered if she were willing or not, because *she* didn't matter."

"I just can't believe it."

"What you don't want to believe is what that bastard did to that poor girl," Pearl snarled. "Damn! The more I think about it, I shoulda just gone ahead and killed him."

While Hallie couldn't bring herself to agree with Pearl's wish that she'd killed Chester, she knew her friend was right about one thing; it was hard for her to imagine what Mary had been through. Each of them had her own cross to bear; maybe Mary's was the heaviest of all.

"Where will we go now?" Hallie asked, her voice weak with worry.

"We'll go wherever this road will take us."

"But how will we know? How will we ever be able to—"

"We'll manage," Pearl insisted, taking the younger woman's hand in her own. "All that matters is that we've left Whiskey Bend. When we get somewhere else, when we find a place to settle, we'll just *know* that it's the right place for us. Then we'll do our best to carry on and start over. Besides, not a one of us will be alone."

"You're right." Hallie nodded and she knew it to be true in her heart.

"Damn right, I am."

As they moved further down the road, a slight breeze rustled the thick green leaves on the trees and parted the high grass like waves roiling the ocean. Hallie sighed. Even though she felt comforted by having Pearl beside her, she knew that she wasn't as strong as the older woman. She couldn't do what Pearl had done many times before; she couldn't just let it go.

Turning slowly, she looked over her shoulder, giving one last look back.

* * *

Hallie woke from a fitful dream, her hand clutching her chest. In her nightmare, there was Chester, spittle forming on his lip as he cursed them, a smoking rifle barrel, and then dark crimson blood. Even as she fought to catch her breath, she swore that she could still smell the copper tang of Chester's wound.

Will I ever get a good night's sleep again?

Looking to the sky, she took in the blanket of stars that covered her. Nestled among them was a quarter-full moon. To the east, there was a dab of light on the horizon; it would soon be daylight. Hallie was tired and uncomfortable. Even in the midst of a hot summer, nights like this were cold. She shivered, rubbing her hands along her arms, trying to stimulate some warmth.

Suddenly, a stick cracked behind her.

Hallie turned to the sound, frantically searching the darkness for some sign of what had caused her heart to hammer like a rabbit's. In the predawn light, she could make out only some of her surroundings; Pearl lay on the ground next to her, both of their backs to the wagon in which Mary lay. Her first thought was that the noise was caused by the horses, but they were tied to a copse of trees in front of her; the sound had come from the opposite direction.

Has Chester caught up to us?

Everything they did since leaving Whiskey Bend was calculated to keep them safe. Even now, they had stopped only because she and Pearl were exhausted, unable to keep their eyes open for a minute longer. Fearful that they were being followed, they'd even forgone a fire, choosing instead to settle and eat cold food by the natural light of the night.

"Stay calm, Hallie," she whispered to herself.

Even though her hands were shaking, she found that she couldn't sit still and simply wait for whatever was out there to find her. She thought of waking Pearl, of facing this unseen menace together, but found she could not; whatever was out there she would deal with if she could. Her breath caught in her throat, but she rose to her feet on quaking legs.

Another stick snapped, followed by shuffling sounds.

With utter certainty, Hallie knew that they were not alone. In the sliver of light that the moon gave, she scanned the ground for something, anything that she could use as a weapon. Finally, her eyes lit upon a thick stick that she snatched up greedily, its bark rough against her hand.

It's up to you now, Hallie. You have to be brave! You have to be strong! Gasping raggedly through clenched teeth, she took her first step toward the sound.

Rounding the wagon, she peered into the gloom. They'd stopped for the night in a small clearing; little bushes dotted the ground, their tiny leaves ghostly in the moonlight. Hallie stopped as she heard the rustling of branches and another footstep. She wanted to cry out, to ask who was out in the darkness, but fear had trapped her voice in her throat.

Then, suddenly, all was revealed.

Standing between two bushes not ten feet away, a young coyote regarded Hallie warily. It remained stock-still as it stared, its small ears straight up and alert. In what little light there was, the animal's eyes glowed mischievously. Somewhere over the coyote's shoulder, she saw even more movement and knew that this hunter was not alone.

"Go on! Get out of here!" she called, but the coyote stood its ground.

It wasn't until she took a menacing step forward, brandishing the stick as if she intended to use it, that the animal skittered away. Still, it only moved a bit farther out of range before stopping and staring again. It was far less afraid of her than she was of it.

Hallie knew that these coyotes weren't a real danger, but what they represented filled her with dread. They were the unknown, the unseen that lurked just beyond her vision. They were much like Chester himself; they were predators in search of prey and they would follow that prey until they seized it with their sharp teeth. She and Pearl and Mary would never be able to stop watching, would never be able to stop worrying about the next creature to fall upon them out of the darkness.

As the sun began to color the horizon, Hallie allowed herself to cry.

Chapter Six

"Goddamnit, Doc! That bullet hurts like hell!"

The words tumbled from his mouth, and Chester Remnick winced as a thunderclap of pain rumbled its way across his head. Lights danced before his eyes and he felt dizzy; if he hadn't already been sitting, he might have fallen. To ease his discomfort, he did the only thing that felt right and brought the half-empty bottle of whiskey back to his lips and drew hungrily from its neck.

As the booze burned its way down his throat, Chester looked around the tiny space. The doctor's office in Whiskey Bend was nothing more than an attic room above the mercantile. The small cot upon which he lay was stuffed into one corner, vying for space with the room's other bits of furniture: a cracked bureau, a wobbly nightstand, and a rickety chair. A cabinet with bandages and medical equipment stood against the opposite wall. It wasn't much of a doctor's office, but it would have to do; too much depended on his surviving for him to die in such a filthy place.

"The bitches!" Chester hissed under his breath.

A little more than a day had passed since his very life had been torn asunder, and Chester still struggled to contain the fury that roiled through his body and mind. Still, there was a part of him that *didn't* struggle, that embraced the anger; after all, it was the anger that had kept him alive.

As he had watched Mary stagger off in the company of those two whores, the fury that raged in his gut made the gunshot wound in his leg little more than an annoyance. He kept his tear- and sweat-streaked gaze locked on the three women for as long as he could, certain that Mary, who was *rightfully* his, would come to her senses and return to him, where she belonged. He diligently watched for hours, but she didn't return.

Through grunts and curses, he managed to crawl his way back to the dark interior of the cabin and set about cleaning the wound. Where the bullet had penetrated the skin, the hole was small but tender to the touch. Blood had steadily seeped out, coloring his trouser leg a deep and ugly crimson. Even though he feared losing consciousness, he somehow managed to make a tourniquet out of one of Mary's blouses that he gleefully shredded.

Even then, as darkness fell and the pain in his leg

throbbed with the intensity of the absent sun, Chester did not think of going for help. On the contrary, he resigned himself to wallowing in his anger, his only solace the bottle of whiskey he somehow managed to retrieve from the table. As the moon rose and then fell, he refused the embrace of sleep, choosing instead to drink steadily, his mind racing and contemplating with relish all the things he would do to those two bitches when he finally laid hands on them. Even Mary did not escape his wrath; the last beating he gave her would seem mild compared to what she'd get for leaving him.

"Mary," he mumbled and cursed her loud and long.

When the morning sun cracked the horizon, Chester knew he needed to act if he wanted to live. With every beat of his heart, his wound throbbed in agony, and he knew that getting to a doctor soon was the only way to keep his leg from being cut off. He'd somehow found the strength to crawl from the cabin to the small barn at the edge of the property, hoist himself atop his mangy horse, and amble on it to Whiskey Bend. Every jostle and jolt of the ride hurt nearly as badly as being shot. He passed out in front of the saloon and was dragged inside.

"I ain't kiddin' here, Doc," he said through clenched teeth as another wave of pain washed over him. "Ya gonna get to this or are ya just gonna let the damn thing kill me?"

Munroe Jenkins had been Whiskey Bend's doctor for the past ten years. The job was his not out of respect for his educational background or bedside manner but by default; there simply wasn't anyone else for miles around who had any medical experience. Dr. Jenkins had been a field surgeon during the Civil War, a time when a patient was more apt to die at his surgeon's hands than because of the injury that had brought him there in the first place.

The doctor's unkempt snow-white hair, bloodshot eyes that danced behind pince-nez, sagging jowls, and nervous tics and twitches did little to inspire a patient's confidence. Chester swallowed hard. He felt as if he had brought himself to the undertaker by mistake.

"Quit yer goddamn bellyachin'," Doc Jenkins cackled, releasing breath that stank sourly of whiskey. "You keep on like that, and I'm a-gonna stitch yer mouth up fer my own peace a mind!"

"Just get on with it," Chester snarled.

"Medicine ain't nothin' to be rushed, boy."

The old man busied himself, gathering a mixture of knives, strange-colored liquids in jars, and other curiosities. Once, when turning his squat body for yet another sharp instrument, he bumped against Chester's leg, causing him to yelp in pain.

"Stop yer complainin'," the doctor admonished him, intent on his work. The last item he brought to the table was a long saw, its serrated teeth gleaming in the scant light coming in the room's lone window.

"What in the hell is that for?" Chester barked, recoiling from the tool.

"Hold yer wad, son." The doctor smiled, revealing brownish-yellow teeth that would not have looked out of place in a dog's mouth. "If there's one thing I done learned in all my years a doin' this, it's that a doctor ain't worth his salt if he ain't prepared for any and all problems that may arise."

"There better not be no—"

"Shut your mouth." The command was loud and harsh and louder when he said again, "If'n you hold yer tongue, it'll be over before you know it."

The older man firmly pushed Chester until he lay flat on his back on the small cot. Snatching the whiskey bottle from the wounded man's grasp, the doctor took a long draw, then wiped his mouth with the back of his hand.

"For courage." He winked before offering the bottle back. "I reckon takin' a slug or two more off a that bottle might do ya a bit of good, son. If nothin' else, it'll keep yer mouth from flappin'."

Chester took the man's advice and a deep gulp of the amber fluid. Out of the corner of his eye, he watched as Doc Jenkins selected a long knife from the table, holding the blade to the light. As he bent down toward the bullet wound in Chester's leg, something that could have been glee filled the doctor's face.

"Just keep on a-drinkin'," the doctor said. "This is gonna hurt a bit."

*   *   *

It was well into the night when Chester finally stumbled from the doctor's room and into the saloon. All around him, men shouted and swore, swilling cheap beer and whiskey and covering the room with a blanket of cigar smoke. Here and there, a whore tried to interest a prospective client in her wares. All in all, it seemed to be just another ordinary night in Whiskey Bend. No one paid him any attention as he slowly, achingly made his way to the bar.

Once he'd settled into a position that left him only *hideously* aching, he fished into his trousers for a coin and slapped it down onto the counter where it was quickly replaced by a bottle of whiskey. Greedily, he pulled out the stopper and drank as if he were a man dying of thirst. Even if it took all night, he swore that he would drown the pain.

Try as he might, he couldn't seem to forget the raw hurt he had felt with the first cut. From that moment, pain had been perched on his shoulder like a crow on a barn. He'd occasionally passed out, only to awaken long enough to slip into unconsciousness yet again. When he had last come to, he'd found himself alone, his leg crudely bandaged, and the bullet that had caused so much trouble lying harmlessly in a pan of blood.

Squeezing his eyes shut when another bout of pain seized him, he downed the last of the drink and brought it down hard onto the bar. His leg still hurt like hell, but he did feel *better*.

" 'Nother?" the bartender asked.

"Goddamn right."

Chester stared ahead, gazing deeply into the grime-streaked mirror that hung behind the bar. Through the dirt and dust, as well as the pain and alcohol that clouded his head, he could see the anger blazing in his eyes.

Slowly, a thin smile curled the edges of his mouth.

This raw anger, the fire that drove him, that threatened to consume him, would be very hard to quench. He had no idea where the two whores had taken Mary, but he was not a man without resources. It would take time and it would take favors, but he knew if he were persistent, he would find them. Then, sated by revenge and blood, he would be able to rest.

Chester Remnick had never been a religious man. Still, it would take one hell of a fool not to think that he'd survived through the grace of some sort of miracle. He'd been given a chance, a chance to make right all the things that had conspired to strike him low. In the end, he knew that one chance was all he would need.

As laughter broke across the saloon, he laughed along through the pain.

Chapter Seven

"Why can't we stop here?"

"Because it ain't safe, Hallie," Pearl explained. "There ain't but a couple of saloons and a store down there. There ain't even a church. I've heard of this place. It ain't nothin' but a nest of *rattlesnakes*. Their eyes would pop right out of their heads if they saw three women coming into town. We'd not stand a chance there, no more than we'd had in Whiskey Bend. You know that."

Hallie frowned and turned her gaze back to the small town. From where the wagon had come to a stop at the top of a high hill on the northern slope of the long valley, the view was breathtaking. Nestled between two towering crags as if it were a baby in its mother's arms, the town of Lancaster was as pretty as any picture; a small stream wound and curved lazily, and tall stands of trees dotted the countryside. The sounds of birdsong and the smell of pines drifted on the cool breeze. Even the clumps of dark clouds that mottled the sky, like deep bruises on a pale blue skin, did nothing to take away from the beauty of the scene.

In short, it seemed the perfect place to settle and build a new life.

"I don't know any such thing," Hallie protested.

"Yes, you do. You're just too stubborn to admit it."

Hallie wasn't sure if it was that she was too stubborn, but she was certain she was *tired* enough to admit to just about anything. It had been five long days since they had left Chester Remnick writhing in the dirt, his curses chasing them into the distance. They'd only made stops to cook a hot meal, to rest the horses, or to grab a few fitful hours of sleep. On and on they had moved, fear nipping at their heels as if it were a pack of wolves. The thought of bringing their travels to an end was appealing.

"We don't know that it's not safe," Hallie continued to argue even if her heart told her that Pearl was probably right. "How can Chester follow us, let alone manage to track us all the way here? Not after what you did to him."

"Do you want to take that chance?" Pearl prodded her friend. "It'd be one thing if you wanted to risk your own hide or even mine, but do you really want to put Mary's life on the line? She's suffered enough without us stoppin' on account a bein' tired."

As Hallie let her friend's words sink in, she stole a

glance at the rear of the wagon. Mary lay huddled amid the blankets and their other belongings, her head turned in such a way that she might have been listening, but Hallie couldn't be certain. The woman's shoulders were slumped, her hair a tangled mess, and her eyes were smudged with deep, dark rings. Thankfully, she'd begun to eat a bit but like a bird, pecking at this and that and consuming very little. Her sobbing and crying, while still a daily occurrence, had lessened. More disturbing was the way in which she still spent all of her time staring into the distance behind them. *Was it in fear that Chester could be coming after them?* Hallie wondered.

"We can't run forever," she finally said.

"You're right."

"What place is ever going to be safe enough?" the younger girl continued. This was the question that had been plaguing her for days, nagging at her when she was most tired, hungry, or fearful.

Pearl sighed deeply, her eyes turning to the sky for a moment, as if she were looking for some kind of divine inspiration. When she spoke, her voice was calm but as firm as a preacher's. "I don't know the answer to that, Hallie. I really don't.

"There ain't a lot I do know in this here life," Pearl continued, "but what I'm sure of is that this place," she began, one arm sweeping over the town of Lancaster below them, "don't seem right just yet. The next one might not neither. We've just gotta keep goin' till we find that special town, that right place to quit runnin'. Somehow, I'm sure we'll know it when we get there."

As Hallie stared into her friend's lined face, she knew that the older woman believed she was telling the truth. From the very first moment that she had met Pearl Parsons, Hallie had been struck by her confidence, by her unshakable belief in herself. If Pearl thought that this town wasn't right, then it simply *wasn't right*. They'd just have to move on to the next one. Now was not the time to begin doubting.

"All right," she agreed.

"It's for the best." Pearl slapped the reins against the backs of the tired team.

As the wagon lurched forward, Hallie stole a last look at Mary. The girl's eyes never lifted, she never so much as blinked, as she was carried off yet again as effortlessly as if she were a branch caught in the currents of a mighty river.

Somewhere off in the distance came the deep, guttural roar of thunder.

An hour before dusk the storm finally caught up with them. Constantly peeking over her shoulder, Hallie had watched, her nerves growing more frayed by the moment, as it had approached as steadily and relentlessly as a wolf stalking a wounded deer. No matter how hard they pushed the horses, the storm proved much swifter, and she realized that there was no shelter in sight.

The speed of the storm was matched by its fury. The sun had long vanished behind a wall of darkening clouds, and the only light by which they could see was provided by long forks of lightning that flashed, one after another, across the broad sky; the peals of thunder following them were as deafening as cannon fire. The air felt heavy, damp, and pregnant with the gale. When the rain finally fell upon them, it was preceded not just by the smell—a sharp moistness that stung the nose—but also by sound; it was as if thousands of booted feet were being stamped at once.

"This ain't gonna be pretty," Pearl said, her face turned anxiously skyward.

The first drops of rain struck Hallie's face not with the gentleness of a soft spring squall but as if she were being pummeled by fists. The storm was angry even at its beginnings; gusts of wind yanked insistently at her clothes and seemed to want to pull the very air from her lungs. Sheets of rain came across the ground toward them as if they were soldiers marching off to war. Try as she might to be brave, Hallie was afraid.

"What are we going to do?" she gasped.

"I don't know!" Pearl shouted over the storm.

"We have to get out of this!"

"But where are we gonna go?"

Anxiously, Hallie peered into the storm. As her gaze swept through the inky darkness, she hoped to find something, *anything* that could provide them with shelter.

She knew that the land in which they found themselves had little to offer. After leaving Lancaster behind, they'd passed through a gap in the soft hills out onto a flat, rolling plain of tall grass broken only by staggered copses of trees. As the last light of the day had been squeezed by the coming storm, she'd even seen the faint outline of a river in the distance. But what she *hadn't* seen was a single farmhouse or ranch, anywhere they could go for help; and the chance of finding one now seemed impossible. In the storm's oppressive gloom, she could barely see her hand before her face.

Suddenly, a long tongue of lightning streaked from the sky, crashing hard into the earth below. Even though it struck miles in the distance, the air seemed to shudder. Light filled the sky; it was as if someone had lit a hundred candles in a darkened room.

"Sweet applesauce!" Hallie cried.

"Holy shit!" Pearl exclaimed.

Even as the last of the deafening thunder rolled off into the distance, Hallie's eyes were locked on the sight that had greeted them in the lightning's scant illumination; the wagon still sat in the wide, open plain of grass, but a long stand of trees lay only a couple of hundred yards in front of them. *If we can just reach their cover . . .*

"Straight ahead, Pearl!"

"What?" The older woman turned to her, shouting to be heard over the raging storm. "What are you talkin' about? What's straight ahead? I can't see nothin' in all of this here rain!"

"Right there in front of us," Hallie explained excitedly. She pointed toward where their salvation had been, even though the inky black of the storm had returned. "There are trees we can get under!"

"Where? I don't see a damn thing!"

As if the storm wished to prove that Hallie had not imagined the trees, another fork of lightning lit the sky.

"Do you see?" Hallie shouted, nearly jumping from her seat.

Without uttering a word in answer, Pearl cracked down hard on the reins, and the two horses, both spooked by the coming of the storm, practically leaped at the chance to run. The wagon took off with a lurch, skittering off the narrow road and out over the uneven ground. Hallie feared that they would lose a wheel or that they would become bogged down in the mud, but the horses never slowed for a moment. With the thundering of hooves and the creaks and cracks of the wagon over every bump, they raced headlong for the trees.

Every passing second, the storm grew in intensity. Hallie's clothes stuck to her skin with cold wetness. Her hair was soaked and stringy, matted against her face. As rain pounded against the wooden wagon in an incessant drumming, it shook like a child's toy. Hallie held tightly to the long seat with one hand while shielding her eyes with the other.

"Almost there!" Pearl yelled.

Ahead of the wagon, the dark outlines of the trees suddenly loomed. As she tried to steady herself through all the rocking and tipping of the ride, Hallie had to strain to see them. When another lightning bolt pierced the sky, she could see how close they were to shelter, but she worried that they'd be no less safe. Branches swung wildly to and fro in the fevered wind as if the trees had come to life and meant to do them harm. The sound of the rain striking the leaves and limbs was different in pitch but just as steady.

Then, just as more lightning turned the black storm into the brightest day, they passed under the tree's wide canopy, and the deluge seemed to have been left behind them.

"Thank heavens," Hallie exclaimed.

"My daddy always done said that the last place you'd want to be in a storm was under a tree, what with the lightnin' and all." Pearl laughed, shaking the rain from her arms. "But I ain't so sure that if he found hisself in a storm like this one, he wouldn't be right here beside us!"

Hallie couldn't answer. As she sat on the wooden seat, the water of the storm running off every part of her body, she felt chilled to her very bones. Even under the shelter provided by the trees, rain still fell on them, traipsing its way off one leaf and then another before finding them at the bottom. The weight of everything they had been through, from the confrontation with Chester to the mad dash through the deluge, seemed to press down on Hallie all at once. She had been pushed to this, forced to accept what life had to give without any choice of her own. This time, when the tears came, she felt a touch of anger mixed with the fear.

"What's the matter?" Pearl asked when she noticed that Hallie was crying.

Try as she might, Hallie could not quiet the voice of frustration that rose in her chest. She knew that it would have been better to simply hold her tongue, to swallow the whole sordid mess, but she found it an impossible task. Tears streamed down her face, mixing with the rainwater. When she spoke, her voice was little more than a whisper. "We should have stopped."

"What was that? I can't hear you."

"We should have stopped back there!" Hallie suddenly exploded; to her own ears, her voice sounded as loud as any of the peals of thunder that had rocked the countryside. "If only we had stayed in Lancaster, if only we had quit all this running, we wouldn't be here, Pearl! We wouldn't be caught out here in this storm!"

"I told you, girl, we needed to get as far away as possible and—" Pearl began, but Hallie wouldn't let her.

"When is it ever going to be far enough?" she pleaded. "When are we ever going to feel that we've gotten far enough away from all the madness behind us? How can we ever really be safe again? All we've done is move from one strange place to the next and then the one after, until I just can't bear to run anymore!"

To all Hallie's questions, Pearl gave no answer.

"As much as I hate myself for even thinking it, I wish you'd just killed Chester, Pearl!" Hallie declared. "I wish you had shot him and that he had died! If he was dead, we wouldn't have to keep looking over our shoulders at every turn, fearful that he'll be there, never knowing a moment's rest! But I know that he's not dead and that changes everything! I know we're doing this for Mary but I just—I just . . . can't," she finally concluded.

Before even the first sobs could rack Hallie's body, Pearl was there. She pulled the younger woman to her and held her tightly.

"Hush now," Pearl whispered into Hallie's ear. "There ain't nothin' wrong with wishin' for somethin' we can't have every now and again, but it just ain't good to dwell on it."

"Oh, Pearl," Hallie sobbed. "I'm sorry for all that—"

"Just put it out of your head," the older woman soothed. "You was sayin' what you thought needed to be said, that's all. To be honest, I can't say I like this any more'n you do, but what's done is done. When we get to where we need to be, then all this'll have been worth it. We'll put it behind us and you, me, and Mary will start livin' again."

At the mention of Mary's name, Hallie's tears stopped falling. All that had happened, all the turmoil that she and

Pearl had suffered through failed to compare with what Mary had endured at Chester's hands. Shame washed over her at the thought of her own selfishness. For Mary's sake, they had to keep on.

"You're right." Hallie nodded, wiping away a stray tear. She turned on the bench to face the wagon's rear and began, "Oh, Mary! Forgive how selfish I've—" but what she saw there stopped the words in her mouth.

There was no one in the back of the wagon. *Mary was gone!*

Chapter Eight

HALLIE COULDN'T BREATHE. In the darkness of the storm, she looked for Mary. In those split seconds, she thought the gloomy blackness was merely playing tricks on her, that her friend *was* still there. But when another splinter of lightning lit the sky, she knew that she was holding on to false hope. Panic swept over Hallie like a brush fire.

"Mary!" she shouted. "Mary! Where are you?"

"What?" Pearl screeched, a cold fear touching her voice as well.

"She's gone! Oh, Pearl, Mary's gone!" Hallie's eyes searched all around the wagon for a sign of the girl, but in the inky darkness she could see nothing. The sun had almost certainly set, and the veil of night had settled like a blanket. Through it all, the storm still raged.

"Where on earth could she be?" Pearl wondered aloud.

The first thought that leaped to Hallie's mind sent shivers down her spine; that Chester had stolen up behind them and snatched Mary out from under their noses, but she knew that the idea was only fear playing on her nerves. Even with the driving rain, she was certain that they would have heard someone approaching. Besides, Chester had a fresh bullet wound in his leg and, if he hadn't died from it, would be in no condition to chase after them, certainly not fast enough to have already caught up to the wagon. Shaking her wet hair, she pushed the idea out of her head.

Then where is she?

"Maybe she fell out of the wagon," Hallie said. Even though she couldn't see more than a couple of dozen feet, she looked back in the direction from which they had come. "When we crossed from the road to here I had to hold on to the seat to keep from being jostled this way or that. Maybe it was worse in the back. She could have been thrown out of the wagon!"

Pearl pondered the idea for a moment, her jaw set tight. "You could be right," she finally agreed. "I wasn't pushin' the horses *that* hard, but I can't say for certain that I wasn't neither. We'll have to go back and look."

"It will be impossible to find her in this storm," Hallie fretted. "Mary could be *anywhere*. What if she slipped out of the wagon after we pulled under the tree cover? She could be wandering around in the woods right beside us and we'd never find her!"

"We'll find her."

"Then I'll stay here and wait. She might come back," Hallie suggested.

Before Pearl could offer a single word of protest, Hallie leaped from the wagon to the ground below. Her booted feet slipped on the wet grass and she fell hard on her knees in the sloppy mud. The pain was stinging, but she quickly stifled her cry. Ignoring the ache, she rose gingerly back to her feet.

"We'll find her," Pearl said confidently. "I know we will."

"I pray you're right."

"I am."

The older woman whistled shrilly through her teeth, snapped on the reins, and urged the horses forward. The wagon creaked and she hurried back the way they had come. Soon they were swallowed by the night. A scant moment later, even the sound of the horse's hooves was lost.

Without Pearl beside her, helplessness descended on Hallie. For several minutes, all she could do was stand and stare, unable to move even an inch. Mary was gone and finding herself alone in the woods was frightening. Darkness closed in from all sides as the storm intensified, and the noise of the wind whipping the trees was disorienting.

The sky was suddenly lit by a succession of lightning bolts, their tendrils flickering like a serpent's tongue. If she hadn't been frightened nearly out of her wits, she might have found it beautiful. For what seemed like a full minute, all that was dark became light; it was as if she were under an endless barrage of photographer's flashes.

Turning her head this way and that, Hallie used the storm's illumination to the best of her advantage. At first, the extra light showed her nothing, but in the scant seconds offered by the very last bolt, her heart leaped with hope. There, not more than thirty feet away, was Mary. Like Hallie, she was drenched, and her clothes stuck to her body. She stood along the tree line, her body small but tense. To Hallie, it looked as if she were a wild animal, ready to flee to safety at a moment's notice.

"Mary!" Hallie shouted. "Over here, Mary!"

Just before the lightning vanished and the darkness returned, the first roar of thunder echoing across the land, Hallie saw the other woman stiffen at her cry. Without a single word, Mary turned her back and plunged into the woods, leaving Hallie alone yet again.

Without any hesitation, Hallie followed, stumbling over the uneven and muddy ground. Even in the murky gloom of the storm, she'd kept her eyes locked on where Mary had disappeared into the trees. When Hallie reached the spot, she looked cautiously into the blackness beyond, took a deep breath, and plunged into the woods behind the fleeing woman.

"Mary!" she shouted plaintively. "Come back!"

Passing through the forest's curtain, Hallie found herself in a world that was darker and scarier than the one she had left only seconds before. Trees of many shapes and sizes crowded together and towered above her, the stormy sky all but completely obscured by the thick shelter of leaves and branches. The space between the tree trunks was filled with choking scrub and prickly brush. With every hesitant step, Hallie held her arms before her as a means of protection, but she was soon covered with scratches and welts. Every time that she pushed aside a wayward branch or passed through some leafy undergrowth she was showered by the rainwater that had clung to it.

"Mary! Wait for me, Mary!"

While every rolling growl of thunder still startled and unnerved her, Hallie almost began to look forward to a new tongue of lightning. In each flash, she would catch a glimpse of Mary as she wove and cut through the woods. Try as she might, Hallie couldn't seem to make up any ground; it was as if Mary were always being held just out of reach.

Whether it was fear that drove her—fear that Chester would somehow find her or fear that the two women were spiriting her away from the life that she knew—Mary seemed utterly incapable of controlling the emotion that coursed through her. *Why else was she running blindly through this nightmare of a storm?*

"Mary!" Hallie called.

Before she could shout another word, she was struck hard in the mouth by a thick branch. In the scant light of the dense forest, she hadn't seen the limb in her path and had collided with it blindly. As the copper tang of blood filled her mouth, she whimpered in pain. Still, she kept moving forward, stumbling along until she could regain her bearings.

Though she was soaked to the bone, tired from running, and aching from all the cuts and bruises, Hallie was determined not to quit the chase. Taking the easy way would be akin to abandoning Mary in her time of need, and that was something she simply could not do. She and Pearl had not been able to abandon Mary after seeing Chester strike her in the streets of Whiskey Bend and she wouldn't do so now! She would continue until she reached her friend or collapsed from exhaustion, whichever came first.

"Mary! For God's sake, Mary! Please stop!"

As she ran, Hallie became aware of a deep roaring in her ears. At first, she thought that it was just another sign of the raging storm, but the noise didn't rise and fall in intensity as the thunder did, or whistle like the wind, but instead grew louder with each passing second. Soon, the roaring became deafening, nearly drowning out the sounds of the storm itself. It was as if she were running right into the jaws of a monster, a monster that she could not see but only hear.

Hallie ran with all her might. Though it was hard to see what was in front of her and she feared another collision, she somehow knew that the time to reach Mary was running out. She passed through a thick stand of tall elm trees; crossed a small clearing; and, as she pushed her way through the tangle of a berry-laden bush, the source of the roaring noise revealed itself to her startled eyes. There, at the bottom of the hill upon which she stood, was a raging river, its wide body swollen to flood stage by the storm. The noise had indeed come from a monster, a monster that had proven to be horrifyingly real.

Try as she might, Hallie could not pull her eyes away from the fury of the flooded river. In the intermittent flashes of lightning, she watched in horror as the roiling brown water sped by, lashing and snatching at anything unlucky enough to be within its reach. Here and there, treetops bobbed furiously in the water, victims found further upstream and now speeding to an unknown future. It was as if the river were a starving man, desperately snatching at the morsels presented to him.

Even where she stood, atop the sharp rise of a hill some fifty feet from the frenzied water, Hallie felt unsafe. A shiver raced through her. *This is the gentle river I saw in the distance earlier in the day now grown as dark as the skies above.*

Suddenly, something moved in the distance, catching Hallie's eye. *There, standing no more than a few feet from the churning water was Mary!* Amid the fury of nature exploding all around her, she seemed particularly small and frail.

"Mary!" Hallie shouted, her voice almost lost in the din of the storm.

All the fear that had gripped her seemed to vanish in the face of the danger now facing her friend. Hurrying down the slope of the hill, she managed to take only a couple of steps before one of her boots slipped in the soupy mud, sending her crashing down hard onto the ground.

"Ow!" she cried, the pain sharp and stinging.

She'd landed hard on one arm; her face struck the ground, and mud caked her blouse and streaked her cheek. With a filthy hand, she pushed her hair out of her eyes and stared intently at Mary, fearful that she would vanish into the storm. Clawing up fistfuls of rainwater and mud, Hallie pushed herself back to her feet and continued forward.

"Mary! Don't move, Mary!"

Hallie halted ten feet from the other woman, the pain in her side hot and raw, her breath coming in ragged gasps, her heart trying to leap out of her chest. She was about to speak, to try to calm Mary, when another bolt of lightning split the sky, immediately followed by a peal of thunder that seemed to shake the very air. Even as she cringed at the sound, Hallie's eyes never left the other woman. Mary was like a wild animal whose eyes were wide and haunches tense, desperate for any means of escape.

"Mary," Hallie began, trying to be calm and soothing. "You need to step away from there and come back with me to the wagon. We need to go back to Pearl and—"

"There ain't no goin' back," Mary cut in, her faint voice somehow audible through all the noise of the storm. Hearing her speak was almost startling; it had been days since Hallie had heard any sounds other than sobs or moans. "If I go back now, he'll kill me . . . he'll kill me and you and Pearl."

"No, no, Mary," Hallie said, shaking her head. "We won't take you back to Chester. We're taking you *away* from him! We left Whiskey Bend to find a new place to live, a place where we can start over, a place for all of us!"

"There's nowhere to hide."

"I won't let him find you. I promise!"

Mary shook her head violently. Hallie couldn't be certain, but she thought she could see tears streaming down the young woman's face. "You don't understand what kind a man he is. He ain't never gonna let me get away! He ain't never gonna rest until he finds me and then when he does . . ."

"Mary, please," Hallie pleaded, reaching out her hand and taking one small step forward. "Whatever danger we face, we'll face it together. You, Pearl, and I will take care of one another and make sure that we're safe. That's what friends do—they watch out for each other."

For the briefest of moments, it seemed to Hallie that Mary would accept her offer, but then another round of lightning and thunder exploded around them and all Hallie's hope vanished. Mary's mood changed. Stepping closer to the edge of the raging river, she said, "If I ain't around, maybe the two of you'll be safe."

"Don't do it, Mary! Please! For the love—"

Before Hallie could say another word or even take a step toward her friend, Mary walked into the dark water and was gone. The force of the swift current grabbed hold and pulled her in, tossing her about as if she were nothing more than a toy in a tornado.

Hallie screamed, "Mary!" She dashed along the riverbank, mindful of her footing, yet desperate to keep Mary in sight. She watched in horror as the woman's head bobbed once or twice on the brackish surface before the river's flow pulled her into the dark night and she was lost. Through it all, Hallie never heard her utter a single cry for help.

Mary was gone!

Chapter Nine

ELI STOOD IN the saddle, peering out into the depths of the storm. All around him, thick sheets of rain came down from the dark clouds churning above. Water poured off the brim of his hat, further blocking his vision. His mood was as miserable as the weather; he was soaked to the bone, and he grumbled with the same deep base as the thunder.

"Wallach should be out here with us," he growled.

Hank chuckled beside his nephew. As another long tongue of lightning shot across the sky, he gave his buckskin horse a reassuring pat on its thick neck. "You know as well as I do that that boy couldn't find his ass if he was usin' both hands," he said. "If he'd come out here with us, we'd have ended up searchin' for him."

"Then what the hell good is he?"

"Wallach ain't too bright, but I ain't never seen no one

that could shoe a horse or handle a brandin' iron any better than him," Hank explained. "Replacin' him wouldn't be no simple matter—that's the honest truth."

"Too bad he hasn't enough brains to keep the gate shut!"

"Yeah, it's a mite too bad," Hank echoed with a noncommittal shrug.

Eli grunted in anger. As the summer storm descended upon the Morgan family ranch, all the hands, himself included, went about latching the doors, buttoning down every window, and securing the animals. Strong weather was a common occurrence and their precautions had become routine. As he watched the dark clouds billow ever closer, he felt that they would ride the storm out with little damage.

With the coming of the crackling lightning and echoing thunder splitting the sky, several of the cattle became spooked and burst forth from an unlocked pen; three head were unaccounted for. By the time the loss was discovered, hours had passed, but the gale still raged on in all of its fury. It had been Tom Wallach's responsibility to make sure that the gates were locked. Even though Eli had wanted nothing more than to punch the man squarely in the jaw, he and Hank grabbed a pair of mounts and sped off after their missing property. They'd been at it for over an hour but had yet to find a single head.

"They couldn't have gotten this far from the ranch," Eli observed. Their search had brought them to the north edge of their land, a gently sloping valley of elms and maples and abundant game, all of it laced by the Cummings River.

"If it weren't for this storm, I'd agree with you," Hank said, spitting a wad of tobacco onto the muddy ground. "But they'll keep movin' like all the thunder and lightning was on their tail!"

"Could they have gone farther down the valley?"

"Probably," the old rancher mused, rubbing a hand over his stubble-covered chin. "My guess is they'll keep right on runnin' until somethin' stops 'em, and the only thing in these parts that'll do that is the river."

"Then let's go take a look. Maybe we'll get lucky." With a sharp snap of his horse's reins, Eli sped off down the hill, with Hank right behind him, mud flying from their mounts' hooves.

As much as he grumbled about being out in the storm, there was a part of Eli that wouldn't have chosen to be anywhere else. In the two weeks since he'd returned, he found that life back on the ranch was as comfortable to slip back into as an old warm coat. Even though he and his mother were no closer to breaking the thick distrust between them, and he still hadn't managed to get used to Abe's transformation, he rediscovered his love for the hard work that had filled his younger years. Spending the days alongside Hank had its own reward; nearly every evening, after another day of sweaty work, they hunkered down on the long porch, shared a smoke and a drink, and talked long into the night.

Still, the matter of Caleb's death dogged him, tugging at the back of his mind. It was hard for him to be back home among the familiar sights and sounds, all the memories of a youth shared with his two brothers. He kept expecting to see Caleb's bright smile and hear his quick laugh. He felt the bitter sting of loss all over again. Soon, he knew he would have to go to town and start asking questions, to try to learn what had actually happened.

But not now . . . now I have to find those damn steers!

Strong gusts of wind tugged insistently at his coat, and Eli scanned the ground as his horse rode hard into the storm's teeth. Even with the intermittent flashes of lightning, it was hard to see much of anything. Hope occasionally rose in his chest when he glimpsed a shadow here and there, but closer inspection revealed them to be nothing more than a large bush, a solitary rock, or simply a trick of the night.

"It they were struck by lightning, we could at least butcher them—if we could find their carcasses, that is," he said over his shoulder.

"Let's go on down the valley," Hank said and led the way.

They rode the valley's slope until the ground began to level. Tall clumps of trees were lit by the lightning flashes, their boughs bent and swaying in the wind and rain. Slowly, a roaring noise made itself heard over the wind, growing louder as they trotted along.

"That'll be the Cummings," Eli said.

"Probably as plump and overflowin' as a fat lady's bosom." Hank whistled. "If'n any of them cattle made it this far, there's as good a chance as any that that'll be where we'll find 'em."

As they approached the river, the noise of the rushing water became deafening. Eli guided his horse to a small rise that had an unobstructed view of the Cummings River between two large clumps of oak trees and brought the animal to a halt, his uncle alongside.

"Would you look at that." Hank nodded. "Angrier than a hornet's nest."

"I don't know if I've ever seen hornets *that* angry."

Normally a calm river laced with a bounty of fish, its cool, clear blue waters inviting and fresh, the Cummings was now as ominous as the storm that had riled it to a frenzy. Amid the whipping wind and heavy rain, Eli couldn't see all the way across its swollen breadth, but he knew that the whole river was in turmoil; frothy peaks of brackish water were crashing together, pulling anything that they could reach into the river's fatal grasp.

If anything were to fall in . . .

Eli frowned. "Let's hope that none of those cattle managed to make it this far, 'cause if they did, they're as good as dead. All it'd take was one bad step and they'd be miles downstream before they knew what happened."

"Then let's hope they ain't as dumb as the fella that forgot to lock their pen," Hank said. With a click of his tongue, he prodded his horse forward, talking over his shoulder. "It won't hurt us to walk up and down this here shore for a bit to find out."

For the next half hour, the two ranchers rode along the riverbank, ever mindful of where their horses stepped. For as far as the storm would allow him to see, Eli looked into every crevice; peered behind every upturned tree; and hoped for some sign, some movement, to reveal the missing cattle. He was just about to suggest that they give up when something up ahead caught his attention.

At first, he thought it was yet another trick of the lightning, showing a dark shape that became a boulder or a bush under closer inspection. *But this was different . . .* Near the waterline, far closer than he would have ventured, there appeared to be some*one.* As he stared through the inky darkness, waiting to see if he wasn't just imagining things, he saw the person stumble and fall to the ground, then rise slowly on shaky legs. Eli's heart pounded hard against his ribs as his heels dug into his horse's flanks.

"Come on!" he shouted to his uncle before charging down to the figure.

Bringing the horse to a quick stop, he sprang out of the saddle, held steady in the muddy ground, and was beside the figure. *He could hardly believe his eyes.* It was a woman, her face and upper body caked dark with grime, her eyes wide as saucers in the scant light of the storm. Her clothes stuck to her tenaciously. When she took sight of him, her small body flinched, recoiling as if with shock.

"Miss?" he asked tentatively. "Miss? Are you all right? What are you doin' out here in the storm?"

She seemed to take him in cautiously, her feet shuffling quickly backward in the sucking mud. Fear was apparent on her face as plainly as the words written in a book. Her mouth opened and closed; but if there were any sounds coming out, they were lost to Eli's ears in the din of the pounding rain and the never ending roar of the river.

"Miss? What are you doin' out here?" he repeated. "Are you hurt?"

"It—it—it's . . ." she stammered, still skittering away from him. "It's Mary . . ."

"Mary? Is your name Mary?"

"Sh-sh-she's—she's gone—gone into the—the river—"

From behind him, Eli could hear Hank pulling up his mount and leaping to the ground. As another sharp crack of lightning lit the sky, sending a shiver of fear through the woman as she moved even further backward, his uncle moved up beside him.

"Sweet Christmas!" the older rancher exclaimed. "What in tarnation is that gal doin' out here! I can understand why them cattle ain't got enough brains to stay out of this weather, but why a person would choose to be here don't make no goddamn sense!"

"Keep it quiet!" Eli chided his uncle. "She's scared enough as it is without you going on with such nonsense." Turning his attention back to the woman, he added, "I can't tell if she's been hurt or not, but from what she's said, I think her name's Mary."

The woman began to shake her head vigorously. Eli couldn't be certain, but he thought that there were tears running down her face. When she spoke, her voice was cracking with emotion. "It—it's Hallie. My—my name . . . is Hallie," she struggled. "Mary—Mary is my friend . . . and—and I don't—I don't know where—where she is . . ."

"What're you doin' out in this storm, little gal?" Hank asked.

Hallie remained silent. Eli could see the hesitation in her eyes as she took the two men in, weighing whether she wanted to tell them what they wished to know. She was skittish, uncertain of what to say or do. Something horrible had happened to her, something so bad that she wasn't even willing to trust those who were willing to help.

Eli took a small step forward and held out his hand to her. "Tell us what happened, Hallie," he said as soothingly as he could. "There's nothing more for you to be afraid of now. You're safe. We'll do everything we can to help you find your friend."

"You'll help me?" Hallie asked uncertainly.

"I'm Eli Morgan and this is my uncle, Hank."

"Eli," she repeated slowly, as if she were looking over his name for some blemish or mark that would tell its true nature. In that moment, he knew that it wasn't just the storm that had frightened her but something else. Still, he stood fast, never letting his offered hand waver. Finally, when she had found the answer to her unspoken question, she stepped forward, reached out, and placed her trembling hand in his, her trust given.

"Tell me what happened, Hallie," he repeated as he held her hand gently; he was surprised by how warm and soft it was, even with all the rain and mud that caked her skin.

"We'd—we'd been traveling for days . . . when the storm started," she began, her voice growing stronger and steadier with every word. "We made it to shelter, but then I realized that Mary was gone! I—I looked for her . . . but then when I found her, she kept running away from me. I ran and I ran but I couldn't catch her! I followed her all the way to the river . . . but then . . . but then . . . Oh, I can't believe this has happened!"

"It's all right, Hallie," Eli coaxed her. "Go on."

"What happened at the river, girl?" Hank prodded.

"I tried to tell her . . . that he wouldn't find us, but she wouldn't listen!" Hallie cried. Her hand shivered in Eli's palm. "She took a step . . . a step into the water and then she was gone!"

"Into the water?" Eli asked. "She went into the river?"

"That's why I'm looking for her!" Hallie pleaded. "I've been running along the bank . . . trying to find any sign of where she might be! Please, help me! Please, help find Mary!"

"If she's in this here river," Hank began, his arm sweeping out over the expanse of raging water, "there ain't gonna be nobody to find."

"We'll look," Eli interjected, cutting the older cowboy off. He knew what his uncle was saying was the truth; it was impossible to believe that anyone who fell into the Cummings River during a storm could survive. *You'd have a better chance of surviving a lightning hit!* But as he looked into Hallie's soft eyes, the way that they implored him to do something, *anything*, he knew that he would have to try.

"With the way this storm is goin', she could be miles from here," Hank said.

"We have to look."

For a moment, it seemed as if Hank wanted to protest the point some more, but then a grin broke out across his wizened face and he gave Hallie a nod. "Reckon you're right. Who knows, maybe we'll even stumble across them wayward cattle we're lookin' for."

Eli was about to turn to his horse to begin the search when an insistent tug on his hand made him stop. Hallie stared hard into his face, large tears welling in her eyes. He was struck by the realization that even now, her face streaked with mud and her hair disheveled from the storm, there was a true beauty about her.

"Thank you, Eli," she said.

He held Hallie's shaking hand for a moment longer before releasing his grip, mounting his horse, speaking to Hank for a moment, and then disappearing into the depths of the storm.

The sounds of the pounding rain and the roaring of the river were so overwhelming, so complete, that Eli felt as if he were deaf. As he strained to hear any sign of the missing woman, he felt covered in a blanket of sound, a cover that wouldn't allow any competing noise.

His uncle and he had agreed that Eli would travel downstream while Hank would take Hallie with him and move upstream in hope that the traumatized woman had simply walked past her friend. Either way, Eli knew that it was a long shot. They had better odds of finding the missing cattle.

"This is hopeless," he muttered to himself.

The thought of disappointing Hallie stung. The sight of her, distraught, was an image he could not get out of his head. He could still hear her voice imploring him to help. Absently, he rubbed his fingers together as if he could still feel the touch of her soft hand in his own.

Ahead of him, the river bent sharply to the east and disappeared from sight. The water had come up so far over the banks that many of the trees that normally lined the shore were several feet deep in the muddy soup; it was as if a cemetery had been planted along the river's shoreline. Some trees had become weakened by the flood, so unsteady in the river's ever-strengthening grasp that they had toppled over into the flow, their leafy branches tossed this way and that.

He was about to turn from the river, to head back from where he had come to deliver the sad news to Hallie that her friend was gone, when a long fork of lightning lit the sky like fireworks on the Fourth of July. The show of nature was so forceful that even the sound of the storm seemed to pause in awe.

"Shit fire and save matches," Eli swore, then the words froze in his throat.

As the last tongue of lightning disappeared from the sky, Eli's gaze locked on the image that had been revealed to him; there, draped limply over the branches of a tall tree that had fallen into the Cummings River, was a woman's body, her long hair trailing down into the water.

Chapter Ten

From where he stood, Eli couldn't be certain whether the woman was alive or dead. Her body was draped over the branches facedown, but it looked as if her head might be out of the water. Both her legs and one arm were submerged in the filthy liquid, the other arm wrapped around the tree limb. She clung to the branches upon which she had been caught, her long hair floating on the relentless flow.

"What the devil?"

Indecision racked his body and mind. There was little doubt that this was Mary, the woman he had set out to find. *But now that I've found her, how in hell am I going to get her out of the river?* Shouting out to her would be futile; it was obvious that she was in no condition to help free herself from the leafy, waterlogged prison in which she was trapped.

His first thought was to head back upstream and find Hank. The two of them would have a much better chance of getting her out before she drowned, but any minute the river could snatch her away and send her hurtling further downstream to certain death. Also, he had no idea how badly she was hurt; the pounding that the river had given her might have resulted in broken bones or other injuries. There wasn't time to get help. Even one minute too long might make the difference between life and death.

Dismounting, Eli moved cautiously toward the bank of the swollen river. Near the tree upon which Mary clung, other trees had met a similar fate; oaks, ash, and maples of all sizes lay broken and dying. But in their demise Eli found hope; because of the way in which they had fallen, their trunks and branches formed a sort of dam, pushing away the heaviest flow of the river. Although the current was still swift and strong, Eli estimated that there was a chance he could reach the woman.

Retrieving a long length of rope from his saddle, Eli knotted one end of it to his waist. At first, he thought of tying the other end to one of the still-upright trees but decided otherwise. *If its brothers had already fallen prey to the predatory river, what would keep any tree safe?* Instead, he secured the opposite end of rope to the pommel of his horse's saddle. Gently, he patted the black and tan's long face. Of one thing he *was* certain; this strong animal would do everything in its power to keep from entering the water.

"Don't let me down, boy," he said softly.

Tentatively, he moved to the river's edge and cautiously put one boot into the black water. With that one step, he found himself up to his knee in the flood wash. Even though the weather was warm, the water was shockingly cold. Once he was sure of his footing, he tested the rope's strength with a tug and began to move forward.

Although he was only a few feet from the shore, Eli still felt the tug of the strong river current at his boots. He had to move slowly, testing each and every step for fear that his feet would fly out from under him and the Cummings would attempt to carry him away.

With his every step, the dark water grew deeper and more threatening; the water rose from the middle of his thighs to his waist and then up to his chest in only a matter of seconds. To the elements, he was just another potential victim, another thing to be uprooted. Placing a hand on the wrinkled trunk of one of the fallen trees, Eli calmed his racing heart before taking another step.

"Hang on, Mary," he whispered through chattering teeth. "I'm coming."

Using one of the fallen trees for guidance, Eli positioned himself away from the strongest flow of the Cummings's current. He had entered the raging river slightly upstream from where the girl was pressed against the tree trunk by the swiftly moving water. Now, at the end of one tree, with Mary's body only about ten feet away, he could see that he would have to surrender himself to the storm-crazed water if he wished to reach her.

"Damn it all," he cursed.

Before him, in the short expanse of water he would have to cross, the brown-black liquid rushed past. In its grasp he saw leaves, branches, even what looked to be part of a door. It would be tricky to get over that expanse of water. But he knew he had to do it.

Quickly checking the strength of the knot around his waist, Eli gave one look back to where his horse stood on the shore before pushing off the tree and plunging into the roiling river. His hat flew off his head like an eagle diving after a mouse; it seemed to be above him, beside him in the water, and then lost from sight all in the time it took to take one gasping breath. He pushed and kicked and fought to cross the chasm of water, but he still felt alone and helpless, ready to vanish from sight forever.

"Ughh." He coughed as a mouthful of the river caught in his throat.

Suddenly yet thankfully, his arm latched on to a tree branch, and he held to it with the tenacity of a child to its mother's breast. Drawing a quick breath, he blinked through the storm and found that he had reached his intended destination none the worse for wear. Even though it had taken only seconds to cross the heaviest flow, his muscles ached from the exertion.

To his right lay Mary. As he inched his way closer,

he was struck by the fact that she was far more the doll tossed by the storm than he could ever have been. Her tiny body seemed to float on the water anchored only by the arm she had wrapped around the tree branch. He wasn't sure if she was conscious. Her face was turned toward him and, even in the scant light of the storm, Eli could see the blood that oozed from her hairline, the rest of her skin as pale as porcelain.

In that moment, Eli found his thoughts returning again to Hallie. It would be hard to tell her that her friend had drowned. Pushing further along the tree, Eli worked his way to Mary's side. Here, the incessant pounding of the water battered his back and shoulders. Through it all, Mary didn't move or make a sound, her hair and clothes soaked wet and clinging to her skin like bark to a tree. Eli could see no rise and fall of breath. Softly yet firmly, he placed a hand on the woman's shoulder and gave her a gentle shake. There was no response.

"Mary," he called into her ear. "We've got to get out of here, Mary."

Still no answer.

Gently, Eli placed his hand against the young woman's cheek. He had hoped to feel something, the warmth of life or the faint pounding of blood still pumping through her veins, but he found only a coldness that, even in the chilling water, sent a shiver through his body. He knew that *if* she were still alive, Mary needed to get out of the water immediately.

Sliding one muscled arm around her thin waist, Eli held tight and pulled the unconscious woman steadily toward him. With her body as limp as a rag doll and her clothing soaked through with water, she was far heavier than he had imagined and he strained hard with the effort. Still clinging tenaciously to the fallen tree, Eli slowly turned her in the raging river until he grasped her beneath her arms, her chest against his, her head nestled into the crook of his neck so as to keep her face out of the water. Through it all, Mary never moved a muscle or offered a single word of protest, as helpless in Eli's arms as she had been at the mercy of the storm.

"Now for the hard part," he muttered into Mary's hair.

Eli knew that it would be impossible to make it safely back across the quick moving stretch of river he had crossed to reach Mary. It had been hard enough without the added weight of an unconscious woman. Once he let go of the tree branches, they would be at the mercy of the Cummings. He would have to trust in the strength of the rope and then pray.

With a deep breath, Eli clasped both arms around Mary and pushed off into the water. As if it were a starving dog pouncing upon wounded prey, the river latched on to him and began to toss him this way and that. They traveled swiftly in the current until being yanked to a sudden halt. The rope dug into the flesh of Eli's sides but held tight. Blood hammered furiously in his ears as he struggled to keep both their heads above water. As they bobbed and churned, he peered toward the shore and saw his faithful horse struggling to hold his ground, his hooves digging into the soft earth of the bank.

With an anchor of sorts on the shore, Eli knew that they would move like the pendulums he had seen while in the military. The force of the river would steadily buffer against them, constantly pushing their bodies closer to the shallower, ever-safer waters from which he had come. It seemed to take forever, but his patience bore fruit as the waters began to slowly calm and he was able to put one foot into the muddy riverbed and hold steady.

Slowly, carrying Mary's limp body, Eli trudged toward the shore. Every muscle of his body ached with a ferocity the likes of which he had never known; his hardest working days driving cattle on the Morgan family ranch paled in comparison. Still, he refused to surrender. Even if she were dead, he would bring Mary back to the friend who sought to find her.

The final twenty feet were like walking a mile. Summoning the last ounces of his strength, Eli pulled Mary from the murky water and laid her down on the shore. As his horse whinnied beside him, he barely managed to undo the biting rope around his waist before crashing down into the muddy earth himself. Spent and exhausted, he lacked the energy even to check on Mary's condition, to verify that there was indeed nothing he could do for her. Eli was able to take only a couple of ragged breaths before he heard the sound of a rifle being cocked nearby and words that made his heart beat even faster than it had while in the river.

"What the hell are you doin' with Mary, you son of a bitch? You took her out of the wagon, didn't you?"

Through the mud and water that danced across his eyes, Eli looked up into the face of a slightly older woman, her lined mouth pulled back in a snarl, her eyes dancing as wildly as the lightning in the sky. Her clothes, while strange and colorful, were as wet as his own. A worn rifle was held tightly in her hands, its barrel never wavering from his head.

"I asked you what you was doin' with Mary!" she demanded again.

"Well, what in the hell does it look like? I just pulled her out of the river." Eli's exhaustion made him short of patience. His time in the Cummings had overwhelmed his ability to speak in a decent tone of voice.

"Bullshit!" the woman shouted as another song and dance of lightning and thunder buffered the stormy evening. "Don't you dare lie to me! All you done is recover your prize! Spiritin' her outta the wagon weren't as easy as you planned, now was it?"

Try as he might, Eli couldn't make heads or tails of what the woman was saying. He was being accused of an offense he couldn't even begin to understand; he had risked his life to save this woman and was now being blamed for putting her in the river in the first place!

"I don't know . . . what the hell you're talking about!" he managed to say between ragged gasps of air that were cool against his burning lungs.

"How much is Chester payin' you for this?" she barked, ignoring him.

"Chester?" he echoed. "Who in the hell is Chester?"

Before he could say another word, the storm was split by a thunderous blast, and the muddy earth in front of him exploded in a shower of dirt. Even with the storm still raging around him, the noise was earsplitting. He looked up to see a tendril of smoke rising from the rifle's barrel.

"Don't you play dumb with me!" the woman barked. The end of the weapon never wavered, never moved from its target—him! "I'd just as soon shoot you as look at you!"

Eli didn't doubt her words for a moment. The danger he'd been in when he'd entered the raging river was nothing compared to what he faced now. The only means he had of defending himself was the rifle slung across the saddle of his horse; he was far too exhausted to make a move for it and, even if he hadn't just survived the Cummings, he knew that she'd shoot him down like a dog before he'd managed half the distance.

"I've never heard of this Chester fellow," Eli said as calmly as he could, his eyes never leaving the rifle. "I was out in this storm with my uncle, looking for our lost cattle, when we came across a woman. She was upset, searching for a friend of hers. She said her name was Hallie."

At the mention of Hallie's name, the woman's stony visage seemed to crack. She peered over the stock of the rifle, confusion and indecision written on her face. "What did you do with her?"

"Nothing," Eli shouted. "I just told you. My uncle and I found her walking sick with worry along the shore of the river. She told us that her friend had fallen into the water and had vanished from sight. Hallie went with my uncle to search upstream and I went the opposite way. I found the girl lying unconscious out on the end of one of those fallen trees. There wasn't time to get help, so I went in for her myself."

The woman stared hard at Eli, as if she were a city banker weighing nuggets of gold, trying to figure out what his words were worth. Time seemed to stand still as she stared intently at the man lying on the ground before her, her jaw knotting and unknotting as she thought. Slowly, the rifle barrel lowered, and he sighed with relief. But before he could utter a grateful word, there was a rustle in the bushes, which parted to reveal his uncle and Hallie.

"Pearl!" Hallie shouted and ran forward. "You found her."

"I didn't—he did." She jerked her head toward Eli.

Gathering her younger friend in her arms, Pearl held Hallie tight. "Oh, honey! I didn't find no sign of Mary and I'd just come back toward the river when I run into this here fella fishin' her out of the water. I thought for sure that he was one of Chester's cronies come to spirit her back to Whiskey Bend!"

"I thought I'd lost you both," Hallie sobbed.

"Thank God, we got Mary back."

As the two women rushed to where Mary lay on the ground, Hank hurried over to where Eli sat and knelt beside his nephew. Pushing back his hat, he wiped his brow with one wrinkled hand and looked over to where Mary's body lay. "I see you had better luck lookin' than we did." He sighed. "Although I reckon you ain't none too pleased with what you found."

As Eli stared at his uncle through the rain, he remembered the cold feel of Mary's skin when he had first touched her. *Surely, she must be dead! No one could possibly spend that much time in the Cummings and hope to still be alive.* Still, he wasn't certain. The thought that the girl could still be alive suddenly raced across his mind, and he found himself scrambling to his feet—sore body be damned—and hurrying over to where she lay upon her back in the grass.

Mary's eyes were closed, wet hair and dirt plastered to her face; she looked to be sleeping peacefully. Eli Morgan was certainly no doctor, but he'd spent enough time in the army to know how to discover if death had arrived. Placing one hand above the woman's left breast, he felt past the cold of her blouse and the skin beneath, searching for a sign that her heart still beat.

"I'm afraid there ain't gonna be much of a point in all of that," Hank said as he stepped in behind him. "I've seen about the same on calves that have been caught unawares in a flood."

Anger flared for an instant in Eli's chest and his words were harsh. "Hush that talk! It's hard enough to hear through all this without you babbling on!"

Hank nodded. "I reckon you're right about that, son."

Eli became aware that Hallie and Pearl were beside him. Neither of the women said a word, although both of them were clearly racked by emotion. As he looked up into Hallie's tear-filled eyes, he was struck by the thought that he never wanted to see her cry again.

"Is she gone?" Hallie asked, but he couldn't bring himself to answer.

Even as the storm continued to rage and pound the earth all around him, Eli searched for some sign, some faint pulse that would tell him that Mary still lived. All around him was noise; especially loud was the pounding of his own heart. Still, he kept on. He wasn't going to quit until he was sure that all hope was lost.

He felt something under his fingers.

At first, he worried that he had imagined it, something that he had wanted so badly that it had become real. But as he continued to hold his hand in place, he felt another beat and then, after a long pause, yet another. He couldn't deny that it was real and that that particular truth had meaning.

Mary was still alive!

Chapter Eleven

As the long night gave way to dawn, exhaustion weighed on Eli as heavily as iron shackles. The last several hours had offered no relief. As soon as they had been certain that Mary was still alive, the women had stripped their friend of her wet clothes and wrapped her in a dry blanket. They'd laid her on some evergreen boughs placed close to the fire that Hank had built in a clearing back from the river under an overhang. There they had waited for the rain to finally let up. When it had, they'd loaded Mary into the wagon and headed for the ranch.

Now Eli pushed the team of horses forward. They had been riding hard for over an hour, froth and foam covering the mounts' mouths. The storm had moved farther to the north and east. In the distance, a thick band of dark clouds still stretched across the sky, while above them and ahead only a couple of dark bruises remained to mark the passing of nature's fury.

Eli shivered. He'd tried to gain warmth beside the fire, but it seemed that his best efforts had been for naught. Even with a lukewarm wind blowing, a sign that with the passing of the rain it would be another scorching summer day, a damp chill pervaded his body. Beside him in the wagon seat, Hallie sat huddled in a blanket.

Eli stole a glance into the back of the wagon, even as the wheels pitched and rolled over the rocky ground. Mary lay on a layer of blankets they'd arranged in the wagon bed, Pearl hovered over her, whispering words of care and concern. The girl had improved little since he'd managed to pull her from the swollen river. *It was a miracle she had made it this far.*

"Is it much farther?" Hallie asked.

Eli turned to her and took in her face and all its details. Even in the early morning light, he swore that he could see for miles in her eyes, eyes that were clouded with weariness. Her arms hugged the blanket tightly to her. She was small but strong, a woman a man would want to take care of, to cherish and call his own.

"We're almost there." Ahead, he could see the familiar signs of the Morgan ranch come into view; the gnarled oak that he and his brothers had spent hours climbing as boys and then the splintered fence post he'd used as a target for his rifle. "The ranch is just up and over the next couple of ridges. We'll be there soon."

"Oh, thank goodness. I'm so worried."

"As soon as we manage to get her settled, I'll fetch the doctor. He'll know what to do," he said, trying to give it a weight of confidence. "But I still don't reckon just why she'd have gotten into that water."

"It—it was because of . . . a man," Hallie explained hesitantly.

"Her fella?"

"He thought himself to be." She nodded. "But he was not the sort of man to treat her right. He was . . . so cruel to her that she left. We were afraid he might manage to kill her."

"Couldn't you have gone to the law?" he asked.

"There isn't any law to be found in Whiskey Bend," she answered with a stiff shake of her head. "Not the kind that does right. The sheriff was just about as rotten as any of the lawbreakers."

As he listened to Hallie's words, a strange feeling washed over Eli. In that moment, all he wanted was to tell this woman that she and her friends would be safe at the Morgan ranch. *Safe*. The fact that he cared so deeply was a sensation that was entirely new to him. But at the same time, he didn't know if she would be made welcome. His mother was unpredictable. *Surely she wouldn't refuse shelter to someone so clearly in need!* Swallowing deeply, he tightened his grip on the reins, snapped the leather straps, and pushed the team forward.

Hank rode his mount beside the wagon, leading Eli's

black and tan. He was the first to sight the Morgan ranch. "I was beginnin' to wonder if'n I was ever gonna lay eyes on this here ranch ever again," Hank shouted. "But I guess even this here old fool's prayers can be answered!"

As they rounded a small bend, the Morgan ranch came into view. Even with all the difficulties Eli had had since his return, this was still his home. Each and every thing that he saw was a welcome sight: the long ranch house, smoke pouring from the chimney; the cattle pens, with the sounds and smells that only heads of steer can bring; the barn, its eastern wall already gleaming wet in the early morning sun.

"Is this where you live?" Hallie asked as her eyes took it all in.

"Yes. This is my family's ranch," he replied. "We'll get Mary into the house and in bed and give her something hot to eat and drink."

"I don't know how to thank you."

"Not necessary," he answered and meant it.

Hank led the way around the cattle pens and brought his mount to a stop in front of the house. Eli positioned the wagon before the steps and hopped down. The two men were lowering the wagon gate when the front door of the ranch house banged open and angry steps thudded across the porch.

"Just what do you think you're doing?" Adele Morgan's voice carried shrilly in the quiet morning. As Eli turned to face his mother, her face mirrored the passed storm: Her graying hair was piled high on her head like the most menacing of clouds, her jaw was set with the rigidity of thunder, and her eyes flashed with the anger of lightning.

"This woman was hurt over at the Cummin—" Eli began.

"I nearly worried myself sick waiting up the entire night for the two of you to return," Mrs. Morgan interrupted. "Only the Good Lord Himself could have known what was happening to you in that storm. Then, instead of bringing home the missing cattle like you were supposed to do, you show up here with these women! Were you carousing all night?"

"Carousing?" Pearl shouted, her dander rising.

"We don't have time for this," Eli said with exasperation. Nodding to Hank, he reached into the wagon and gently pulled the blanket holding Mary's limp form toward him. He was just beginning to lift her when his mother's words rang out.

"You will not bring that woman into my house!" she declared loudly.

"You can't mean that!" Eli barked, the words exploding from his chest.

"I most certainly can! And I do!" his mother answered him pointedly. "I am not the sort of woman that just lets any harlot, split tail, or dance hall whore come traipsing through her front door."

Eli could not believe the words that were coming from

his mother's lips. He knew her to be a stubborn and difficult woman; when her dander was up, she could be as unmovable as the most obstinate of mules! But this—this was something he would never have thought her capable of.

"Are you callin' my friend a whore?" Pearl yelled, her face a crimson mask.

"Pearl, please!" Hallie pleaded, stepping in front of the older woman as her friend took a menacing step toward the stairs. She knew Pearl to be willing to resort to violence to protect those that she cared for; the bullet lodged in Chester's leg was testament to that fact.

"We don't have to take this shit from her!"

"Yes, we do," Hallie explained to her friend tearfully, her voice choking with worry and fear. "Mary is badly hurt! All the time she spent in that cold water could be the death of her! It will be if we don't get her to a warm bed and a doctor to her side. There isn't time to get her anywhere else—it has to be here!"

"But that old bag ain't gonna let us in!"

"Adele, please," Hank interjected, trying to reason with his sister. "What these gals is sayin' is nothin' but the out-and-out truth. If'n we don't get her to warmth quick, it's gonna be too late—fetchin' the doc or otherwise. It ain't the right and Christian thing to keep her out here."

Adele's face twisted in anger. "Don't you dare talk to me about the right way of doing things! I haven't forgiven you for sending that telegram to Eli and dragging him back into our lives. You never have learned not to meddle in other's affairs!"

"Be reasonable, Adele," Hank continued.

"I don't want to hear your lame excuses!"

"Please, ma'am," Hallie said, stepping slowly forward. "I realize that this is a great imposition, but my friend is awful sick. She needs care. As soon as she is well enough to travel, we'll leave."

"Just stop yourself right there, missy," Adele interrupted. It certainly would have taken a hard person to not have been moved by Hallie's words, but Adele's stony expression never once softened. "You don't need to worry about imposing upon me because you won't be! You just hop yourself back up in that wagon and drive it off of this here ranch. This is my land and I say who is going to be on it and who isn't!"

Eli was stunned into silence. A roaring anger raged through him. It burned so brightly, so fiercely, that it threatened to consume him. At that moment, he didn't give a good goddamn what his mother's wishes were. He was taking Mary into the house and that was the end of it! He was just about to make his demands known when the front door opened for a second time.

"What is all this commotion?"

Abe Morgan strolled out onto the porch to stand beside his mother. Even after a few weeks back home, Eli was still in a state of shock at how much his brother resembled the former president. The surprise was especially great now, at this early hour. Abe wore a black, double-breasted suit with buttons that shone brightly; his thumbs were planted firmly in the coat pockets. The thick beard that covered his jawline but not his upper lip was trim and neat. Even the way that he carried himself was formal, presidential.

"What in the hell?" Pearl exclaimed.

"I'm afraid I'll have to ask you to be a bit more cautious with your language, young lady," Abe reprimanded her. "I come from people who, in their backwoods lives, were prone to speaking with a loose tongue, but I can assure you, it's certainly not very becoming as you get older. I dare say it's a habit you should rid yourself of."

For a long moment, all was silent. The strangeness of what they had seen, of Abe's sudden appearance, seemed too great for Hallie or Pearl to comprehend, let alone to give voice to their thoughts. In the end, it was Abe who spoke again.

"Now what seems to be the matter?"

"My friend almost drowned," Hallie blurted, the spell of silence broken. She quickly moved over to where he stood at the edge of the long porch. "She fell into the river and has a cut on her head."

"That's quite enough!" Adele said angrily.

"Madam, please. I ask of you—" Abe began.

"I told you that I have made up my mind and that I expect you to leave!" Mrs. Morgan continued, deaf to her other son's words. "Just get back in that wagon and go!"

Abe held up a hand to silence her, his voice loud and firm. "Madam, if you please! It is my duty to hear all the concerns of the people. If I did not, what kind of president would I be? After all," he added with a gentle smile and a wink in Hallie's direction, "I can't rightly have them going back home and telling potential voters that I am deaf to their concerns, now can I?"

Mrs. Morgan looked as if she wished to protest further, her mouth opening and then quickly closing, but she held her tongue.

"Please continue, my dear," Abe prodded Hallie.

"My friend is badly hurt," she told him, hope leaping in her eyes at the thought of someone listening to her plight. "She fell into the river and would have drowned were it not for Eli braving the waters. If Mary doesn't see a doctor soon—"

"Mary?" Abe asked worriedly. "Did you say her name was Mary?"

"Why, yes, she—"

Without another word, Abe made his way down the steps and to the wagon's side. The look on his face was one of dread and confusion. Reaching into the wagon bed, he clutched one of Mary's limp hands to his own and held tight.

"Oh, my beloved Mary! My dear sweet, Mary!" he exclaimed. "What in the name of Heaven has happened to you?" Turning to Eli and Hank he ordered them to action. "Generals, Mary is in dire need of medical attention. The two of you bring her into her quarters at once before fetching the top army surgeon. Act now or you will find yourself in the guardhouse!"

Without hesitation, Eli and Hank lifted the unconscious woman from the wagon and carried her gently but quickly up the stairs. All the while, Abe stayed at their heels, offering words of encouragement and admonition. When they passed Mrs. Morgan, Eli never even glanced at her, his body coiled for any words of disagreement, but she gave none. Then they were in the house and out of sight. Finally, the older woman followed, slamming the door closed with a bang.

"What in the name of all the stars above just happened?" Pearl exclaimed. "That fella acts like he's Abraham Lincoln. On top of all of that, he seemed to think he knew who Mary was, but that just ain't possible!"

Suddenly, the answer dawned on Hallie. "He does know her . . . in a way."

"Don't tell me you done gone crazy too. How is that possible?"

"It's really quite simple," she said, turning to Pearl with a smile. She was suddenly thankful that she'd read as many history books as she had. "Mary was the name of President Lincoln's wife!"

An hour later, Eli walked into the barn with Hallie at his heels. As she entered, the sharp smell of manure and hay filled her nostrils and she absently rubbed her nose.

She took in all the sights: ranching instruments of many shapes and sizes that lined one wall, the airy loft piled high with straw, and the three stalls sunk deep into the back of the building. It was to these that Eli walked with a bedroll under each arm.

"I'm sorry my mother was so disagreeable," he said over his shoulder.

"We're the ones who should be apologizing," Hallie disagreed, "because we are imposing upon her. As soon as Mary is able, we'll do just as I told her and leave."

After all the fuss of their arrival, Mary had been safely put into a dry, warm bed in an unused room. They'd found her a loose gown and done their best to settle her. Pearl had begun to fret that Mary was running a fever. It was decided that the doctor should be fetched just as soon as possible.

While Mary was being cared for, Adele Morgan had silently smoldered. At her first chance, she had managed to make her demands known: Only Mary would be allowed to stay in the house, and the others would have to sleep in the barn. As long as Mary was to be provided for, Pearl and Hallie had no objections.

Through it all, Abe had steadfastly remained at Mary's bedside.

"I'm sorry I didn't warn you about my brother's . . . strange appearance," Eli continued. "It's hard enough for me to get used to. I can only imagine what you must have thought."

"I have to admit that I was startled," Hallie replied. "I couldn't quite believe what I was seeing. But as soon as he spoke, I knew that he was a good man. My grandmother used to say that what matters is a person's heart; and from the look of things, his is in the right place."

"Indeed it is."

Hallie paused for a moment, unsure whether she should give her thoughts voice before finally asking, "Has he always been this way? Has he always believed that he was Abraham Lincoln?"

"No, not always," Eli answered with a shrug. "But my older brother was the sort who would go his own way no matter what was expected of him. For that and many other things, I always looked up to him. He'd always loved school and books and had studied Lincoln. After his illness, he awoke believing he was the president . . . and does to this day."

They walked to the farthest stall in silence. Eli knelt and spread the bedrolls out beside each other. Fetching an old oil lamp from where it hung on the wall, he blew the dust off the cover and checked the wick.

"It's not much, but I reckon you'll be better off than you were in that rain."

"Thank you, Mr. Morgan," Hallie said, taking the offered lamp. "Thank you for all that you have done. Without you and your uncle, I don't know what would have happened to us. I do know that Mary wouldn't have a fighting chance, and for that I will always be grateful."

"I only did what was right," he said. "But you're welcome all the same and, please, call me Eli."

Even in the deep gloom of the barn, Hallie could see Eli's eyes drinking her in. As he continued to stare at her, she returned his gaze, not out of fear or even of shyness but because of something . . . different. In that moment, she was glad for the semidarkness, if for nothing more than to hide the deep crimson that had covered her face.

"Hank and I'll be going to Bison City to fetch the doctor for Mary," he explained. "If I were you, I'd try to get a little rest. You need it after all you've been through."

"I'll try," she answered.

As he turned and strode out of the barn, Hallie watched him. Her heart beat a little faster, and she could feel her breath quickening. One thing was painfully clear to her: In all her years, in all her travels, she was certain that she'd never met a man quite like Eli Morgan.

Chapter Twelve

Bɪsᴏɴ Cɪᴛʏ ʟᴏᴏᴋᴇᴅ as if it were bursting at the seams. Farm and freight wagons, buggies and saddle horses clogged the town's main thoroughfare. The boardwalks that fronted the stores were crowded with a motley lot: old mixed with young, tall with short, well dressed with those barely covered by an untorn stitch. Once the small town could have been described as calm and sedate; it was now busy and boisterous. As Eli brought his horse into town at a canter, he strained to find a face that he could recognize.

"Can it really have changed this much?"

"Like I done told ya before," Hank answered, "time has a way of changin' things."

"I reckon you're right."

Since the day he had arrived on the train, Eli had not set foot in Bison City; life on the ranch was complicated enough without confusing it any further with a visit *here*. Hank or one of the other ranch hands was always willing to go to town for supplies. But now that Eli had finally arrived, his eyes couldn't drink up the changes fast enough.

New houses nestled against new businesses, all of them populated by new folk going about their daily lives. Several of the sights were the same; Malek's Mercantile remained, although its banisters and awning were sagging and worn. But much was new, and everywhere he looked he saw something different. A barbershop, a saloon, and a telegraph office were all bunched together along a street that simply hadn't been there before.

"I'm beginning to think I don't know this place anymore."

"A lot of it you don't." Hank chuckled before pointing further on up the street. "Doc Holland's place is right where it's always been, just up the way and around the corner."

Eli gave his uncle a nod and urged his horse toward the doctor's office. He knew in the pit of his stomach just why he had hesitated to come to Bison City: Somewhere on these streets, his brother had died alone in a pool of blood. He couldn't help but glance down each narrow alley, wondering if that had been the spot or if it were the next. Anger and sickness raged in his gut. He had always felt that a part of him had died alongside Caleb that night; and now being here, where it had actually happened, the feeling was raw.

Doctor William Holland's office wasn't much—a two-room building fixed to the back end of the postal station just off the main street. Eli and Hank tied their horses to the hitching post and went in.

"Afternoon, Sawbones!" Hank hollered just inside the door.

Doc Holland peered over his shoulder at his visitors. He was thin as a reed, with thick-lensed glasses and sparse, white hair that he combed over his bald pate. William Holland had been the physician for Bison City for as long as Eli could remember. He was always seen about town dressed to the nines, in a suit coat and tightly knotted tie, his wife of forty years on his arm.

"We ain't bargin' in on nothin', is we?" Hank asked.

"As a matter of fact, gentlemen," Doc Holland replied. He stepped to the side to reveal a middle-aged man sitting on a long table, a look of excruciating pain written on his weathered face. Eli recognized him immediately; Jefferson Hughes had been a distant neighbor of the Morgans for years. A large man in both appetite and heart, Jefferson had been a close friend of Eli's father and had spent many a night at their kitchen table, laughing until his ample belly heaved and rolled. At the moment, there was no laughter in his eyes, his right arm cradled gingerly against his chest.

"Sweet Christmas!" Hank exclaimed with a wide grin. "What the devil happened to you?"

"This ain't no laughin' matter," Jefferson protested with a frown. "When a man gets hurt he goes to the doc to get fixed up. He ain't supposed to be made a fool of."

"That depends on what you did!" Hank said.

Turning to Eli, Jefferson said, "Good to see you again, young man." He gave a wink and added, "It's really a damn shame you're related to this cantankerous bastard. I wouldn't spend too much time around him or folks might get to thinkin' just as badly of you!"

"I worry about that myself." Eli chuckled. "That arm looks like it's giving you a lot of pain. One of those horses of yours didn't up and kick you, now did it?"

Jefferson looked down at his cradled arm and wrinkled his nose as if he'd just taken a whiff of rotten meat. " 'Cept this is on account a me fallin' off the ladder I got in the barn. I was movin' along as right as rain when I turned, took a step, found out there weren't nothin' there, and fell on my arm!"

"Ya fell off 'cause you couldn't see past yer gut!" Hank cackled.

"Just keep on laughin', Hank!" Jefferson growled, even though Eli thought the old rancher could see the humor in it all. "You mark my words . . . the next time you so much as fall on your ass, I'm gonna be there a-laughin' my head off!"

"You'd have been fine if'n you'd fallen on yer head!" Hank kept on teasing.

Eli butted in: "I'm sure the doc'll fix you up fine."

"I was about to do that very thing when you two characters barged in," Dr. Holland explained. As he spoke, his hands sank into a large bowl of a thick, white liquid. Sheets of cloth swam in the murky fluid like ships on a misty lake. Eli recognized the plaster used to set broken bones from his time in the army. "It'll take a while for it to heal," the doctor continued. "But he'll mend."

"And the first thing I'm gonna do when it's off is punch Hank in the chops!"

As the two old friends continued to tease each other, Eli slid over beside the doctor and said, "I'm afraid this is more than just a friendly visit, Doc. We've got ourselves a bit of a problem out at the ranch."

"What seems to be the matter?"

Eli told the physician about Mary; from finding her half drowned in the Cummings River to Hallie and Pearl placing her in a bed at the ranch. When he had finished his tale, he said, "I was hoping you could come out and take a look at her."

"I've got to get Jefferson's arm set and the cast dried before I can turn him loose," he said, nodding to where his patient and Hank continued to argue. "By the time I get finished with him it will be afternoon. Go on home and I'll be out as soon as I can."

"Is there anything we can do until you get there?"

"Do what you're doing," Doc Holland answered, stirring the contents of the plaster pot with both hands. "Keep her warm and comfortable and let her rest as much as she wants. When she does wake, give her something hot to drink—tea or soup, if you've got it. After the ordeal she's been through, she's likely to be as weak as a kitten and need to get her strength back."

"Anything else?"

"The hard part is already done—you fished her out of the river."

Eli grinned down at the small man. "If the water had been running any faster, neither one of us would've needed your attention. All we'd need is a pair of pine boxes!"

"I lucked out there." The doctor smiled, finally making a joke of his own.

"So did I, Doc."

"You best make sure someone takes ole Jefferson home, Doc," Hank said with a laugh. "He's liable to put the wrong foot in front of the other and end up back here for you to fix his other arm."

"And *you* best get out of here before I give you a reason to stay!" Jefferson barked, shaking his good arm in mock anger.

Back out on the street, Eli lifted his hat and wiped the sweat from his brow with the back of his arm. The day was going to be another scorcher. Squinting, he looked up into the cloudless sky, the sun hanging directly above. He'd been on the move since they had set off after the missing heads of cattle, and he could feel the ache of fatigue in his bones. The sooner he got himself home and managed a bit of sleep, the better.

"I sure do love givin' Jefferson a heapin' pile of grief," Hank exclaimed.

"It'd take a blind man not to see that you do."

"It's the most fun I've had in weeks."

Eli was untying his horse from the hitching post and preparing to climb back into the saddle when his uncle snapped his fingers and swore. "Damn. I told your momma that I'd get her a couple of somethin' or others from the mercantile when we was in town and I 'pert near forgot!"

"Good thing you remembered." Eli nodded. "She's already madder than a hornet's nest being poked with a sharp stick. You come home empty-handed, and we're all gonna be sleeping in the barn."

"I'll walk over and get what she needs and then we'll get on home."

As Hank crossed the busy street to Malek's, Eli leaned back against the hitching post and pulled his hat down over his eyes. He lazily watched two dogs playing with a stick in the dusty street. He tipped his hat as a woman passed by carrying a baby, a small boy hanging onto her skirts. A smile had just colored the edges of his mouth when he was suddenly grabbed hard about the waist from behind.

"What in the hell?" he barked in surprise.

Flipping back his hat, Eli was dumbfounded to find a woman pressed tightly against his back. The arms of her blue dress peeked out on each side and the strong scent of a floral perfume enveloped him. As he tried to turn his head to get a glimpse of the woman's face, she clung to him tenaciously, refusing to give up her identity.

"Who—who in the . . . ?" he muttered.

As suddenly as he had been grabbed, the woman holding him let go and took a step back. Just as quickly, Eli spun around to face her. The face that looked up at his was plump and round, with high cheekbones and a pert nose. Bright green eyes blinked under long lashes, and an ear-to-ear smile flashed brightly.

"Fa-Fawn?" Eli stammered.

"Oh, Eli!" she squealed. "I can't believe you're here!"

As she spoke, her eyes shining brightly, Eli realized that hers was the name he'd guessed, although she was a little plumper than he remembered. Try as he might, he could never seem to rid himself of Fawn Billings.

"I didn't recognize you for a moment," he managed.

"Oh, you silly, silly goose!" she exclaimed as she playfully batted his shoulder with one gloved hand. "I was just walking about and watching the goings-on when you trotted out of the doctor's office right in front of me! It was as if not a single day had passed since I last saw you! I just had to come over and say hello."

"Hello . . . yourself," Eli said, not knowing what else to say.

Fawn Billings had been born in the same year as his younger brother, Caleb, and had grown up beside the Morgan boys, attending school with them in the one-room building at the edge of town. Her father, Jonathan Billings, ran the Bison City Bank and Trust, and was, by default, an important town figure. One trait that Fawn had acquired early was an air of self-importance. Incredibly vain and needy, she was used to getting what she wanted. Unfortunately for Eli, what she had made clear she wanted most of all was to be Mrs. Elijah Morgan. No amount of persuasion had ever convinced her that he did not share her dream.

"I'd thought that maybe you might come back to town, after what happened to your father," Fawn continued sweetly. "And I was right! How come you didn't let me know you were home?"

Eli was about to speak, to offer up some reason that didn't involve going into his dislike for the town that killed his brother, when a deep baritone voice spoke from the shadows of the boardwalk.

"Well, look who's here."

Eli immediately recognized the man who had spoken; his was a voice that he could never forget. Stepping out into the sunlight, his long, thick, muscular form looking smart in his dark suit was Seth McCarty. Nearly half a head shorter than Eli, with thinning black hair and a close-cropped mustache, Seth had also grown up alongside Eli and Fawn. But unlike Fawn, he held nothing but hatred for the Morgans.

"Eli." The well-dressed man nodded.

"Afternoon, Seth," Eli offered coldly.

"I was beginning to wonder if you were ever going to acknowledge me."

Eli could hear the disdain and dislike that dripped from every word Seth uttered, but he could care less if the other man was put out. From the first moment that they had met, Seth McCarty had rubbed him the wrong way. Seth was a bully in every sense. He'd taken great pleasure in picking on the other children of Bison City, but he had held a special enmity for the Morgan brothers. They'd had more than their share of scrapes when they'd been boys, and many a nose had been bloodied or cheek bruised. In the end, Eli had always seemed to get the better of his rival. But, like a true bully, that hadn't been good enough for Seth. Not content with being on the losing end, he had turned anger upon a victim who had had a harder time fighting back: Caleb.

It had begun with a shove here, a kick there, until poor Caleb, five years Seth's junior, was as terrorized as a rabbit in a forest of foxes. One day, when Eli had come upon his younger brother wailing a flood of tears, blood streaming from his nose, Eli had had enough. He'd found Seth behind the mercantile, laughing about what he'd done, and proceeded to thrash him mercilessly. If Abe hadn't managed to pull him off Seth, he might not ever have stopped. From that day on, Seth had let Caleb alone, but the anger that filled his heart had grown right alongside the boy himself, never blowing over as boyhood rivalries tended to do. It was as clear as the sun in the sky.

Seth hates me still.

"I didn't see you standing back in the shadows," Eli replied.

"I suppose I can't fault you for that." Seth snorted, his lips curled in a wry smile. "After all, far more sophisticated men than you have found themselves overwhelmed by Fawn's attentions."

"Now, you just hush that kind of talk," Fawn admonished, her voice as rich with honey as it always was. "I haven't seen Eli in what—four years at least—so it should be easy to see how I might be overcome with emotion seeing him again, isn't it?"

"Quite frankly, I can't imagine why anyone would miss such a man, let alone be happy to see him," Seth said with a sneer. He gave Eli the once-over and, from the expression that crossed his face, he didn't like what he saw.

If it weren't for the fact that he was waiting for Hank to return from the mercantile, Eli would have mounted his horse and ridden out of town, rather than stand and take Seth's abuse. *The man is a silver-tongued snake.* Seth would keep biting and biting until Eli had had enough and bit back. If Seth kept on, he just might get what he wanted.

"Tell him," Seth said evenly.

"Oh, Seth, dear . . . ," Fawn said nervously. "I don't know if—if—"

"I said, tell him!"

"Tell me what?" Eli asked, annoyed.

Fawn was silent for a moment longer, and it looked as if she might protest a bit further, but her head dropped and she said, "Seth and I are to be married in the fall. Ever since he came to work for Papa, he's been courting me, and when he asked for my hand in marriage, I accepted."

From her tone, Eli could see that Fawn was reluctant to tell him the news and did so only because of Seth's insistence. On the other hand, Eli was thrilled. Hopefully, that would take care of the attentions she had been directing toward him. Although what Fawn could see in Seth was truly beyond him.

"So I'm telling you to stay clear of Fawn," Seth stated firmly. "It wouldn't do to have my future wife be seen talking with someone like you. Just think of the scandal that would take place if loose lips began to flap. I have a reputation to uphold in this town."

"Now, just wait a goddamn minute," Eli shot back. "Only one man ever told me what I could or couldn't do and I had enough trouble abiding by him, so there's no way a dressed-up peacock like you would manage!"

"Oh, Eli!" Fawn practically purred. "Don't fight over me!"

"There's no place for you here anymore, Morgan," Seth said with a sneer as he took a menacing step forward. "When you left here with your tail between your legs, life went on without you. We've kept on building our lives in this town. When the day comes, God forbid, that Fawn's father has to step down as head of the bank, I will be the man to take over. You best watch your tongue around me. Just imagine how your words would weigh if you needed a loan to keep that pitiful ranch of yours going!"

"Now, Seth!" Fawn admonished again.

Eli's pulse raced and his fists were clenched tight in anger. With all that had happened in the last few days—with his time spent in the flooded river and the hurt that filled him just being in the town that had taken Caleb from him—Eli could stand no more. He'd had to put up with Seth's bullying, his insults to his family, and his cocky attitude for longer than he cared to imagine. By God, he wasn't going to take any more!

If it's a fight that Seth's after, it's a fight he's going to get!

He had just taken the first step toward slugging the bastard in the mouth, to teaching him a lesson he wouldn't soon forget, when he was stopped by the familiar voice of his uncle.

"Well, I'll be a weak-kneed calf," Hank crowed. In his

hands were a couple of jars he'd brought from the mercantile. "Do this old man's eyes deceive me or is it that pretty little Fawn Billings I see?"

"Mr. Gallows." She chortled happily. "It *is* a pleasure to see you."

"Seth." Hank nodded to the other man.

As a reply, Seth simply grabbed Fawn by the elbow and pulled her back onto the boardwalk and began walking away. Fawn peeked back over her shoulder at Eli. They were soon lost among the many faces that crowded the boardwalk.

"I reckon I finished my business at just the right time."

Eli didn't answer and instead unhitched his horse and swung up into the saddle. He led the way out of town. With every step of the black and tan's hooves, Eli's anger grew.

Chapter Thirteen

"What do you want now? Haven't you already asked for enough?"

In the face of Mrs. Morgan's resentment, it was all that Hallie could do to hold her temper in check. Standing in the ranch house kitchen, she forced herself to turn away from the older woman, allowing her gaze to wander around the room; it passed over the cookstove, the small pump that sat at the end of a long counter, the trestle table and chairs, the tall kitchen cabinets that held the flour bin and the dishes and bowls, and even lingered on the pie safe, all to escape looking at that woman for one moment longer.

Even as she tried to formulate her sentences, Hallie couldn't help but wonder if she shouldn't have become used to the older woman's abuse by now. Over the course of the five days that they had been staying at the Morgan ranch, the family matriarch had done everything in her power to make their stay as uncomfortable as possible. There had been sharp, biting words and angry stares from hooded eyes, all mixed with a generous air of contempt. Each confrontation seemed to be worse than the one that had come before.

"I'm terribly sorry to have to inconvenience you, Mrs. Morgan."

"Not a one of you dirty trollops would even begin to know what it means to inconvenience a Christian woman like myself!" the older woman snapped. "You just waltzed right in here and took over the house like you owned the place!"

"We wouldn't have asked to stay here if Mary hadn't needed—"

"Mary this and Mary that!" Mrs. Morgan said angrily, refusing to hear Hallie's explanation. "That's all I've heard since you got here. I will not be at your beck and call. What do you think this is—a hotel? I hope I never see the likes of you again!"

Hallie sighed silently. It was hard to believe that *this woman* was Eli's mother. They were complete opposites: Eli was a kind and considerate man, while his mother was a shrew. From the way she acted, you would think Hallie had asked her for the deed to the ranch!

Still, there was a part of Hallie that understood Mrs. Morgan's anger. The three of them *had* intruded upon her and her family. *Wouldn't I be put out by complete strangers being thrust upon me?*

"I'm sorry to have to bother you, Mrs. Morgan," Hallie explained in a voice that she'd always reserved for speaking with children, calm and easy, "but I need a pan I can fill with water. My friend is still running a fever and I'd like to be able to cool her. The sooner her fever goes down and she is able to eat a bit, then the sooner we can move on."

Her last words seemed to give the older woman pause and her eyes narrowed. Her jaw was still clenched and her arms folded over her chest, but Hallie thought she could see Mrs. Morgan had softened a bit. When she spoke her voice was not *completely* laced with venom.

"Over there," she said, nodding in the direction of the pantry.

"Thank you."

When Hallie turned away a faint smile curved her lips. *My mother had always told me that you could get much further in life using honey instead of vinegar!* But she had taken no more than a few steps toward the pantry when Mrs. Morgan's biting tongue began to lash her yet again.

"Don't think for one second that I ain't been keeping track of all you've been borrowing," she said snidely. "I'm wise to how your sort operates! If you think I'm just going to let you waltz on out of here with everything but the stove, you've got another thought comin'!"

Hallie spun quickly on her heel, anger rising hotly in

her chest, and stared defiantly at the woman's wrinkled face. "Are you saying that I am a thief, Mrs. Morgan?" she managed, her voice trembling.

"It's obvious to me that you're no saint!"

"I've never pretended to be a saint, but I *am* a decent woman."

Mrs. Morgan paused, letting the aspersion linger over her like the smoke over a battlefield. Hallie could see satisfaction written across the older woman's face for having delivered a wound to her pride. "If there's even one spoon missing, I won't hesitate to call upon the sheriff."

Hallie's heart caught in her throat at the woman's accusation. After all that had happened to them, after all of the insults Mrs. Morgan had already leveled at them, she still found herself shocked at being labeled a criminal.

"I am not a thief!"

"Oh, I struck a nerve there, did I?" The older woman smiled maliciously, her hand rising to her chest in mock apology. "But don't go acting all upset on my account, girlie. I know it's more likely you're put out by my guessing what you really are."

"I'll have you know that in my hometown I am respected!"

"And what town is that?" Mrs. Morgan said quickly as she took an aggressive step toward the younger woman. An inquisitorial look filled her eyes as she mirrored Hallie's stare, seeking for something, for some truth she did not yet know to reveal itself.

"Akron, Ohio. My father is a minister."

"Minister, ha! From the moment you showed up on my step, I haven't heard one word about what sort of woman you are, or any other damn thing about you. So tell me, what respectable woman travels across the country in a wagon without menfolk to look after her?"

"I told you what kind of woman I am. I don't . . ." Hallie began but held her tongue. The fact of the matter was that the older woman was simply baiting her, wanting the argument that would inevitably ensue just as badly as she herself wanted to avoid it. But even silence proved not enough to halt Mrs. Morgan's relentless assault.

"What's the matter, girlie? The devil got your tongue?"

Hallie's mouth moved slightly, opening and closing slowly, but the only noise she heard was the rapid pounding of her heart as it threatened to burst from her chest. What held her silent had nothing to do with the devil; *what kept her quiet was the truth.*

From the moment she had first encountered Eli along the swollen banks of the Cummings River, she had been filled with a great fear of the many questions she felt certain would be asked. *Where are you from? Why were you out in that storm? Where were you headed?* Even her joy at finding Mary alive was not enough to overwhelm her apprehensions.

Later, upon their arrival at the Morgan ranch, she had braced herself, steeling her resolve and preparing to provide answers that, while not quite out-and-out lies, would still fail to mention the true horror that was Chester Remnick or the gunshot that had forever changed all their lives. When she had spoken to Eli of what had befallen Mary, she hadn't been entirely forthcoming, even if her evasions settled uneasily on her heart.

But those questions had *not* come and it seemed as if her fear was misguided. With each passing day, Hallie had begun to hope that perhaps the inquiring words would *never* be spoken. Now, standing in Mrs. Morgan's harsh gaze, her hope had proven to be nothing more than an illusion.

"What were you doing in that storm?" the older woman asked.

"We were caught in the storm by accident," Hallie finally answered.

"Where were you coming from?"

"We were coming . . . from the east. We left because I needed to find another job teaching school."

"That's a lie."

"It is not."

"It's a lie if I ever heard one," Mrs. Morgan declared adamantly.

For the briefest of moments, Hallie thought of telling her the truth—not only of what had happened with Mary and Chester but about how she and Pearl had desperately wanted a new start of their own, of what had happened between herself and Zachary Wall. But in the end, she kept quiet. Now was neither the time nor the place for all her story to be told.

"Whether you believe me to be telling the truth or not, Mrs. Morgan, doesn't make me a liar," she said confidently. "We needed jobs and were bold enough to take risks to find them. Unfortunately, in the course of doing so, we found ourselves caught in a storm. We could have died if not for the kindness of Eli and his uncle."

At another mention of Eli's name, Mrs. Morgan grew even colder. She wrinkled her nose, almost as if she had smelled something rotten. "I curse the day he came back here almost as much as I do the moment you and yours appeared on my steps. The sooner you're all gone, the better."

With that, the older woman went out onto the long porch, banging the door loudly behind her. Hallie sighed to herself before fetching the pan and water and retreating to the bedroom where Mary lay.

Mary lay on the small bed, her skin hot to the touch, her limbs twitching from time to time. In the five days that she had lain in the tiny room at the back of the ranch house, her eyes had been closed for most of the time, and the only sounds she had made were an assortment of moans but no words. She had never regained enough consciousness to eat, although she had taken in water through a damp cloth pressed to her lips and squeezed;

it was as if her body was struggling to cling to life, even if her mind were not.

"The old battle-ax gave you the pan, I see," Pearl said when Hallie entered the room.

"Not without an argument."

"Argument courses through that woman's veins like blood itself."

"I believe you're right."

"I am," Pearl said with a nod. "That cantankerous old biddy ain't gonna give an inch."

Hallie hesitated for a moment, unsure whether to give her worries a voice. When she did speak, it was little more than a whisper. "She asked about the storm . . . about what we were doing out in weather like that. She wanted to know where we came from and where we were headed. She finally let the matter drop, but I expect her to return to it soon."

"Ain't none of her business," Pearl answered.

"I'm not so sure about that. We are living in her house. She has the right to know about us."

"And I'm tellin' you that it ain't her concern," her friend repeated as she pushed a wayward strand of hair from her face. "What happened out there is between the three of us. It ain't the affair of nobody else, except maybe that weasel I shot."

"Don't you think she has some right to know *why* we are here?"

"If'n she knew what had passed between us and Ches-

ter, the first thing she'd do would be to fetch the sheriff
and see what he makes of the situation. Odds are, he and
I would disagree."

"She wouldn't do that! Eli wouldn't allow it!"

"You willin' to take that chance?" Pearl stared. " 'Cause
I ain't."

"But this is her home that we're staying in," Hallie
persisted. "We are eating her food, burning her candles;
everything we need is being provided by her and hers.
Even this pan and water belong to her. Even if it's not the
whole story, she deserves to know something."

"But we ain't livin' under her roof, Hallie," Pearl argued. "Not really. Until the time comes where she lets us
sleep in normal beds like we was real honest-to-God persons, instead of makin' us curl up in the barn like we was
just some of her cattle, until then . . . she don't deserve
to know nothin'."

With that, Pearl took the pan of water from Hallie's
hands and made her way to Mary's bedside. She wet a
long strip of cloth that she'd scavenged from an old dress
at the bottom of her traveling trunk and draped it across
the unconscious woman's hot forehead.

"A wise decision, nurse," a deep voice spoke.

Abraham Morgan sat beside Mary's bed in a rickety,
high-back chair. From the moment that the three women
arrived at the ranch, he had steadfastly remained by
Mary's side. He had taken all his meals in the small room
and had slept in the old chair, a blanket pulled up to his

bearded chin. Even though fatigue was written across his face, he refused to budge from his vigil.

"It is a boon that she is receiving such excellent care," Abe continued.

"We're doing the best we can."

"Quite so . . . quite," he mused, rubbing long fingers through his coarse beard. "But I will have you know that my Mary is a fighter in her own right, indeed. No calamity, even one as persistent as this, will be able to fell her great and God-loving spirit. Of that, I can assure you."

Pearl let her eyes wander over the man who believed himself to be President Lincoln. Hallie could see a softness in her look, something almost maternal. "Maybe she'd want you to get some rest of your own," she soothed. "After all, ain't no point in you both bein' laid up."

"She would expect me to rest; you are quite right about that." Abe nodded to her. "But I remember a moment shortly after we were married, when I was the one felled by a great illness. Even in the haze of my condition, I still recall opening my eyes to find her at my side, willing me to get well. She never wavered, staying by my side until I was back on my feet. I hope to be here to give her the same inspiration when she wakes. It is the very least that I can do."

"I reckon you know what you're doin', then."

Hallie couldn't help but marvel at Abraham Morgan. When she and Pearl had first met him on the steps of the ranch house, they had been filled with shock and wonder and had worried greatly about his desire to be so close to Mary. But at Eli and Hank's insistence, they had relented and allowed him to stay by their friend's side. From that time on, they had watched as he cared for her as if she were really Mary Todd Lincoln, the long-dead president's wife.

As the days had passed, Hallie found Abe's strong spirit and optimism to be infectious. Where she had once feared that her friend would surely die, she now believed that Mary had a chance, that she was hearing Abe's words of encouragement and drawing strength from them, the strength to live.

"Thank you for all your help, sir," Hallie said truthfully.

Abe turned in his chair to look at her, his eyes holding her fast with such soft intensity that she would have sworn that he was who he thought himself to be. "This woman is my wife, miss. For her, I would do anything, even if it meant the loss of my own life."

Hallie nodded; she believed him.

As Abraham turned his attention back toward Mary, Pearl rejoined Hallie. "We're gonna need fresh bedding before too long," she said. "She's done soaked those so deep they feel as if they done gone in that river on her back."

"I suppose I could ask Mrs. Morgan for more . . ."

"Don't you worry none about that old bat arguin' with you," Pearl shot. "I ain't got no problem with walkin' out there, tellin' her what we need, and settin' her straight about the matter if she gives me any guff!"

"No, Pearl. I'll do it," Hallie said quickly. "You just stay here and I'll take care of it."

The truth was that Hallie hoped to keep Pearl as far away from Mrs. Morgan's sharp tongue as possible. Their staying at the Morgan ranch was tenuous at best; if Pearl and Mrs. Morgan were to butt heads, she and Pearl could easily find themselves back out on the prairie roads with a sick girl and in even more danger than before.

"Just don't tell her nothin' about where we come from or where we was headed," the older woman lectured. "Remember that it ain't none of her business."

Hallie was just about to open her mouth, to agree with Pearl, when a loud crash split the hot summer afternoon air and was immediately followed by a bloodcurdling scream.

Chapter Fourteen

As Hallie rushed from Mary's room hard on Pearl's heels, any number of possible calamities filled her head as to the source of the crash and scream, each one of them involving Chester. *Has he found us?* In those short seconds, she was sorry that she had ever stumbled across kindhearted Eli on the riverbank, sorry that she had allowed him to bring them to the ranch, sorry even that she and Pearl had hatched the plan to spirit Mary away in the first place.

She and Pearl raced down the short hallway and, when they burst into the kitchen, gasped at the sight that greeted them. Mrs. Morgan lay on the floor writhing in pain, one wrinkled hand pressed tightly against her hip. Her face was a contorted mask, her eyes pinched nearly shut in agony, aged teeth bared in a grimace. She was sprawled next to an overturned chair, with fragments of glass from a lamp sprinkled all around her on the floor.

"What in the hell?" Pearl exclaimed.

"Oh, my word!" Hallie said.

"Ahhh," was all that Mrs. Morgan could manage in response.

At the sound of the older woman's agonized moan, Hallie rushed past Pearl and knelt beside Mrs. Morgan's twisted body. Up close, she looked like a child's doll, tossed awkwardly upon the floor, fragile enough to break at a touch. Obviously, she had suffered more than just a simple fall and bruise.

"Mrs. Morgan," Hallie began, gently reaching a hand to place on the woman's shoulder. "Are you—"

"Don't . . . you . . . dare . . . touch me," the woman hissed through tightly clenched teeth. Her eyes glared holes into Hallie; it was as if Hallie were offering the woman poison instead of aid.

"Mrs. Morgan, we're only trying to help you!"

"I . . . I don't . . . need your . . . help . . ."

"Are you hurt?"

"That ain't too hard to figure out," Pearl remarked, putting it all together as she looked around the room. "She must have been tryin' to reach the shelf above the pantry when she lost her balance. When she fell, she might have busted her hip."

"We've got to get her off the floor," Hallie observed.

"Her room's just over yonder," Pearl said, nodding

to the first door off the kitchen. "She ain't gonna weigh more'n a bunch of sticks, so the two of us ain't gonna have no problem gettin' her there."

But before either of them could move even a single inch, the injured woman's shrill protest filled the room. "Don't either . . . of you whores . . . so much as lay . . . one of your filthy fingers . . . on me! I won't . . . won't stand for it!"

"You ain't gonna be standin' ever again if'n you don't let us get you off this here floor," Pearl admonished her.

"I'd . . . I'd rather die . . . ," Mrs. Morgan explained, each knot of words punctuated by a quick draw of breath, "right . . . right here on this . . . floor . . . before I let either . . . either one of you . . . put hands on me!"

"Suit yourself."

Pearl gave an absent shrug of her shoulders before turning to walk back to Mary's room, resigned to leave Adele to her fate. But before she could go very far, Hallie scrambled to her feet, hurried after Pearl, and grabbed her friend's arm.

"Pearl, wait!" Hallie exclaimed. As much as Mrs. Morgan's harsh words, angry glares, and all-around disdain had grated on her nerves, Hallie knew that she could never turn her back on someone in need. "We can't just leave her here!"

"You heard it straight from the horse's mouth," Pearl said with a frown. "No matter how bad she's hurt, no matter how long she'd have to lay there, she don't want our help."

"Just because she doesn't *want* it, doesn't mean that she doesn't *need* it."

"Ain't much difference."

Hallie turned and looked over her shoulder to where Mrs. Morgan lay in pain. The older woman was struggling, trying to raise her body onto her side, but the agony was too great. She gasped air in thick gulps as a lone tear slid down one wrinkled cheek.

"We have to get help," Hallie said simply.

For a brief moment, Hallie thought that Pearl wanted to argue the point but finally, she blurted, "Oh, what the hell! I suppose you're right and we should help the old witch. But if she ain't gonna let us so much as touch her, what in the hell do you think we can do?"

What could they do?

Even if they were to fly in the face of Mrs. Morgan's shouts and curses and attempt to move the woman against her will, odds were that she would fight them.

For the first time since she and Pearl had burst from Mary's room into the wreckage of the kitchen, Hallie realized that Abe had not followed them. Even after hearing the crash and his mother's scream of pain, he had still chosen to remain by Mary's side. While he would have had the strength to move his mother, Hallie knew with certainty that no amount of prying would get him to leave the woman he firmly believed was his wife. The answer to the problem was obvious.

Find Eli and send someone for the doctor!

"She won't let us help her, but that doesn't mean she won't allow someone else," Hallie explained. "I'll find Eli and he can decide what to do."

"And in the meantime I get to watch the mean old hen."

"Can you handle it?"

Pearl chuckled. "Somehow I don't think the old biddy is in any condition to give me any guff!"

Bursting out onto the long porch, Hallie was met by a thick wall of heat. The yellow summer sun hung high in the blue sky, relentlessly blazing down on the earth below. In the face of such heat, it was hard for Hallie to believe that there had been a powerful storm only a few days earlier.

With one hand shading her eyes, she looked out over the ranch grounds for any sign of Eli or Hank. She looked out across the busy cattle pens, the weathered barn in which she and Pearl slept, and the other outlying buildings that were dotted about, yet she could see no sign of either man. She thought of shouting out, of yelling Eli's name, but she could barely hear herself think over the bawling cattle, barking dogs, and other sounds. No, if she were going to get Eli to help his mother, she would have to search for him.

Making her way down the steps, Hallie ran over the hard-packed ground, the heat already pressing down on her as if it were a blanket, smothering her and forcing her to breathe in gasps. She felt instantly wet with sweat, her blouse clinging tightly to her skin.

Rounding a bend between two cattle pens, Hallie came across a group of men struggling with a partially open gate. Two of the ranch hands were pushing with all of the strength they could muster on the loose end, while another pair leaned against the fence posts frantically waving their hats and whistling shrilly. Inside the pen, an enormous black bull reared its thick neck and horns skyward, bellowing a guttural sound and scratching the ground with one monstrous hoof. The sheer power and ferocity of the animal transfixed Hallie, freezing her in her tracks and forcing her to stare in wonder.

"Miss Hallie!" A man's voice cut through her daze.

Turning, she immediately recognized the ranch hand who had shouted to her. Buck was a man Eli had introduced to her only the day before. Tall as a cornstalk with sandy blond hair and a gentle face, he'd been full of laughter and smiles when they had first met. Now his face was a mask of concern.

"You best get on out of here, Miss Hallie!" he warned.

"But, I—" Before she could say another word, the humongous bull roared and charged the fence, its thick horns crashing into the wood and shaking the entire frame. The two ranch hands who had been leaning against the boards scattered like ants shaken off a leaf by a gust of wind.

"Goddamn son of a bitch!"

"Hurry up and get that damn gate shut!"

"You can't stay around here, Miss Hallie," Buck persisted among the other men's shouts.

"But I need to find Eli," she finally managed to say. "It's urgent."

Briefly, she thought about telling Buck what had happened to Mrs. Morgan, to try to enlist his help in helping her, but she held her tongue. Even if Buck weren't busy with the raging animal, she wondered if the older woman would be willing to even accept his help. *No, I need Eli.*

"Do you know where I can find him?" she implored.

"He and Hank are in the barn. You best look there."

"Thank you!" she shouted, running away before the last word was even out of her mouth.

With every step, the heat of the day seemed to become greater. The palms of her hands grew slick with sweat and she had to struggle to maintain a hold on her skirt as she ran. Breathing hard, she approached the barn. She couldn't tell if it were a mirage caused by the heat, but by the way that the building shimmered, it seemed as if the barn were getting farther away.

Finally, Hallie arrived at the side of the barn, and ran around to the front and in through the large double doors. After the glaringly bright summer afternoon, it took her a moment for her eyes to adjust to the murky interior.

Once she could see clearly, she spotted Eli, Hank, and another man bent over a calf that lay on the ground. The two Morgan men held the animal still as the other man applied a glowing hot iron to cauterize a cut in the calf's shoulder. The iron was held for only a few scant seconds but the barn was soon filled with the cow's plaintive cries. When the hot metal was removed, the calf jumped to its feet.

"There you go, little lady," Eli said as he patted the side of the calf's head.

Hank added, "You'll be right as rain in a few days."

"Easy for you to say." His nephew chuckled. "You weren't the one got burned."

"Let's get you on back to your mama," Eli said, preparing to lead the young animal out to the pens. He looked up and saw Hallie standing in the open barn doors, her face covered in sweat as she gasped for air. Letting go of the calf, Eli hurried over to her. He held her firmly in his grip for fear that she would collapse.

"Hallie!" he said urgently. "What on earth's the matter?"

"At . . . at the house . . . ," she gasped.

"Has something happened to Mary?" he asked.

"No . . . no! It's . . . your mother!"

Even inside the gloomy barn, she could see Eli's face

blanch, his eyes narrow and his jaw growing firm. Even his grip on her shaking arms seemed to tighten. "My mother?"

"Somethin' happened to Adele?" Hank hurried over to join them.

"She . . . she was up . . . on a . . . chair when . . . when she fell," Hallie explained, the words catching drily in her throat. "We heard . . . her scream out . . . and came . . . came running."

"Is she badly hurt?"

"I . . . I think so, but . . . I don't know," Hallie admitted to him. "We tried to get her . . . off the floor but . . . she wouldn't let us touch her."

"That woman is stubborn as a mule!" Hank declared.

"Is she still on the floor?" Eli asked, ignoring his uncle's remark.

"Yes!"

Before the sound of her voice faded, Eli rushed out of the building and into the hot summer sun, his destination the ranch house, Hank only half a step behind. Drawing a deep breath, Hallie lifted her skirt and ran after them.

Eli and Hank bent low over Mrs. Morgan's body, concern and consternation written on their faces. They had taken a door from its hinges and laid it beside her on the floor; they intended to use it as a makeshift stretcher to move her. Adele lay where she was when Hallie left her.

"I told you not to bother! I don't need your help!" she protested.

"Now, sister," Hank soothed, "this ain't no time for stubbornness."

"I said not to bother and I meant it!"

"I don't give a good goddamn," Eli barked, his patience worn thin by his mother's objections. "I'm not having the doc out here to visit and find you lying on the kitchen floor! We need to get you to bed and that's the end of it!"

"Don't you dare fetch Doctor Holland! It's not as bad as that!"

"Argue all you want," Hank said with a wink, "but I don't think the boy's gonna listen."

"Damn right, I'm not."

As Hallie watched the scene unfold before her, she felt relieved. While she and Pearl would have relented in the face of Mrs. Morgan's sharp words and arguments, her son refused to wilt and instead simply did what was needed.

Pearl looked on from where she leaned against the doorframe leading down the hall, trying to hide the smile that threatened to spread across her face.

"When we lift her up, Hallie, slide the door underneath her," Eli directed as he and his uncle positioned themselves around the fallen woman. Every time they moved, broken glass crunched beneath their boots.

"Let's go," Hank said and nodded.

"Don't you go jarring me," Mrs. Morgan protested, but before she could utter another word, Eli lifted her shoulders and Hank her knees. The only sounds she now seemed capable of making were cries of pain.

"Easy now!" Eli said firmly over his mother's screams.

Once the woman was up off the floor, Hallie slid the door quickly beneath her so that when they lowered her, she came to rest on it instead of the floor.

"Weren't nothin' to it," Hank exclaimed.

Even as Mrs. Morgan resumed her complaining, the two men each grabbed an end, hoisted the door up, and proceeded out of the kitchen and down the hall to her room. Through it all, the sound of her complaints bounced from wall to wall.

"Thank goodness that's over," Hallie said to Pearl.

"Over? What in tarnation makes you think it's over?"

"But they were able to get her up and off the floor," Hallie explained, her voice full of confusion at Pearl's questions. "Now the doctor will come. Surely, her life's not in danger now!"

"I ain't worried about the old bat dyin'," her friend said with a chuckle. "But now that she's gonna be on the mend, she ain't gonna be up and about like she's used to. Someone's gonna have to help her along . . . gonna have to tend to her every need."

The truth of Pearl's words struck Hallie and made her mute. *Someone* would have to take care of her, much as

Mary was being cared for. *Someone would have to listen to her complaints morning, noon, and night.*

It would be *Hallie and Pearl.*

Chapter Fifteen

"I CAN'T BELIEVE you expect me to eat such slop!" Adele shouted, her voice echoing around the small room. "Why, I wouldn't be one bit surprised if the cattle turned their noses up at it!"

Hallie sighed softly to herself. As she lifted the dinner tray from where it lay across the older woman's lap, she put her tongue between her teeth and gently pressed down, fearful that she might use it to defend herself. As her grandmother had once told her, *silence is golden*.

Several long hours had passed since Adele's accident, several fewer from the time of the doctor's visit. Dr. Holland had declared her unfit to move and consigned her to plenty of rest in her bed in the ranch house. Her mouth had never once quit complaining. Now, well after the setting of the summer sun, her vigor and ire remained aloft and blazing.

"If you'd been the cook for a wagon train bringing folks across the plains," she complained, "they'd have just as sooner shot you than to try to choke that down!"

When the doctor had left for Bison City, Hallie had approached Eli and volunteered to be the one to care for Adele. It was a difficult decision to make, but she made it unflinchingly. She had many reasons for making such an offer: to repay the Morgans for their generosity in welcoming them into their home to care for Mary; to prevent the job from falling to Pearl, whose patience with the woman wouldn't have lasted even two minutes; and, she had to admit to herself, she had done it for Eli. He had begun to inspire feelings in her she couldn't quite name. In the face of Adele's rabid tongue-lashings, she had begun to doubt the wisdom of her decision.

"What was all that ruckus I heard before you brought me that slop?" the older woman asked as she tried to raise herself in the bed, failing miserably and noticeably wincing. Despite the doctor's proclamations about her health, she'd continued to insist that she was fine. "It sounded as if a herd of buffalo was loose in there!"

"I'm not familiar with the kitchen and made more noise than necessary finding what I needed," Hallie explained, unable to maintain the silence she preferred in dealing with Mrs. Morgan. "I was just looking in the cabinets. I'm sorry if I was too noisy. Were you trying to sleep?"

"Sleep." She snorted. "Sleep when I'm hurting like hellfire. You were nosing around in my kitchen as if you belonged there. I don't want you rooting around in my things!"

"Yes, ma'am."

"Women who travel around from town to town are up to no good. Most of them are no more than whores, cheats, and thieves."

Hallie bit her tongue to keep from saying things that she would regret later. But even in the face of Hallie's self-imposed silence, the injured woman was more than happy to keep right on ranting.

"You and that other'n will probably steal everything in this house that ain't nailed to the floor! Are you after Eli and *her* after Hank? I wouldn't be surprised if the two of you don't poison me to get me out of the way."

Now she is accusing us of trying to kill her! What next? Hallie's blood pressure rose. *The very idea!* Mrs. Morgan had accused her of a lot of things, but this was the first time she had gone as far as to accuse her of attempting murder. She was just about to loosen her tongue and show the woman she could give as well as she got when a knock sounded on the door.

"Are you all right, Ma?" Eli asked evenly as he leaned against the wooden frame, his arms folded across his broad chest. Hallie couldn't be certain, but when he glanced her way, she saw mischief dancing in his eyes. His gaze lingered on her, and Hallie was certain she was blushing. She wondered what he would think if he knew that his mother thought she was trying to kill her.

He wouldn't believe it, would he?

"Doc left some laudanum," he continued, staring coolly at the woman who had given birth to him. "He said that if you got to hurting too bad, we can give you some."

"I don't need any of his damn medicine," Mrs. Morgan shot back defensively, obviously not as happy to see her son as Hallie was. "I'm perfectly fine, I tell you! I am perfectly capable of caring for myself. I don't need any help, especially not from such trash!"

"You should be glad Hallie is willing to take care of you," Eli replied calmly.

"You must be touched in the head. They'll eat us out of house and home and I'll get damn little care from either one of them! They can't even cook," she snorted.

"The meal I had was as fine as any I've had in a long time," Eli offered in Hallie's defense.

"I'm sorry you didn't like the soup, Mrs. Morgan. Is there something else you would prefer?" Hallie interjected. Her heart leaped at Eli's praise, even if she wasn't sure if he meant it or if he was just trying to placate his mother.

"What I'd prefer is for you to leave me, leave this house, and leave the whole damn state of Colorado!"

"My preference entirely." Eli smiled, took Hallie gently by the elbow, and led her from the room, shutting the door behind them. Even from behind the wooden door, Mrs. Morgan's rantings continued to hammer like hail.

*　　*　　*

Out on the long porch, Hallie marveled at the night sky. The moon hung low, bright and fat on the horizon, so large that she felt she could reach out and touch it with her fingers. There were no clouds in the sky, the night as clear as the day that had come before. Thousands of stars filled the inky blackness above, sparkling like jewels and seemingly twice as precious.

Eli's boots echoed across the wooden planks of the porch until he came to a halt beside her. Resting one hand on the railing, he ran the other through his thick black hair as he followed her gaze skyward. "Nowhere in the world is the night sky as beautiful as it is in Colorado."

"It is lovely," she agreed.

Hallie was surprised by just how comfortable she felt around this man. He was almost a stranger, yet she felt she had known him all her life. She was struck by a sudden urge to confide in him—to tell him about Chester, the gunshot and their mad dash to freedom—but she didn't want to burden him with her troubles, certainly not in the face of his mother's accident. Instead she waited for him to speak, happy to gaze at the sky beside him.

"Are you cold?" he asked.

"No, I'm just fine, thank you."

Even with the summer sun having set hours earlier, the night still managed to retain some of the day's warmth. A gentle breeze blew here and there. The only sound that Hallie could hear was the soft rustle of the cattle moving in the pens and the pounding of her own heart.

"I'm awfully glad you're here, Hallie, and not just to help take care of my mother. I'm sorry you have to listen to all of her hurtful words."

"I'm afraid I've heard far worse." She smiled.

"I'd hate to think that's true. With her salty tongue, my mother could hold her own with the roughest of trail drivers," he said with a chuckle. Even as he tried to laugh, Hallie could sense that the subject was difficult for him, even a little embarrassing.

"She carries on, bossing everyone around as if this was a palace and she was the queen," he continued. "It's always been this way, but not to this extent. My father was very patient with her. It must be hard for someone outside the family to hear . . . It always has been for me, but I guess I got used to it. Even on her best days, she can be as stubborn as any mule. I can only imagine how she'll be after four or five more days cooped up in bed."

"It's all right," Hallie said quickly.

"Don't lie now," he chided her.

"I'm not!"

"Hell, yes you are!" He laughed. "Remember, she's *my* mother."

Hallie couldn't help but join his laughter, even if it was restrained. "Really, her mouth doesn't bother me much. I guess that I've gotten used to it, too. After all that you've done for us—taking us into your home and allowing Mary to stay here—it truly does seem like the very least we can do is help with your mother."

"I'm hoping that she'll be up and around in a week or two."

"I hope so, too."

For a few moments, they stood in silence. As she looked up, entranced by the night, Hallie saw a star streak across the heavens, its trail brilliant one moment and then swallowed by the dark the next. It was a sight she had seen many times before, but tonight it was *different,* it was *special.* She turned quickly to Eli, but he was no longer standing beside her. He had turned and was sitting on the long wooden railing, shifting his gaze from the heavens and fixing it squarely on her. Even in the gloom of the evening, she could feel his eyes searching hers, racing over her skin, asking questions for which she had no answers. She felt as if she were back in the storm, held in check by a force greater than her will. Even if she had wanted to, she couldn't look away.

"Some things are difficult for a man to hold on to," he said simply.

"What?" she asked in confusion.

"Especially when it's about his kin, his flesh and blood," Eli kept right on.

"I don't understand what—"

"Let me tell you, Hallie," Eli said softly yet firmly, his voice holding her every bit as tightly as his eyes. "If you're going to stay here at the ranch, if you're going to care for my mother, there are some things you should know. There are things about the Morgan family, *secrets* that will make it easier for you to understand why my mother is the way she is." He paused for a moment longer, as if he was uncertain how to continue, but he found his voice once again and added, "None of these things are going to be easy for me to say, but I *want you* to hear them."

"All right"—she nodded—"but you don't need to tell me anything."

"I think I do. I want to."

Waiting for Eli to speak, she was filled with both anticipation and dread. *What kind of secrets is he talking about?* She could tell that whatever they were, they hung heavily on his heart and that telling her was not an easy task.

"Four years ago, my brother Caleb was murdered."

"Oh, Eli!" she gasped. His words were so strong, so powerful, that she had to fight the sudden urge to rush to him and put her arms around him.

"It happened around this time of year, on a night just about like this one—starry, clear, and the air still warm with summer," he pressed on, looking up into the sky. With determination lining his face in the growing moonlight he told her about his brother's death, his going into the army, and his parents' disappointment. "After I left, sorrow was heaped upon sorrow when Abe became ill. He survived but was changed forever. All of this broke my father and made my mother bitter. If only . . . if only I hadn't left . . ."

Hallie asked, "But why did you go?"

"Because I'm a stubborn ass," he spat angrily. "It's because I'm just like my mother in the end, just like the woman who shouts and bitches at every turn. I get my mind made up and that's just the way it's gonna be, no matter who I hurt in the process."

"But that's not the person that you are," she said quietly, suddenly angry with him for berating himself. When he had begun to tell Caleb's story, she'd been rooted in place, frozen like the moon in the sky, but now she felt full of emotion, her hands moving expressively as she spoke. "The person who rescued us and brought us to safety isn't stubborn or selfish. If it weren't for you, Mary would have drowned in that river! You saved a life."

"One rescued for one taken don't make it even."

"What?" she asked incredulously. "What are you talking about?"

Eli sighed deeply. As reluctant as he had seemed to speak about his brother, the unspoken words now seemed to pain him. Hallie knew that *this* was what was truly causing him anguish.

"Tell me, Eli," she prodded.

At her words, his eyes seemed to embrace her. She could see him steeling his courage, readying himself for something, *an admission* that hung heavy on his heart.

"It's my father," he said.

"What happened?" she asked, but felt a knot in the pit of her stomach.

"When I left here—left the ranch, Bison City, and all my old life—I had no intention of ever coming back," he explained, his hands balled into tight fists. "Even when I got out of the army, I stayed on in Texas and began to build myself a new life, one that had nothing to do with ranches or cattle. I did my best to make my peace with all that had happened. But then I got a wire from Hank telling me that I should come back and, like a fool, I listened. When I arrived, I found that my father had died."

Hallie was quiet. Her first thought was surprisingly of Adele Morgan. For a woman to lose both a husband and son was far more than she should ever have to bear. Her heart ached for Eli, but even though she wanted to comfort him, to soothe his hurt, the words she wanted to say did not come easy.

"My mother blamed me for what happened. She said that I was the one who killed him," he continued, his voice cracking with emotion. "She said that he waited and waited for me to come to my senses and return to the ranch, but she claimed that he was a fool for waiting in vain for an ill-begotten son like me. My mother believes that it was my stubbornness, my selfish desire to stay away, that killed him."

"But that's not true! Your mother is wrong!"

"I don't believe that it's all my fault, but I'd have to be some sort of fool if I didn't think some of it was true," he answered, showing some of the stubborn streak he claimed to have. "Ever since I've been back here, I've done my all to avoid facing it, working hard at Hank's side, helping keep the ranch going. I've never even been to my father's grave, or my brother's either for that matter, and I don't know if I'll ever have the stomach for it."

"But you must go there!" Hallie insisted.

"I think I've given it—"

"Mark my words, Eli"—she cut him off—"if you don't, you'll always be filled with regret."

"How do you reckon?" he asked, interested in what she had to say.

Cautiously, she stepped toward him, reached out, and took his hands gently in her own. His fingers and palms were rough and weatherworn, but she was pleasantly surprised to feel a strong warmth emanating from them. Squeezing his hands together in her own, she looked directly into his eyes.

"I left my home in much the same way that you left here," she said as a breeze rustled her long hair. "My parents had a life chosen for me that I did not want and I rebelled. I left as quickly as I could, certain that I would never return. Two years after I left, I heard from an aunt that they had both died."

"Hallie, I'm—" he began, but she hushed him.

"Now it's your turn to be quiet."

He nodded his head.

"Ever since then, all I've wanted is to stand before their graves and tell them that I loved them, that my leaving wasn't about rejecting them but was about making a life of my own." As she spoke, hot tears began to slide gently down her cheeks; she had no desire to stop them.

"I wanted them to know of my life, to know of my successes and failures. If I could have even one minute to stand before their graves and speak to them, I'd take it in an instant."

For a moment, Eli was silent. Then he gently removed one hand from her grasp and wiped at the tears staining her face. When he spoke, the heat of his breath against her face sent shivers down her spine.

"Maybe you're right," he said. "Maybe I should go to the cemetery."

"I'll come with you if you need me."

"I wish you would."

Hallie was about to speak, to tell him that she would do anything she could to help him ease his pain, when he leaned forward and brought his lips to hers. She was momentarily startled but soon melted into his arms, their kiss growing in intensity with each beat of her heart. She clung to him tightly as his mouth explored hers. When he broke the embrace, she smiled at him, happy that he still held her by the elbow for fear that she might fall, dizzy with the passion that washed over her.

"So tomorrow morning, then?" he finally asked.

"Tomorrow morning?" she echoed, uncertain as to his meaning.

"To the cemetery. I'll pay my respects," he explained. "That is, if you'll come along."

"I will, Eli." She smiled at him brightly. "I will."

Chapter Sixteen

Hallie sat beside Eli in the wagon, a smile on her face as bright as the early sun that had just begun to shine in the morning sky. Scant, wispy clouds hung low on the horizon, stretched so thin that the clear blue of the day shone through. What little breeze blew wasn't enough to stir the leaves. A lone hawk soared in the already growing heat, a silent judge looking down upon them as they slowly made their way to Bison City.

She woke in her hay bed in the barn, and dressed carefully by the scant light of the lamp Eli provided for them. A smile was the first thing she put on, even if her trip wouldn't be a cause of joy for everyone. Pearl initially grumbled at having to care for Mrs. Morgan and Mary by herself, but soon agreed to do so; the knowing wink and nudge she gave turned Hallie's cheeks a deep red. After a quick meal, she climbed into the wagon's seat, and, with a hitch of the reins and a click of his tongue, Eli drove away from the ranch house.

As glad as she was to be away from Mrs. Morgan's watchful gaze and biting tongue, Hallie was even happier at the idea of spending the day with Eli. *Everything about him is so different.* She'd scarcely been able to sleep a wink after their kiss; the merest thought of his lips pressing against hers was enough to send shivers racing across her skin. Still, she tried to balance her own happiness against the reason for their trip.

Today is the day Eli is to visit his father's and brother's graves for the first time and he wants me to be with him!

As the miles went by and the sun rose ever higher in the sky, Hallie was pleased at how easy it was to talk with Eli. She was never at a loss for words. As they rode along, they bounced from subject to subject as naturally as the wagon bounced from rut to rut on the dirt road. He told her wild tales of how he, Abe and Caleb, as boys had run over the hills that surrounded the ranch, of how he had once nearly burned the barn to the ground, and also of his time in the army. He showed her trees, creeks, and wildlife; once, a coyote paused on a hilltop just long enough for Eli to point it out before it scampered into the tall grass and disappeared from sight. Through it all, Hallie was rapt. She drank in his words, happy to hear him speak and relieved that she was required to offer so little of her own past in return.

"Before long, you'll know me as well as I know my-self," he said with a laugh.

"Then you'll just have to tell me more," she prodded him.

"I would"—Eli shrugged—"but we're about out of road."

As if he were a traveling magician lifting the veil on his newest sleight of hand, he guided the horses around a wide curve in the road, and there was the town of Bison City suddenly coming into view. Hallie's eyes took it all in; building abutted building along the town's main street, more of them spilling off in nearly every direction; storefronts with large signs advertised services of every kind, some of their owners on the long boardwalk hawking their wares. Crowds were everywhere, on foot, wagon, and horseback; and the train's shrill whistle announced the arrival of even more goods and people. The town seemed alive, hustling and bustling.

"This, for better or for worse, is Bison City," Eli said with a wave of his hand in the town's direction. "It isn't much. Probably not very different from where you came from, I'd bet."

To that, Hallie had no answer.

Since she'd first laid eyes on Bison City, the only thought that had filled her head was how different it all seemed from the town she *knew*, from Whiskey Bend. Taverns, drunks, and fights were her former residence's greatest assets. It wasn't the sort of place folks took the train to visit; it was the kind of town people did their best to avoid. She suddenly wondered why she had stayed there for as long as she had. Still, she couldn't bring herself to give voice to these thoughts.

I can't tell Eli my tale . . . not yet.

"It seems so busy," she finally managed.

"Wasn't always that way, but, as Hank keeps telling me, things have a way of changing whether you're here to watch or not." He smiled warmly. "I suppose that holds true for places just as much as it does for people. Hell, when I came back on the train, I wasn't sure I recognized the town."

"Maybe it didn't recognize you, either."

"Let's hope not." He winked as he snapped the reins and hurried them along.

On Bison City's main street, the hustle and bustle Hallie had glimpsed from the distance was far greater, far *louder* than she had expected. Horses and wagons jostled for space on the street. The sweet smell of woodsmoke, tobacco, and food hung on the air like clothes on a line. Peals of raucous laughter spilled from the open door of the saloon. Even as Eli cursed a man leading a pair of meandering cows that had wandered directly in their path, she couldn't help but smile.

"That man hasn't got the sense of either of those damn animals," he declared.

"He may lack sense, but he seems to have manners."

"How do you figure?"

"At least he knows better than to curse in a woman's presence."

"You're only saying that because you haven't talked to him."

They slowly made their way past a hardware store and a blacksmith shop. Hallie marveled at the strength of the men who pounded away at the glowing hot steel inside, sending sparks flying around the darkened interior. *How could they work in such heat?* She was just about to ask Eli that very question when she glanced up to find a man staring *directly* at her.

He leaned against one of the white pillars of the tavern, a brown bottle held limply in one hand, an unlit cigar in the other. He was heavyset, his girth straining against the buttons of his dirty blue shirt. His fat face was covered in a long, mangy black beard; but his eyes peered out at her from beneath the brim of his hat, staring with the intensity that an alcoholic gives his latest drink. From where he stood on the boardwalk, raised above the street, his gaze was nearly level with her own; when the wagon moved past, his head turned slowly in their direction, never wavering from her.

A sudden, strong wave of fear washed over her. *Certainly, I've never seen this man before in my life, but that doesn't mean that he hadn't seen me!* Dread grasped at her heart and pounded at the door of her mind. She thought of Chester, of the hatred that must be overflowing his heart for all three of them, and then of all the riffraff he called friends. He would have his pals scouring the ends of the earth, looking for her and Pearl and Mary, searching for some sign that would let Chester catch up with them to extract his revenge.

Is this man one of Chester's friends?

Is he looking for me?

Is he even now thinking of confronting me?

"Why don't we stop by the mercantile now," Eli said, breaking into her thoughts and forcing her to turn at the sound of his voice. "The cemetery is on the far western edge of town, and coming back through all this mess doesn't sound like much fun to me. It'll be easier now than later."

"All right." Hallie nodded, quickly looking back to the tavern. Where the man had stood only seconds earlier, there was no one. She looked all around, scanning the faces of the people on the boardwalk and the street, but saw no sign of the man. She tried to reassure herself that she had only been imagining things, that the man had simply been watching the young ladies parade by, but the way that her heart pounded in her chest told her that she had about as much belief in those hopes as she did in Father Christmas.

"Let's get what we need and get out of here." Eli frowned.

Eli brought the wagon to a stop in front of the mercantile and leaped down to the ground. Hallie followed quickly. As she bent down to straighten the hem of her dress, she heard footsteps pounding across the wooden boardwalk. Looking up, she feared seeing the strange man again but was instead surprised to see a pretty young woman dressed in a bright red and black dress, her blond curls bouncing with every step, heading right for them.

"Eli!" she shouted as she ran. "Oh, Eli!"

He turned at the sound of his name. For the briefest instant, Hallie could have sworn that a look of dislike passed across his rugged face. Whatever it was, it only lasted for an instant before the woman crashed into him, wrapping her arms around his body and holding him tight.

"Morning, Fawn," he grumbled.

"Thank my lucky stars that I decided to step out for a bit this morning," the woman shrieked. "Why, if I had waited until later in the day, I would have missed you altogether. And here I was wondering if you were ever going to set foot in town again."

"You weren't the only one."

Hallie could not help but marvel at the woman before her. Everything about her carried an air of privilege; the fine cut of her dress, the scent of perfume that wafted from her in the summer heat, and even the assured tone of her voice all spoke of money. Even though she had not said a single word to the woman, Hallie felt uncomfortable in her presence. *Fawn? Did he call her Fawn?* As she watched, she was surprised to feel a pang of emotion that could be nothing but jealousy.

Over the top of the woman's blond head, Eli looked at Hallie. His eyes seemed to show embarrassment and offer an apology at the same time. Gently but firmly he pulled the woman's arms from about his waist, freeing himself from her grasp. Once he was disentangled from her, he looked about them as if he were expecting someone else to be present, but there was no one other than the bubbly young woman.

"Fawn, there's someone I'd like you to meet." With a nod of his hat toward where she stood, he said, "This is Hallie Wolcott. She and some others are staying out at the ranch."

Slowly, Fawn turned to face Hallie. Her look was piercing yet distant; it was as if she were becoming aware of the other woman for the very first time, so intent had she been on rushing to Eli's side. As Hallie met her gaze, she saw an expression wash over Fawn's face similar to the one that had passed over Eli's only moments earlier. However, while Eli's look had been one of simple dislike, the one that scorched a path over Fawn's was different; *it was one of pure unadulterated hatred.* Hallie nearly recoiled at the sight but, as quickly as the hurtful look had appeared, it was gone, lasting only a few beats of her heart, replaced by a sugary sweetness she found nearly as upsetting.

"It's so nice to make your acquaintance," Fawn sang

as she rushed across the boardwalk to her. She took Hallie's hands and squeezed them together tightly. "I'm Fawn—Fawn Billings. My daddy owns the bank, so if there's anything you need, anything at all, don't you dare hesitate to ask!"

Slightly taken aback, all that Hallie could say was "Thank you."

"There are just no thanks necessary. I've been so close to Eli Morgan for just about forever! My whole life, least-ways." She smiled happily, but Hallie could hear the edge of a threat lurking just beneath her words, as if it were a dull knife being slowly dragged over a whetstone. "Any friend of his just has to be a friend of mine!"

"That's nice," Hallie managed.

But suddenly, the storm clouds over the woman's face reappeared. Stepping back, Fawn looked Hallie up and down, a furrow knitting its way across her brow. "I'm full of so many questions I could burst!" She took a deep breath and began, "Where did you come from? How on earth did you come to know Eli and why are you staying on the ranch?"

Hallie was shaken by Fawn's questions. She opened her mouth to speak, but before she could utter a sound, Eli's voice cut across the busy boardwalk.

"It's none of your concern," he said simply.

"Now don't be that way, Eli," Fawn said as she threw a glance at him over her shoulder and batted her lashes. "You can't blame me for being curious, now can you?"

"My companions and I had a bit of trouble with the storm a few nights back," Hallie interjected, willing to give Fawn a nibble of the truth without letting her sink her teeth into the whole story. "Eli and his uncle thankfully came upon us and were kind enough to allow us to shelter at their home."

"Eli to the rescue!" Fawn exclaimed, her words mocking.

"Everything's all right now," Hallie said lamely. She would be no more willing to embrace Fawn's confidence than she would a snake.

Deceit was written all over this woman.

"Well, I'm sure that some time spent in the care of Mrs. Morgan will be just what you need to get yourself back on your feet and on the road again," Fawn declared, her words sounding more like an order than advice.

"You're probably right," Hallie murmured.

"But whatever brings the two of you into Bison City this morning?"

"Just got something to . . . attend to," Eli answered hesitantly, picking over his words in a manner that matched the delicate nature of his business. "We're going to stop at the mercantile for a few things and then we'll be on our way back to the ranch."

"Well then, why don't I just come along with you?" Fawn beamed, her hands flying to her chest in excitement. "I don't have anything planned and I'd love the chance to show Hallie our fine town. Don't you think that sounds like a *marvelous* idea?"

Before the last word was even out of Fawn's mouth, Hallie frowned. She felt quite certain that it was most definitely *not* a marvelous idea. Today would be difficult for Eli. Visiting the graves of both his brother and father was something that he had been avoiding. It was a task that she felt awkward enough intruding upon herself; having Fawn along would be too much. *Maybe there is a way I can help him . . .*

"Maybe the two of us could get what's needed from the mercantile," Hallie said to Fawn, hoping to keep her away from Eli so that he could make his visit to the cemetery alone. She caught sight of a frown on Eli's face out of the corner of her eye. "That way Eli would be able to finish what he needs to do and you can show me around town."

Fawn's frown showed that she liked the idea about as much as Eli did. Still, she forced a smile and said, "I guess that would be all right. It would give us some time to get acquainted. That is, if it's all right with Eli."

Eli looked as if he wanted to object but held his tongue and tipped his hat to them. "If that's the way you want it, Hallie, then I reckon I'll be on my way. I'll be back to get you."

"See you later," Fawn called happily.

Briefly, Eli held Hallie's gaze with his own green eyes. In his rugged face, she swore that she could see some sign of disappointment, a hint of unhappiness at the arrangement. In that moment, her feelings from the night before were fanned flame in her breast, and she had to resist the strong desire to run to him, to hold him tighter than Fawn had only moments before. Instead, she merely smiled at him warmly.

"I'll be waiting." She nodded to him. "At the mercantile."

"Afternoon, ladies." Eli turned on his heel and walked away.

Chapter Seventeen

THE INSIDE OF the mercantile was stifling. Even with the open door behind her, Hallie felt as if a wall of heat were pressing down on her. Beads of sweat ran down her cheeks and arms. It was equally gloomy. The only light other than that coming from the door fell from a small high window open to the noon sun, whose orange-yellow beams spilled onto the wooden floor at her feet.

Slowly, Hallie's eyes began to adjust to the difference in light from the sunny day outside. As things began to come into view, she looked about the mercantile. Every inch of the interior seemed to be stocked full of goods. From coffee in sacks to ointments in jars to pomades in tins, the shop seemed to have everything the good people of Bison City could have hoped for. The competing scents combined in the musty interior to make her nose twitch.

"So what is it you need?" Fawn asked, an insincere smile still plastered on her face.

Hallie turned and stared at the other woman. Though it had been her idea, she still couldn't believe that she had willingly volunteered to spend part of the afternoon with Fawn. Everything about Fawn seemed false; from her smile to her clothes and even her manners, all was calculated for effect. Hallie could practically see the wheels turning behind the woman's eyes. Such distrust made it hard for her to find her voice.

"Um . . . we need—we need a sack of flour and one of coffee," she managed to finally stammer.

"That's all you need?" Fawn asked with a laugh. "Why that's hardly worth the time to come to town!" Before Hallie could open her mouth, the young woman added, "I'll tell Mr. Kettle what we need and he'll have it made right up and ready!"

She strode across the wooden floor, the sound of her heels echoing around the mercantile, and approached the man standing behind the long counter, all with the air of privilege, the assurance of a woman used to getting what she wanted.

Hallie was too far away to hear what Fawn was saying, but from the way that the store's owner—a squat, heavy-set man in an apron who sported a huge bushy mustache—was vigorously nodding his head, she knew he would deny nothing to Fawn Billings.

"It's all taken care of!" Fawn exclaimed proudly. "Mr.

Kettle will have your order brought to the wagon and loaded." Then, with a conspiratorial wink, she lowered her voice to a whisper and said, "I also had him put it all on my daddy's tab. With all the work he has at the bank, he won't bother to look over the particulars when he settles the bill."

"Oh!" Hallie exclaimed. "You shouldn't have! Eli won't like it."

"What Eli doesn't know can't possibly hurt him, now can it?" Fawn smirked mischievously. "Besides, Mr. Kettle has already set about his work. It would be rude to interrupt him."

Over Fawn's shoulder, Hallie could see that the mercantile owner had indeed begun to gather her items. He stood before the sacks of flour, his back already hunched over in an anticipation of the strain of lifting.

"Eli would want to thank you just the same," Hallie said.

"Oh, I doubt that very much." Fawn laughed.

"Why on earth would you say that?"

"Because Eli Morgan is the sort who doesn't want anyone to do for him what he can do for himself," Fawn explained with the wave of one finely cared-for hand. "He's been that way ever since we were children. He'd just as soon give me thanks for purchasing your goods as he would thank whoever murdered his brother."

Even in the stifling heat inside the mercantile, Hallie suddenly felt all of the blood in her veins run ice cold at

Fawn's casual words. She knew little about what had happened to Caleb; what Eli had told her about his younger brother's murder and the grief that he still held in his heart over that loss had been painful for her to hear. But the callous way in which Fawn mentioned his death sent chills running up and down Hallie's spine.

Part of her wanted to walk away from Fawn, to turn on her heel and disappear out into the heat of the summer day. But another part didn't want to give the spoiled young woman the satisfaction of knowing that she had gotten under her skin. When Hallie spoke, her back was ramrod straight, her voice cool. "I'm certain that Eli will want to pay for his own supplies."

"I wouldn't accept it," Fawn said simply.

"Why not?"

"Because money isn't the type of repayment that I'm looking for."

"What is?"

At that question, Fawn took a quick step closer to Hallie. Her eyes regarded her with the intensity that a fox gives to a baby chick that has strayed too far from its mother's side. "What I want is to know who you really are, Little Miss Hallie Wolcott from places unknown," she demanded. "I want the truth. I want to know where you came from and why you're staying at the Morgans' ranch."

Now Hallie knew why Fawn had so readily agreed to accompany her to the mercantile; she had jumped at the chance to get her away from Eli and to pressure her into telling her what she wished to know. Hallie, however, was determined not to give Fawn the information she wanted.

"My two friends and I were going to Denver," she began, the words sliding off of her tongue as easily as if they were true. "We had been traveling by wagon, after we left the train, when we were caught in the storm that struck a week ago. If it hadn't been for our good luck in coming across Eli and his uncle, I don't know what would have happened to us."

"Three women traveling alone in a wagon at night?" Fawn asked skeptically.

Hallie nodded with as much confidence as she could muster.

"Why wouldn't you have known enough to seek shelter?"

"The two women who were traveling with me and I are all to be teachers," Hallie lied further, certain that Pearl would have laughed uproariously at the very idea. "None of us had ever been in that sort of weather and didn't know any better. Truly, we're lucky to be alive."

As Fawn listened, Hallie could see her interest growing colder. Certainly, she had wanted something much more salacious, something full of adventure and excitement; what she really wanted was the *truth*. Unfortunately for Fawn, that was something Hallie wasn't prepared to give.

"But then why are you still staying with the Morgans?" Fawn asked, refusing to let go without some form of juicy rumor. "Even if your wagon was damaged, certainly it would have been repaired by now."

"They are still working on it."

"Don't tell me that you're sweet on Eli?" Fawn taunted.

In the face of all Fawn's questions and accusations, Hallie felt herself wilting; it was as if she were a flower shriveling under the relentless glare of the sun. She was certain that Fawn would keep asking questions, would keep hammering away at her, and would hack something away from the facade that Hallie was constructing. It was because of such worry that she inadvertently gave away a truth.

"It's because my companions and I are caring for Mrs. Morgan."

Fawn seized on the information. "Mrs. Morgan?" she exclaimed. "Whatever is the matter with her that she needs your care?"

"She fell the other day," Hallie explained, the slope already far too slippery for her to regain her footing with lies. "It wasn't too serious, but the doctor has asked her to stay off her feet for a while. In the meantime, we're lending a hand."

"You don't say . . ."

A thin smile spread across Fawn's face. *Is she actually pleased that Adele Morgan is hurt?* Hallie's words seemed to roll around in Fawn's head, bearing further fruit with every turn. Absently, she began to walk away from Hallie, suddenly oblivious to the other woman's presence, until Hallie was once again alone, standing at the front of the mercantile.

"Oh, what have I done?" she muttered to herself.

As if in answer, her arm was suddenly pinched in a viselike grip and she was violently yanked to the side and away from the open door. Her feet were pulled out from beneath her and she struggled to hold her balance.

"Hold yer tongue, girly," a man's voice ordered.

In the corner of the mercantile, away from the light of the door and deep into the gloomy shadows, she somehow knew who was speaking to her before her eyes could focus upon her attacker.

It's the man who was watching me out in front of the saloon!

"No, don't—" she began before he clamped his hand down roughly on her mouth.

"Best keep those screams to yourself, little darlin'." He smiled at her through crooked, stained teeth. When he spoke, his breath smelled of whiskey. "Don't be foolish and give me a reason to slit yer pretty little throat."

Eli climbed the last steps of the steep hill to Bison City's cemetery through waves of heat that made the tombstones shimmer and sway as if they were floating adrift in the ocean. He wiped the glistening sweat from his brow with the back of his arm and peeked at the sky from under the brim of his hat. The sun stood at its highest point, beating down without mercy.

"What in the hell am I doing here?" he muttered to himself.

Even as he spoke it, Eli knew the answer to that particular question; it was one that he had grappled with for years, never finding the right answer until Hallie had provided one for him the night before.

I'm doing what is needed.

The cemetery was located west of town, up a steep hill, and nestled in among tall elms, oaks, and pines that sat at the edge of the greater forest beyond. Thick brush filled the space between these sentinels that watched silently over the dead. From where he stood, Eli could look back over all Bison City and far into the valley in which it lay.

For a moment, he simply stood and looked at the tombstones. Most were made of white marble or gray granite, engraved names almost obliterated by the years of pounding rain and blazing sun. They stood not in rows but haphazardly, as if the bodies that they marked had simply fallen on the spot and been buried posthaste. A wrought-iron fence had been built around the perimeter. *Is it to keep intruders out or the spirits within?* Eli wondered.

From his time in the army, Eli had some familiarity with the dead. He'd seen men who had been shot, stabbed, dismembered, or had suffered any other calamity that could befall a soldier. But, somehow, as he stood before the cemetery and the tombstones that were contained therein, he was struck by just how different this all was; these were the graves of his kith and kin. *This is my family!*

Swallowing hard and mustering his determination, Eli stepped up to the waist-high gate and swung it in on rusty hinges that screamed as if in pain. The dry grass crunched under his boots as he stepped among the stones, peering at the worn names that had been carved into them, searching for the ones that belonged to his brother and father.

I wish Hallie were here.

He couldn't help but to think of the soft sound of her voice, the sweet smell of her hair, and the warm touch of her skin against his own. When his lips had brushed against hers, he'd marveled at the way it had made him feel, the fire that it had lit in his belly. She was *different*, special, and unlike any woman he would have ever expected to meet in Bison City.

The type of woman I meet in Bison City is either a whore or like Fawn Billings!

He had hated to leave Hallie alone with her, but he could tell that she was trying to tactfully arrange his visit to the cemetery without Fawn's unwanted intrusion. He felt certain that Fawn would pester her relentlessly, demanding to know things that weren't any of her business. Fawn would fear that Hallie was trying to steal her imagined place by his side. When he had run into Fawn several days previously, it had been obvious that she still had designs on him, her engagement to Seth McCarty be damned.

Eli was grateful not to find Seth at Fawn's side. Remembering the slanderous words the man had spoken on his first visit to Bison City still raised his ire. *It's as if nothing has changed between us!* It would have been hard enough for him to stay his hand if Seth had once again commenced with a tongue-lashing directed toward *him*, but if he had turned his biting comments to Hallie, no amount of restraint would have been enough for Eli to keep from thrashing the man just as he had when they were boys. Then again, maybe Hallie wouldn't have needed his help. She struck him as the type that could more than hold her own.

"After all," he said aloud, "she's put up with my mother for—"

The words died in Eli's throat as he read the name on the tombstone before him. The white rock of the marker was clean, the letters and dates of birth and death just as crisp as the day in which they had been carved by a steady hand. A few loose stones and pesky weeds shared space at the base of the stone, but all these details were lost on Eli, all save the name itself: CALEB JOSIAH MORGAN.

Emotion welled in Eli's chest. Blood pounded in his

ears, and his mouth was as dry as the air around him. His vision blurred as tears came unbidden.

"Brother," he whispered.

In the many times he'd imagined himself standing before his brother's grave, Eli never thought he would be so overwhelmed with loss. Thinking about Caleb's murder had always caused despair and anger to rage within Eli's mind; but now, standing in the cemetery, he felt such a sense of loss that it was as if one of his limbs had been severed from his body, leaving him to go through the rest of his life incomplete.

Tentatively, Eli reached one shaking hand to his brother's marker, desperate for some contact with Caleb, no matter how tenuous. The pale flesh of his palm burned from the heat that the stone held, but he paid it little mind, choosing instead to hold it tighter as penance for a visit withheld too long.

"I'm so sorry, Caleb," he began, the pent-up words falling from his mouth as if they were water spilling from an opened dam. "I'm sorry that you were murdered, sorry that you never got to live the life you wanted, and I'm sorry that I couldn't help the day you were put in this goddamn place! But I just had to get away from Bison City and the ranch and our parents! I had to go or I would've suffocated!"

As the minutes stretched by, Eli spoke of his time in the army, of the life he'd led in Texas, and of his return to their birthplace. He spoke of his confusion at all that had happened with Abe; of his mother's continued obstinacy; and even of Hallie, Pearl, and Mary. He spoke until his voice was hoarse, but still he croaked on, afraid he'd leave something out. As the words spilled out, he was struck by the realization that Hallie had been right: He needed to come and make his peace.

Suddenly, out of the corner of his eye, he noticed the gravestone that lay next to that of his brother. It had been partly covered with leaves so he hadn't seen it before. The marker was smaller and cut from a darker stone, but what Eli could not pry his eyes from was the name: MILBURN SAMUEL MORGAN.

Eli couldn't help but be struck by the irony of the situation: his father and Caleb lying next to each other peacefully in death as they could not in life. All the time that he had been carrying on before Caleb, there his father had lain, as if listening to his every word. Eli couldn't keep a smile from crossing his face.

Releasing his hold on his brother's tombstone, Eli grasped his father's. The stone was equally hot, but he welcomed the pain, rubbing his fingers along the rough rock. Emotion welled yet again; while he wouldn't have to repeat his entire tale, he had more than his share of apologies to make.

"I'm sorry that you and I never got along, Father," he said, his voice cracking. "I'm sorry that you were disappointed in me."

Like a thunderclap issuing from a cloudlessly blue

sky, a sharp crack split the air and echoed off the trees and grave markers. Eli felt a hot, searing pain race the length of his right arm before the corner of his father's tombstone exploded in a shower of stone and dust. He fell on his side, grasping his arm in pain, his fingers wet and sticky, his mind reeling and dizzy.

I've been shot!

Chapter Eighteen

HEAT FAR HOTTER than the summer day filled Eli's arm. In the split second after the shot, the pain had been slight. But after that first moment, after the first beat of his heart, it engulfed him.

"Son of a bitch!" He winced as his fingers probed along his elbow, growing sticky with the blood that oozed from the wound. He couldn't be certain, but he believed that the bullet had passed clean through the soft flesh in the underside of his right arm before crashing into his father's marker. With every new touch, fresh shock waves of agony raced from his elbow to his shoulder and across his chest. The coppery smell of blood filled his nostrils.

From where he lay on his side in the scraggly grass, Eli tried to look around, to gain his bearings. Sighting through the rows of tombstones was difficult; it was as if he were peering through a broken set of teeth, each stump more rotten than the one before.

Who in the hell is out there? Who means to kill me?

Carefully, he raised his head and peered into the scraggly line of trees at the cemetery's edge, in the direction from which he thought the shot had come. He hadn't had time to focus on a single tree or scrub, let alone to find a gunman bent on murdering him, when another shot split the summer day, whizzing past his face and smashing into a weather-beaten tombstone inches behind his head. From equal parts fear and reflex, Eli fell back to the ground, pressing himself into the earth.

"Goddamn it!" he shouted, his anger rising as quickly as the pain. "Who the hell are you?"

No answer.

"Only a coward would shoot a man without showing himself!" he continued, hoping to shame his assailant into at least revealing his identity. "Only a yellow coward would do such a thing!"

Still no answer.

Eli strained to hear any sound over the incessant pounding in his ears. He lay as stock-still as he could manage, his wounded arm pressed tightly to his side, his ears cocked for any noise, hoping that the gunman would reveal himself; but he heard only the gentle rustling of the leaves in the trees.

He felt as defenseless as a newborn calf. While he'd often carried a gun when he'd been in the army, he hadn't done so since. He and Hank went hunting with rifles in the woods near the ranch, but he'd never been the sort to go into town with a holstered pistol at his waist. If he had a gun with him, he could have defended himself— returned fire and, at the very least, made the other man think twice, worrying that he didn't have an easy kill. *Now here I am, an unarmed, wounded man with my life hanging in the balance!*

"Hell of a time for a mistake," he muttered under his breath.

He had to move. To stay where he lay amid the tombstones was to court a certain death; he'd join Caleb at his father's side, where all *three* of them would lie silent and without argument. Eventually, the shooter's caution would run out and he would realize that Eli did not have a gun. At that moment, it would be a simple task for him to walk through the cemetery and put a bullet right in the middle of his chest.

If I want to live, I need to move!

It was too much for him to hope that the shots had been heard in Bison City; the town was too far away from the cemetery. Even if someone had heard the gunshots, he'd believe that a hunter was roaming through the thickets looking for game. With every passing second, the pain in Eli's arm grew in intensity like a raging fire, blazing out of control across his body. Isolated, the only person he had to depend upon was himself.

Once again, he tentatively raised his head, but this

time looked in the other direction, the direction that offered him an escape. He only had a quick moment to scout a path into the woods before another shot cracked across the cemetery and imbedded itself into a wooden marker.

Had that shot come from closer range?

Eli couldn't be certain, but it sounded as if the shot were nearer. He wondered if his adversary was moving closer, inching forward to finish him off. He didn't dare pop up to look for fear of taking another bullet. If he were shot in the leg, if he were unable to get to his feet and run to safety, he was as good as dead.

He had fallen beneath the tombstones of his father and brother. Looking up at their names carved into stone, he felt the fire in his arm spreading to his gut, urging him to get to his feet and to run to save his life. Even as he stared at the reminders of their deaths, his family gave him the courage to fight.

So, too, did the thought of Hallie. He remembered the night that he had first met her along the banks of the swollen river, the chill that ran through his body whenever he was at her side, the passion of the kiss they had shared just the night before, but mostly he thought of the times still to come. To die here in the cemetery, to surrender himself to the mystery gunman, would deprive them both of what lay ahead, and that was something that he would not allow.

Screwing up his will, Eli readied himself to run. His

breath caught hot in his throat, sweat poured from his skin, and his heart pounded as if it were a jackrabbit's. Every second that he stayed there in the cemetery was one second longer for the gunman to find him.

"Move, damn it!" he urged himself. "Move!"

It pained him to move his arm, but he blocked it from his mind and sprang to his feet to race between the uneven tombstones, careful not to collide with one and topple back to the ground. Even though he was no more than twenty feet from the wrought-iron fence, it seemed miles of ground stretched before him. Still, on he ran.

From behind him, shots rang out. He held his breath, waiting for one of the bullets to collide with his back, his arms, or his legs; but instead they slammed into tombstones, or thudded into the earth and spit up dirt. One even clanged against the fence before him, sparks blazing into the sunlight. He strained to push himself faster for fear that the bullet with his name on it was yet to come.

"Keep going," he hissed through clenched teeth.

He leaped over the fence, one boot touching the metal bar, but even as he landed awkwardly on the ground beyond, he held his balance and kept stride, racing for the tree line and the hoped-for safety beyond. The cracks of the pistol continued to come unrelentingly, now ripping into the trunks of the trees and bushes before him. His lungs began to ache from the exertion, but Eli never slowed for an instant, barreling ever forward.

Eli pressed on as he crashed into the deep underbrush

that choked the space between two tall elms. The thick
vines and ensnaring branches snatched his hat from his
head, but he never thought of stopping to retrieve it even
for an instant. Small thorns tore at his exposed flesh, but
the pain was nothing compared to that of his wounded
arm as it brushed against the snapping branches. He
clenched his teeth tightly to keep from crying out.

Then, as quickly as he had entered the deep brush,
he was through it and out into the open spaces of the
woods. He dodged past tree trunks, leaped over fallen
limbs that rotted on the forest carpet where they lay, and
pushed himself until his arms and legs burned and he
had to suck air into his heaving lungs. Still, he never
stopped moving, fearfully certain that the gunman was
right behind him, ready to finish him off.

Finally, the ache of pushing himself became too
much and Eli darted behind a tree trunk and stopped,
his heart deafeningly racing and his fists balled for whatever fight he might have left to give. He tried to listen for
any sound—a footfall or a stick breaking that might give
away his pursuer—but couldn't hear past the rushing of
his own blood.

He waited, waited, and then waited some more before
taking a deep breath and looking out from where he hid
into the forest. His eyes peered from tree to tree, bush to
bush, and then back again for any sign of the gunman,
but he could see none. Instants turned into seconds then
into minutes but still he saw nothing—no movement, no

assailant. Questions raced through his head as swiftly as the bullets that had been shot at him.

Who in the hell is after me?

Where has he gone?

Did he follow me into the woods or is he waiting for me to walk out of them?

Eli knew he had to get away. He had to get out of these woods, back to Bison City, and get himself and Hallie back to the ranch. He'd do it or die trying!

The smell of the man almost made Hallie sick. His clothes were stiff and unwashed, filthy with sweat and food and stinking with the sharp odor of tobacco that clung to him as if it were a blanket. His breath bore the tang of whiskey. Even the air around him seemed to exude rot. Held in place, unable to move an inch, she was afraid she would retch.

But mingled with the sharp smells of the man was that of her own making, the bitter odor of fear. Sweat ran in rivulets down the sides of her face and spine, matting her hair against her forehead. She felt smothered, oppressed with worry and despair that knotted her insides. Even in the heat of the mercantile, shivers raced across her skin.

"Keep your tongue, girly," the man threatened, his scratchy voice little more than a whisper. "If'n you try to yell out, I'm just as likely to cut you from ear to ear as I am to look at ya! Listen to what I'm sayin' and you might live to see another day."

Even if she had wanted to do so, Hallie couldn't have screamed for help, not with the man's hand clamped down over her mouth like a vise. His hand was as rough as bark on a tree, scratching against her skin.

"Are ya gonna listen?"

Hallie quickly nodded her head.

"Then know that I've been a waitin' here in this piss hole of a town for a hint of you or either of them other two bitches," he began, his wet tongue licking her ear. She jerked her head away. "Waitin' for one of you bitches to be stupid enough to show yer face and that's exactly what you done.

"Chester ain't the type that takes kindly to bein' made the fool," he kept on, giving name to the man who terrorized Hallie's dreams. *All of my fears of being pursued have come true in an instant!* "He's gonna be damn happy with ol' Charlie here for bein' the one to find you!"

Even as she listened to Charlie's words, Hallie's eyes looked furtively around the mercantile for someone to come to her aid. An elderly man stood not ten feet away, a tin of some sort only inches from his face as he peered at its label, his wrinkled forehead lined with concentration. Other than him, she couldn't see a soul. She would even have been thankful for Fawn to return, but the woman was nowhere to be seen.

Hallie heard sounds coming from the street: the strong voices of the men greeting acquaintances, the pounding of horse's hooves, and the creaking of wagon wheels. All the sounds were so close but still too far away to be of any help at all.

I am all alone with this monster!

"I wonder if Chester would mind if I did the deed myself."

Hallie's blood froze in her veins at the man's words. Tears came to her eyes and ran down beside the sweat. She felt suffocated and so weak in the knees that they bent; the man's hand yanked her upright and back into place.

"Don't like that there idea, huh?" He chuckled into her ear, obviously pleased that his words had found their mark. "Don't like thinkin' about a knife slidin' all easy like between your ribs, and you bleedin' out onto the floor."

Hallie was shaking, unable to control herself. She thought of Pearl and Mary and all the trouble they had already endured. That harm should come to them *now*, when they had traveled so far was a tragedy that threatened to overwhelm her.

But then she thought of Eli. In her mind's eye, she could see his face just as plain as day. She remembered the joy that she had felt by his side only hours earlier, riding beside him in the wagon. She thought of their kiss again, the familiar waves rushing over her, giving her strength she didn't know she had. No, she would not quit, not surrender to the fear this man inspired. Straightening her back, she managed to stifle her tears.

"Nah, I ain't gonna be the one that does you in," Charlie continued, unaware of the feelings running through his prey. "That's somethin' reserved for Chester alone. But no matter where you run, no matter what you do, it ain't gonna make one goddamn difference in the end, you mark my words. He's gonna gut you and them bitches just the same. Hell, he might even like it more if you run and make some sport of it."

Fear gave way to anger in Hallie's heart. She had been a victim long enough, longer than she could bear. This man wouldn't shake her, wouldn't make her cower in a corner. She was just about to fight, to scratch at his skin or to do anything to free herself, when he spoke again.

"Keep lookin' over your shoulder, 'cause one day he'll be there!"

With that, Hallie was shoved forward, losing her balance and falling hard on one knee. Pain shot up her leg but she ignored it, turning around quickly, ready to fend off another attack, but the man had already gone.

For a few moments, Hallie sat on the wooden floor, her mind racing over all that had happened. *Chester knows where we are!* Try as she might, she couldn't escape that truth. As long as they remained in Bison City, as long as they stayed with the Morgans, their lives and those of all around them would be in danger. *But what can we do?* Mary's condition was such that she couldn't be moved.

"What on earth are you doing on the floor?"

Hallie glanced up to see Fawn standing before her, a look of utter puzzlement written on her face.

Before Hallie could answer, before she could come up with yet another lie to pass off to Fawn, she was once again grabbed roughly by the arm and pulled to her feet. *The mysterious attacker had returned!* She was about to scream out, to ball up her fists, and attack the man, when she looked over and found that the hand that had grabbed her belonged to Eli.

"Oh, Eli! What are—" she managed.

"We're leaving."

"But—"

"Right now," he said gruffly.

He pulled her toward the door of the mercantile so quickly that she could only stumble along. It wasn't until they had passed out into the sunshine that she noticed the blood that soaked the sleeve of his shirt.

"Eli, you're hurt," she gasped. "What happened to your arm?"

"Never mind that," he snapped, unwilling to do anything but herd her to the wagon. "We don't have time now for talking."

"But what about—?"

"Just get in the wagon, Hallie!" he barked.

She did as she was told, unable to keep herself from looking for some sign of the man who had accosted her, but he wasn't to be seen on the busy street. When Eli dragged himself up to the seat with a noticeable wince of pain, she held her tongue. As she looked at him, his eyes spoke not of anger but of caution. They shifted from one side of the street to the other.

What happened to him?

As they rode out of Bison City, she looked back over her shoulder to watch as the town disappeared behind them. The sight that held her gaze the longest was Fawn Billings standing on the steps of the mercantile, her red dress bright, watching them intently.

Chapter Nineteen

Angry and irritated, Seth McCarty walked quickly down the dusty main street of Bison City, his brow drenched in sweat. Absently, he shot his cuffs and wiped a mote of dirt from his sleeve, silently cursing his untidiness. All around him, the town's citizens went about their day, the streets full of laughter, sweat, and swearing. To it all, he paid no heed, his mind as heavy in thought as the revolver that was tucked in his belt, beneath his coat, lying snugly against his back.

"Afternoon, Mr. McCarty!"

"Mighty fine day, don't you think, sir?"

Greetings flew toward him from all sides. Even though he deflected them all with little more than a wave of his hand or a curt nod, he had long ago grown accustomed to receiving such attention. After all, he *was* the public face of the town's bank, a figure known to all. Men and women alike curried his favor, hopeful that they wouldn't be turned down in their moment of need all because they had failed to give a smile or simple acknowledgment. *And why shouldn't they grovel to me?* He was a man with power, quite used to getting all that he wanted.

He'd been stepping out of the bank on business when he'd first spotted Eli and then Fawn rushing to put her arms around the man's waist. In a split second, his heart raced with hatred and thoughts of vengeance. *How dare that cowboy interfere with the life I've built!* He'd retreated into the bank, retrieved his pistol from the desk drawer in which it was locked, and then followed as his enemy parted from Fawn at the mercantile and set off, his path leading out of town and toward the cemetery. He had hung many steps back, careful lest Eli turn and discover him; but the man's thoughts had been elsewhere and he'd blindly led the way, stopping only occasionally to wipe his brow.

At the cemetery, Seth had hid in the thick woods, waiting patiently for his moment to strike; like a spider spreading out its web, waiting for the fly to deliver itself to his bite. He'd watched as Eli knelt before the markers; he had been too distant to make out the words Eli spoke, but he was mindful of the opportunity Eli's back presented.

Do it now, he thought. *Do it while he's distracted!*

He leveled the gun, his sweaty hand as steady as he could manage, took a deep breath, and pulled the trigger. The pistol bucked hard in his hand, but he held it tight, staring through a puff of smoke, expecting to find Eli grasping at a chest wound; but to Seth's chagrin he'd missed the chest and hit Eli's arm.

Fighting a sickening feeling deep in his stomach, Seth tried to remain as calm as he could, waiting for his target to reveal himself from behind the tombstone where he had flung himself after the shot. But as the seconds ticked by, Seth began to worry. He'd watched Eli spring from his hiding spot and hurtle into the woods beyond, and he had fired as quickly as his finger could pull the trigger, but to no avail; he might as well have been cursing at the man for all the damage he had inflicted. There was no way in hell that he was going to follow Eli into the woods in the hopes that he'd achieve what he set out to do, so he left the bastard to his own devices.

Now I'm returning with my tail between my legs!

"Fine day for a walk now, ain't it, Mr. McCarty!"

Seth could only grunt a reply.

The bank soon loomed before him. Without slowing for a moment, he shot in through the front door, passed where the fat sow of a teller peered at him through sleepy eyes, and was in his office, the door slamming shut behind him. He'd be alone until he wished otherwise; all his staff knew far better than to knock on his door when he was in a snit. Two fingers of brandy were soon burning a path down his gullet as he dropped the pistol back into its hiding place and collapsed into his desk chair, cursing his bad luck.

I did it for Fawn!

From the very first moment that he witnessed Fawn rushing to Eli's side in front of the doctor's, Seth knew he would have trouble. From the way she spoke that day to the way her eyes embraced Eli, Seth realized that Fawn Billings was still in love with Eli Morgan—or, to be more exact, that she had never fallen *out* of love, even after all these long years. Since then, when they were together, she talked of nothing but Eli, regaling her intended husband with tales of their youth, about how charming Eli could be, even about how he had spurned her advances. It had simply become more than Seth could bear.

Given enough time, there was no telling what could happen, what damage could be done. Fawn would keep on and on and on, needling and pestering until she finally managed to break down Eli's defenses, getting him to understand that it was *she* that was meant for him and *he* for her. Then, all the hard work he had done, all the time he had spent building a life for himself at the bank, would be lost as if it were nothing more than smoke. *Gone in an instant!* And that, when it was so close to the old man's finally retiring and his becoming the most powerful man in all Bison City, was something that would not do.

He poured another glass of liquor, and it quickly followed the first into the fiery pit of his stomach. Rising from his chair, Seth went over to the window and looked upon the town.

In all his life, he had never feared taking a risk; from his dealings with his drunk of a father to how he conducted his business at the bank, he'd taken every advantage offered to him without a second's pause, ready to make his way or to die trying. What faced him now was no different. Whether she truly knew it or not, Fawn *belonged* to him. She had been blinded by the wily ways of that stupid cowboy who certainly didn't give a good goddamn about her. In the end, the only impediment to life with Fawn, to the future he demanded, the only obstacle that stood in his way, was Eli Morgan. Just as Caleb Morgan had received exactly what he deserved, so, too, would his good-for-nothing brother! Once Eli had been eliminated, no one would ever again threaten what he had worked for.

"Next time you show yourself, you son of a bitch," he threatened, already feeling better about what had happened in the cemetery, "I will kill you."

Just like your goddamn brother.

Chester Remnick leaned heavily against the tavern's long bar, his shoulders sagging and his eyes boring holes into the bottom of a glass of whiskey. Outside, dusk slowly crept up upon the day, the high sky stained a deep purple as the sun clung tenaciously to the horizon. Chester paid no heed to the changing of the guard; night and day had little meaning when you spent all your time in a bottle.

A dull, hot ache still pulsed its way up and down his leg. Even with the bullet removed, pain remained a constant, stinging reminder of what had happened to him at the hands of those whores. Sleep also eluded him; every time he closed his eyes, he could see the flash of the rifle quickly followed by the searing pain in his leg.

Still, no matter how badly his leg bothered him, it was far less than the pain of loss and embarrassment he'd suffered. It galled him no end that he'd been done in by a couple of women. If only the shooter had been a man! While the wound was still painful, he could have held onto the scraps of his dignity and kept his head up. But no amount of wishing would make it so; it had been two women who had brazenly taken what was rightfully his, had stolen his Mary.

When he had asked about for help in finding the runaway women, he'd had no trouble finding volunteers; there were enough men in his debt or in fear of him to stock a small army. But he'd seen the looks, the glances down at his leg mixed with a small curling of the corners of a mouth for him to know jokes were being made at his expense. He was certain that *someone* would find those bitches, but what price would he pay for that success? How much of the fool would he look?

Laughter sounded from behind him.

Chester turned slowly to glance at the tavern's front

door. A portly man, his belly hanging heavy over his trousers, his cheeks red with cracked blood vessels, staggered in and nearly fell. He would certainly have succeeded in pitching forward onto his face had it not been for the tramp on his arm. She wore a gaudy shade of green, her blond hair bouncing at her tits, and she was nearly as drunk as her companion. She seemed to be hanging on his every slurred word, even if she was only half his age.

In his own booze-induced haze, Chester had half a mind to slice the whore's throat from ear to ear, so poisoned was he toward her gender. Instead, he settled for another belt of liquor.

Somebody was gonna pay, goddamn it!

Even when he lay on the floor of his shack, sick out of his mind with delirium from the gunshot, Chester had dreamed of the punishment he would dole out. The bitch who shot him would get what all fat sows got: be gutted and hung up to bleed out. The other one, well, she was a mite on the pretty side, so he couldn't be blamed for having a bit of fun with her before finishing her off. Neither would get less than she deserved.

As for Mary . . .

Chester had come to believe that Mary's leaving with those two cunts wasn't anything less than a betrayal. Even though they'd most certainly coaxed her off, enough time had passed for him to believe she'd chosen *not* to return at all. Part of him wanted to do unto her what he'd inflict on the other two, but something held him back. In the end, he'd let her live, but she'd have to be punished; black and blue from head to toe.

"I reckon you'll be wantin' this," a voice spoke from his side.

Chester turned to find a man loosely holding a scrap of paper in one hand. It took a moment for his eyes to clear through the liquor, but he finally managed to recognize the man as the telegraph operator at the train depot. When he'd spoken to the man earlier in the week, he'd given him explicit instructions of what to do if he were to receive a communication. On that occasion, the telegrapher hadn't seemed so sour, but now it was a different matter entirely; annoyance was clearly written on his lined face at being made a delivery boy.

Chester waited for the operator to hand him the message, but he did not.

"I'll be by to pay up later," he mumbled.

The man simply stared.

"I said I'll be by," Chester said again, the edge of a threat lining his voice.

"Ain't good enough."

Drunkenly, he dug into his pockets and fished about for some coins. He finally managed to gather some which, not bothering to count, he pounded down on the counter as if they were nails to be driven.

The telegraph operator smiled at his impending payment, placed the message on the bar, and reached for the coins. His fingers had no more than touched metal when Chester snatched at his wrist. The grip was as tight as a vise; the man's bones were like twigs waiting to be broken.

"Now listen to me, ya no good son of a bitch," Chester snarled. He tugged on the soft flesh of the man's arm until he relented and turned a sweat-beaded face toward his own. His bloodshot eyes held the operator's, practically daring him to look away.

"Don't ever think I ain't a man of my word," he threatened, the whiskey hot and sour on his breath. A few heads in the tavern turned to watch the show, but Chester paid them no mind; he had words that would be spoken, audience or none. "I ain't the sort that takes to bein' spoken to like a no-good bum. I done killed for less. Don't doubt my word again, or it'll be the goddamn last mistake ya'll ever make."

The telegraph man could only nod and shake, his fear making him mute.

"You understandin' me?"

Chester held the man's gaze a moment longer, finally making certain that there was no doubt as to the truth of his words. The operator's lower lip quivered. Somewhere in the pools of the man's eyes, he could see tears forming, from fear or pain he could not say. When he finally released his grip on the man's wrist, the operator scurried away as if he were a rat, rubbing at his wound, never bothering to retrieve the payment he had once thought so precious. Chester let him go without even a look.

He plucked the message from the bar top and found it to be only two words:

BISON CITY

Suddenly, the pain in his leg that had at one time threatened to pull him under, to drown him, vanished. The cloud of drunkenness that he'd been living under over the last week broke as if it were a storm split by a radiant sun. Even the anger in his gut ceased to roil. A thin smile split his craggy face as he stared at himself in the mirror behind the bar.

I'm coming for you, Mary . . . and hell's coming with me!

Chapter Twenty

Eli tenderly pressed against the soft underside of his bare arm and pain raced down his side. The inside of the barn wobbled for a moment, the setting sun blurring on the horizon, but he steadied himself and stayed upright. The bullet had passed through one side of the tanned flesh of the arm and out the other; the wound itself was more bruise than blood, though a steady seepage had soaked his shirt.

Still, it hurts like hell!

Even though this pain had been his constant companion since the moment he had been shot, he'd done his best to ignore it, particularly in Hallie's company. The ride back to the ranch had been in near silence. He'd kept his jaw tightly shut as each rock and bump in the road rattled him as badly as it did the wagon. For her part,

Hallie had done the same, occasionally looking back over her shoulder in the direction of the town.

Taking the strips of cloth he had scavenged from the ranch house, Eli started to wind them around his arm. Fresh pain struck, and his breath came hard and fast through clenched teeth. *Goddamn that smarts!* He'd have to keep a close eye on the wound to make sure that it didn't start to go bad, but he couldn't dare risk a trip to the doctor, not with an assassin on the loose. He'd have to manage to get by.

What had happened had been no accident, of that there could be no denial. Someone had followed him to the cemetery, far from the prying eyes of the people of Bison City, with the intent to do him in. That his attacker hadn't succeeded would mean another attempt.

Questions raced through his head, neck and neck with the pain.

Who is out to kill me?

Does this have anything to do with Caleb's murder?

"What happened to you in town?" Hallie stood in the barn's open doorway, just as beautiful as an angel, her hair glowing in the sun's waning light. Her face was lined with worry, the corners of her dainty mouth turned down. Eli somehow managed to smile, shrug, and wince all at the same time.

"Not much," he mumbled.

"Don't tell me that," she disagreed with a soft shake of her head. "I'd have to be a fool to believe that, not after the strange way you acted in the mercantile, not after I saw all that blood on your shirt, and certainly not after you were so silent the whole way back to the ranch."

"Hallie, I—" he began, but she cut him off.

"Then, just as soon as we get back, you rush out to the barn and hide yourself," she continued as if he hadn't spoken a word. "Now I find you wrapping up a wound and still you tell me it's not much?"

Without waiting for a response, she went to him and took his hurt arm gently in her hands. Already, a small flower of deep crimson blood had begun to bloom on the white cloth, the makeshift bandages doing little to staunch the still-leaking wound. Hallie gasped. "Someone shot you!"

"I just . . . it was . . ."

With his good arm, Eli pulled her to him, pressing her small body close to him and holding her tightly in place. He was filled with the warmth of her. It was heavenly. Burying his face in her hair, he inhaled deeply, her scent and touch filling him with emotions that he'd never before experienced. Desperately, he wished that *this* moment might go on forever, that they would never need to return to the danger and hurt of the world; but she shuddered against him, a spasm of feeling that shook them both. Reaching down, he gently took her by the chin and turned her face up toward his.

As he stared down into the pools of Hallie's eyes a lone tear broke free and raced down her soft cheek, and Eli knew that he couldn't possibly tell her someone was out to kill him. With all that she had already endured—the nightmarish night at the river and Mary's near drowning—he would not burden her with his own troubles. What had happened to him in the cemetery had its roots in something else, something *older*, that had nothing to do with Hallie Wolcott.

"Don't worry about me," he finally said.

"How can I help but worry," Hallie replied.

"What happened to me isn't something to lose sleep over, mark my words."

She opened her mouth to speak but instead closed it without a sound. As Eli gazed into her eyes, he thought he saw an emotion swim across her face for a moment, some unspoken thing that had nearly come out and revealed itself, but then it was gone just as quickly as it had come.

"Then I guess I'll have to believe you," she whispered.

"Thank you, sweet girl."

Slowly, she disentangled herself from his embrace and pushed away. The words he had spoken had been meant to calm her, but he could see worry etched on her face. She was not convinced, but she did not feel she had the right to press him further.

Hallie turned to go without a word and Eli didn't make a move to stop her.

*   *   *

Hallie stood in the doorway of Mary's room in the ranch house and looked in. Abe sat slumped in the chair beside the bed, his chin down on his chest, the light from the kerosene lamp flickering across the walls. Hallie was about to move on, to avoid disturbing his much-needed sleep, when she realized that he wasn't asleep at all; his eyes blinked several times. He took a deep breath, and bent over to whisper to Mary. It was as if the wind were working its way through a crack in the window, so fine was its sound. But Mary slept on.

Hallie sighed. After her talk with Eli out in the barn, she'd come to the house to find companionship, someone with whom she could talk. The thought of being alone was nearly more than she could bear. Pearl and Hank had been nowhere to be seen so she had come to Mary's room, treading lightly past the barely open door to the room where Mrs. Morgan lay.

Eli lied to me or, at the very least, refused to tell me the truth. She felt shaken, and a strong sense of unease tickled the fine hairs on the back of her neck. Something bad had happened to Eli while they were in Bison City. Of that much she was certain, but the truth remained elusive. *I so badly want him to confide in me!* Leaving the safety of his embrace had been difficult, but she knew that to stay was to crumple into a storm of tears and she didn't want him to see her that way. Still, she couldn't allow her night to end in silence.

Hallie stepped into the room, and Abe turned to her, rising from his seat.

"Evening, Miss Wolcott," he said.

"Good evening." She smiled. "I hope I'm not disturbing you."

"Not at all, not at all." He smiled warmly. "I was simply regaling my sweet Mary with tales of my youth. She was always quite fond of them, so I thought I might lift her spirits while she rests."

"Isn't it difficult to have a one-sided conversation?"

"It is quite ironic that you would put it that way, my dear"—Abe laughed—"as that was what my story was about. You see, as a young lad growing up in the woods around Springfield, a great deal of my time was spent alone with nature, silent as a Sunday at church, my only companions the trees that shaded me, the many animals that lived beneath their boughs, and the gurgling of a stream or two. In those moments I truly began to appreciate the joy one can achieve in the quiet around you."

"This was in Illinois?" Hallie asked, fully aware of Lincoln's true background.

"Yes, it was." Abe smiled as brightly as the flickering kerosene flame beside him. "Life was so much simpler then. I didn't have to worry about the intrigues of politics, the back room dealings and out-and-out lies of Washington, and I most certainly did not have to deal with the many problems of running a war. They were better times."

"It certainly sounds so."

As she watched Abe speak, Hallie was struck by just how convincing he was. If she didn't know better, if she hadn't heard of the story from the Morgans, and if she didn't know what fate ultimately had held in store for the former leader of her nation, she would *swear* that the man standing before her was indeed Abraham Lincoln, the president of the United States of America.

"Isn't it hard for you . . . ," Hallie began, unsure of her words. "Don't you get tired of being the only one to speak? Of speaking of all of the good times, hoping that she will tell a story of her own?"

"Just as it was in my time as a young boy in the woods," Abe began, his tone solemn yet warm, "there is more to a moment such as this than there first appears. Even though I desperately wish for Mary to awaken from her sleep, I take a great deal of joy in her company, happy that she is still with me and that I am allowed to remain at her side. I certainly cannot force her to speak; so I wait, patient in my vigilance, ever hopeful that she will open her beautiful eyes and be with me once again. Until then, I wait for her voice."

"Being patient in such a way would be hard for me," Hallie admitted.

" 'Patience is a virtue' is an adage that my mother passed along to me as a boy, and I have never failed to put it to good use—both in my political life and behind the doors of my own home."

"But waiting is so hard."

"That is only because you do not see the joy in the anticipation."

Suddenly, as if it were a lightning bolt from a clear sky, Hallie was hit by the realization that much of what Abe spoke of in regard to Mary could also be applied to her situation with Eli. For his own reasons, Eli was reluctant to share with her what happened to him in Bison City, much as she was to tell him of her time in Whiskey Bend or of what had happened in the mercantile. *But that doesn't mean that I should spend my time at his side pining for that which is not forthcoming!* On the contrary, she should simply accept that he would tell her when he was ready and enjoy each moment at his side for what it was: a joy!

"I think I do understand," she admitted, truly happy that of all the people she could have found for companionship at the Morgan family ranch, fate had brought her to Abe.

It was as if a great weight had been lifted from her shoulders.

"That's wonderful," Abe said, and she could tell from the smile shining in his eyes that he meant the sentiment. "Now if you would like, I'd be honored if you would pull up a chair and listen as I tell Mary yet another tale of my younger days. Who knows, there might be something else for you to learn."

"I'd love to," she answered.

Yes, coming to this room was a wise decision, indeed!

*   *   *

Even as the sun dipped beneath the far horizon, bidding a final farewell to the day, Hank could see the dark clouds gathering in the southern sky. In the deepening orange and red light, they looked like bruises, purple and angry. Already, the wind had begun to pick up, rustling the trees and pushing the sweet, fresh smell of rain into his face.

Cupping his hand, Hank lit the end of a thin cigar and inhaled deeply. The tobacco burned within his lungs, but he held the smoke for a moment longer before blowing a plume into the night. With another long day finished, now was his time to relax.

"Looks like more bad weather."

Hank turned as Pearl approached him, her boot heels echoing on the wooden porch. Her blouse and skirt matched the painted horizon in color; yellows and reds that captured the eye. Her hair was piled high on her head, a few curls breaking free and falling toward her shoulders.

"Reckon so," he answered.

"Leastways this time when the storm comes, we ain't gonna be out in it. We won't need two heroes dashin' to our aid."

"We just happened to come along, that's all."

"That don't mean I'm not glad for it." She laughed easily, and Hank grinned in response. Her voice was as sweet and welcoming to him as the distant rain carried on the wind.

From the moment he had first set eyes on Pearl Parsons by the swollen banks of the Cummings, there had been something *different* about her that had captured his fancy. His time on the ranch didn't leave him with much left over for socializing, but he'd never met a woman quite so colorful, quite so boisterous, and that, in itself, intrigued him.

"This here's a nice life," she remarked, looking out at the sprawling grounds of the ranch. "Myself, I've always been one for the cities and towns, all of the hustlin' and bustlin', everyone havin' someplace to be. I didn't have no idea what I'd been missin'."

"It ain't the life for everyone," he admitted.

"But it was for you."

"I ain't fit for the town life," he said, then chuckled. "That sort of life ain't never done appealed to me. Runnin' a business or some such, that ain't for me. A tie ain't nothin' but a noose turned upside down, but it'll choke a man to death just the same."

"That's one hell of a way to look at the world." Pearl laughed heartily.

"Ain't it though?"

"As a matter of fact, it is," she agreed easily with him, her eyes shining in the last rays of the day. "Most of the men I've had the displeasure of knowin' were only interested in lookin' at a woman's bare bosom or the bottom of a whiskey glass, so it's nice to hear somethin' a mite different."

"Nice to know I ain't in such company."

"No, you most certainly are not!"

For a moment, Hank was content just to look at the strange woman standing beside him. If he had had more experience with women, he felt almost certain that he would've known what to say, what remark to make to set her laughing again, but the words eluded him. Oddly enough, Pearl seemed just as happy to be silent, letting their smiles do all the talking.

"Mind if I have one of your cigars and share a bit of your company?" she finally said, breaking their silence.

"Not at all."

Hank handed her a cigar and then struck a match, cupping it in his hands to keep the wind from snuffing it out. Before she dipped her face to the flame, Pearl reached out and placed her fingers against his own; and in that instant, it was as if he had touched the match to his flesh, so strong was the charge that ran through him. As he watched her puff on the cigar, the tip glowing red from her effort, he realized that he didn't want the moment to end. When she moved her hand away, he was surprised to find himself disappointed.

They stood in silence as, far in the southern distance, forks of lightning crisscrossed the darkening sky, lacing the horizon with the fury of nature. It took the thunder a few seconds to reach them, but when it did the bass of the storm's fury was as deep as a wild dog's growl.

"Gonna be a storm," Pearl observed.

Hank nodded. Even in the joy of the moment, he felt a twinge in his gut.

Something bad was coming!

Chapter Twenty-one

THE SWEET SMELL of flapjacks mingled with the strong fragrance of coffee as Hallie filled her plate and cup and sat down at the long table. She'd risen early to cook as the ranch had begun to come to life, the morning sun shining a bright orange through the kitchen windows. The heavy storm that had threatened the night before had passed harmlessly to the south, though the first morning air had been scented with the crisp, freshness of faraway rain. But now, only a scant hour later, the day had begun to turn into a scorcher, the heat dry and stifling. She wiped her brow with the back of her arm and began to eat hungrily.

"It's the God's truth, Hallie," Hank said from his place across from her, his mouth still full of food. "These flapjacks are fit for a king, so it won't be no surprise to hear that this old cowboy took a hankerin' to 'em!"

"I'm glad you like them." She smiled as she spoke.

"Darn right!"

"There's plenty, so eat up."

"Don't need to tell me more than once." The cowboy rose to fill his plate from the stack keeping warm on the cookstove.

As happy and as proud as she was to see Hank digging in to his breakfast, it was also as clear to Hallie that there was one person who was *not* enamored of her cooking.

Eli.

He sat quietly beside her at the head of the table, his tanned brow lined with worry, his shoulders slumped as if they were the boughs of an old tree that had spent a night under the pounding rain. His gaze rarely left his plate; the food was scarcely touched. When he had first entered the room, he'd said little, a simple greeting followed by a few grunts and shrugs. Once in a while, his hand would run to his wounded arm, and he winced in pain.

Hallie took a deep breath, trying to draw comfort from all that she had heard from Abe the night before: *He will tell you what is bothering him when he's ready.* Even as she attempted to be patient in her thoughts, to put what she had learned to good use, she found that giving action to such sentiments was far more difficult than she had bargained for. With every passing moment of silence, her desire to rush to Eli, to put her arms around his waist and hug him, became stronger.

Still, his silence had begun to bother her. *Just because I understand he needs time before he can tell the secrets he is holding doesn't mean that we aren't to say a word to each other.* She was just about to break the quiet, to ask him about his arm, the weather or some nonsense, when Pearl came bustling into the room, a plate full of food in one hand, a sloshing cup of coffee in the other.

"I swear," Pearl spat the words as hard and as fast as if they were bullets. She slammed the plate and cup down on the table. "I swear that if the sun ever rises on a day when that woman is happy about somethin', I just might fall dead from shock!"

"What was the matter?" Hallie asked, even though she was fairly certain that she already knew the answer.

"The same thing that's always the damn matter," Pearl declared, her tone as sharp as a railroad spike. She poured herself a cup of coffee and set the pot back on the stove with a ringing clang. "That old biddy ain't happy with nothin' in life, certainly not with this food! She's got venom runnin' through her veins!"

"Come on now, she ain't that bad," Hank interjected with a wide grin.

"Then next time you can serve her meal! Maybe she'll take off a chunk of *your* hide!"

"Think she'd treat me different on account of my bein' her brother?"

"I'd put money on her bitin' your head off just the same!"

Hank seemed to think about it for a moment, opening his mouth to say something; but looking at Pearl, her hands on her hips and spoiling for a fight, he thought better of the idea. "Naw, you're probably right," he agreed with a wide grin. "Even after all these years, I still don't think that she's too fond of me either."

"That's because you're a stinky old goat!"

"I may be old, but I ain't no goat."

Pearl just grinned.

As she watched Pearl and Hank tease each other, Hallie could see that it wasn't done with cruel intent. While her mouth said otherwise, it was clear by the twinkle in Pearl's eyes and the beginnings of a smile that lifted up her mouth that something had come over her. In the presence of the older cowboy, some of the hardness had fallen away. A flood of warm feelings raced through Hallie at the thought of Pearl's finding companionship and contentment.

Because of her own newfound happiness she had kept silent when Pearl had returned to the barn the night before, deciding not to tell her what had happened in the mercantile, how the strange man had threatened them all. She had also held her tongue about Eli and her worries about his visit to the cemetery. It would have been nice to have had another opinion, someone to share her concerns, but she wouldn't have marred her friend's happiness for all of the stars that dotted the sky.

"Maybe you should take in her noon meal," Pearl kept right on prodding Hank.

"I wouldn't mind savin' you the hassle"—he grinned, the laughter bright in his eyes—"but me and Eli got plenty of work to do on the fence line to the east. We're bound to be there till nightfall."

"It'll wait," Eli said suddenly. After his voicing little more than a grunt or two the whole morning, the sound of his voice was so startling to Hallie's ears that she nearly jumped from her seat.

"What'll wait?" Hank asked, confused. "That fence?"

"We can send a couple of the hands to take care of it," Eli explained, his eyes never leaving his plate. "We're not straying from the ranch today."

"Why's that?"

"We're staying here!" Eli suddenly barked, his gaze shooting up and holding his uncle fast. Hallie stole only a quick glance in his direction; his hooded eyes were watery and red, bloodshot in a way that told her he had not managed to get much sleep. More than ever before, she wanted to know what had happened in town, to know what secrets he kept from her.

The heated air of the kitchen captured the silence that followed Eli's outburst. Hallie had begun to wonder if it would ever be broken when Abe surprisingly stepped into the room, his face no less sleep deprived than that of his brother, his hair and beard slightly unkempt.

"Good morning," he said solemnly.

"To you as well," Hank responded warmly, happy for a change in the tone of the room. "I hope you were able to get a little sleep last night."

"I am afraid that it would have been little more than a wink or two," the man who believed himself to be the late president answered. "Watching over my beloved Mary requires a vigilance that leaves little time for my own comfort. I dare not allow myself to waver. One never knows when there will be an improvement."

"Has there been any change?" Hallie asked hopefully.

"Unfortunately not," Abe answered as he helped himself to a steaming mug of coffee and a couple of flapjacks, obviously not as averse to Hallie's cooking as his mother was. "I had hopes that Mary's convalescence would be brief, but she still must rest a while longer as she recovers the strength she needs to rejoin us."

"It won't be much longer, I reckon," Pearl ventured.

"Let us hope not, my dear."

As this casual talk began to replace the harshness of Eli's words, Hallie couldn't help trying to gather their meaning. *Why doesn't Eli want Hank and himself to be far from the ranch? Does it have something to do with what occurred in Bison City?* As hard as it was for her to accept, she knew that the only answers to these difficult questions would come when, or more important *if*, Eli decided to tell her.

"Keep eating. You need to keep your own strength up," Hank told Abe.

"I need little to keep going, but even I require a bit of nourishment from time to time." With a nod to Hallie, he added, "A task much easier on account of our fine new White House cook."

She was about to answer, to thank Abe for his kind words, when there was a knock on the door, followed by the screech of hinges and the sound of booted feet on the wooden floor. All heads turned in surprise at the sight that greeted them.

There, in a bright blue dress, her golden hair pulled up beneath an equally bright bonnet, was Fawn.

For a moment, the air in Hallie's lungs vanished. Sweat beaded her brow and the hairs on her arms and the back of her neck stood on end. It was as if she'd suddenly found herself in a dream, as if she had blinked her eyes and where there had been nothing at all, a second later there was Fawn.

"I'm terribly sorry to be barging in like this," she began, her voice dripping with honey, her smile as bright as the sun rising steadily in the sky. "After all that's happened here, I couldn't seem to keep myself away."

"What on earth are you talkin' about?" Hank asked, puzzled.

"Why, Mrs. Morgan's fall, of course," Fawn explained, her green eyes darting to Hallie's and holding them just long enough for a sickening feeling to begin to spread across her gut.

"Hallie told me about the terrible accident, about how Mrs. Morgan had fallen and was unable to leave her bed," she explained. "Well, the more I thought about it, the more I was certain that it was my Christian duty to come and see about her."

"You rode out here to see about that old bat?" Pearl asked.

"Now, Pearl . . . ," Hank scolded.

"I took my father's buggy at first light," Fawn explained proudly, her chest swelling in her bodice. "I am more than capable of driving myself. I'm not the sort of woman who needs to be chauffeured about as if I were the belle of the ball."

Hallie winced inwardly at the obvious dig at her trip to Bison City. Knowing the truth of the matter, that Eli had asked her to accompany him to town, that she had not needed him to drive her, did little to salve the stinging wound. She gave Eli a furtive glance, but he seemed to be paying Fawn about as much mind as he'd paid his breakfast.

Fawn also seemed to be aware of his lack of interest. Her bright eyes darted from one face to another but always back to Eli, where he sat slumped in his seat, and his back turned to her. Hallie could see the emotions that flitted across Fawn's face: hope that he would pay her notice and exasperation that he didn't. His lack of attention got the better of Fawn and she took a few steps toward him.

"I'm so sorry about your mother, Eli," she offered.

Eli's response was little more than a grunt. Frustration crossed Fawn's face like clouds on a brilliant blue sky, a soft red flushing her pale cheeks. No longer content to be ignored, she reached out and placed her hand on his right arm and gave it a gentle squeeze.

"Fawn, don't—" Hallie began but it was already too late.

"Goddamn it!" Eli roared, the pain in his arm cutting as sharp as a knife blade. He shot up and out of his seat, the blood in his temples pounding, his teeth clenched tight. When his eyes finally turned to Fawn, the emotion written in them was certainly not what she had longed for.

"Eli, I didn't know you were hurt," she muttered, flustered and concerned.

"Don't touch me!" he barked.

"What in hell's the matter with your arm?" Hank asked with concern in his voice, more than a bit confused by his nephew's outburst. "You fall off your horse or somethin'?"

"It's nothing," Eli answered, but it was clear to all in the room that his words were false.

While she had been startled by Eli's anger, it didn't take long for Fawn to recover, the confusion that had been written on her pretty face replaced by a syrupy-sweet mask of helpfulness.

"But what about Mrs. Morgan?" she asked.

"She's gettin' the help she needs," Pearl offered, her tone defensive.

"I have to wonder about that," Fawn retorted. Hallie saw clearly that Fawn Billings was not the sort to take rejection lightly. Even when faced with an obstacle like Eli's anger, she was ready to get right back in the fight, no matter who was the opponent. She considered herself to be a woman of means, cultured, far above the type of woman she thought Pearl to be, too far above her in station to be spoken to in such a way.

"Now just you hold on for a minute," Pearl barked, her dander rising.

But even as she listened to the older woman fighting against her accusations, Fawn's attention had been pulled elsewhere. Her gaze was fixed upon a spot over Pearl's shoulder, farther into the room. Questions filled her eyes as a sly smile broke across her face.

"Abe?" she asked, her voice uncertain. "Is that you?"

Hank and Pearl parted to reveal Abe standing near the stove, a cup of coffee held gingerly between thumb and forefinger. He nodded his tousled head solemnly, as if he were greeting the wife of an ambassador. "Miss," he said.

"Why, I haven't seen you in years." Fawn smiled warmly, her eyes surveying his tall frame, taking him all in, surprise in her reaction. "But why on earth are you dressed that way? You look just like President Lincoln's photo in my father's old books!"

"How I truly hated posing for those photographs,"

Abe said with a chuckle, traveling in his mind back to a distant time that he had never actually experienced. "Having to sit still while the photographer fussed around, changing plates and tossing a black cloth over himself. As bad as it was to pose with my generals, imagine how hard it was with the children!"

Fawn laughed heartily, her tight curls bobbing. "Ever since we were kids, you always were the one that could make us all laugh with your silly stories!" But when she noticed that she was the only person in the room who took his words for a joke, she soon stopped, more confused than ever. Hallie could see the gears of her mind spinning, trying to make sense of the puzzle before her.

"I assure you that it was not meant as a joke," Abe said matter-of-factly.

"Now, Fawn," Hank started, "you gotta understand that—"

"I can't believe this!" Fawn cried, cutting Hank off in mid-sentence. In her eyes, mischievousness danced. "This is the strangest thing I've ever seen! Does Abe Morgan really think that he's President Lincoln?"

"Just hold on now," Hank soothed.

As she listened to Fawn's incredulous words, Hallie realized that the strange calamity that had befallen Abe was one that the Morgan family had borne in silence. They'd kept their secret from friends, neighbors, and, apart from the doctor, all of the townsfolk of Bison City. While Abe's belief that he was the former president was mostly harmless, it was not without its share of difficulties. Looking at the scene with Fawn's eyes, Hallie could see just how ridiculous it all must seem.

"When did this happen?" she pressed.

"I assure you that nothing has occurred with which you need to concern yourself, miss," Abe said, his feathers not the least bit ruffled by Fawn's accusations that he was not who he claimed. "The only person that you need give your prayers is my beloved Mary, to whose side I must now return." Before another word could be uttered, Abe left the room, Fawn slack jawed behind him.

"He's just a bit confused," Hallie tried to explain after he'd gone.

"Confused?" Fawn laughed. "He's more crazy than confused!"

"Watch how you talk about him," Pearl said sharply.

Fawn paid the warning little mind, as she tried to come to grips with all that she had witnessed. Suddenly, she seemed to remember her original reason for coming to the ranch.

"Mrs. Morgan!"

Without so much as a pause, she headed off in the direction in which Abe had gone as everyone scrambled to catch up.

Chapter Twenty-two

ADELE MORGAN LAY in the center of her four-poster, her spindly body covered only by a sheet. The room was both small and meager, as if it had been added as an afterthought on the ranch house. Other than the bed, the only furniture was an old, worn dresser and a washstand, its white bowl nearly empty of water. The hot, sticky smell of sweat clung to the room like a cloud despite the open window.

"What in tarnation is the meaning of all this ruckus?" she demanded, her temper as hot as the room. Her gaunt face had become even thinner; her imposed bed rest combined with her refusal to eat was causing her to waste away. Her hair resembled a rat's nest, tufts going this way and that. Still, she had the air of a lady about her. In a show of modest decorum, she brought the sheet quickly up to her neck and clutched it tightly in two bony hands. "Why are you barging into my room?"

Bounding into the room as if it contained her fondest desire, Fawn paid no heed to the older woman's obvious discomfort at her intrusion. Her buoyant smile had faded into a more concerned expression of worry and sympathy so false that Hallie's stomach roiled. Fawn perched herself on the corner of the bed where, to Hallie's eyes, she resembled a vulture more than a bird of mercy. Fawn's hands pried Adele's from the sheet and held them tenderly.

"Oh, Mrs. Morgan," she cooed, her voice as soft and tender as if she were a schoolmarm soothing a child who had fallen and skinned a knee. "I am so very sorry for all the pain and suffering that you've had to endure! If only I had known what had happened to you, I would have come much sooner. You must be in terrible agony."

"Now, Fawn," Adele began to protest. "It's not—"

"Oh, you poor, poor thing!"

From where Hallie stood in the narrow doorway, with Pearl on one side and Hank on the other, she watched the drama before her unfold as if she were attending the theater, the story clearly make-believe. She wished that Eli would step forward and put a stop to Fawn's show of concern, but he remained silently behind them in the hallway.

"Are they giving you enough to eat?" Fawn asked as she cast a baleful glance back over her shoulder at Hallie.

"The way you're shrinking away, you'll be nothing more than skin and bones before too long."

"I can hardly eat the slop they bring me," Mrs. Morgan said in a self-pitying voice.

"Now it ain't been that bad," Hank argued.

"It's not fit for a dog."

"I guess that makes you the biggest mutt in these parts," Pearl said to Hank under her breath, "what with the way you were gobblin' it up." Her words set the old cowboy to snickering, but he withered back to silence under the harsh gaze his sister flashed at him.

"We haven't heard any complaints from anyone else," Hallie offered in their defense, the ire rising in her chest at Fawn's accusations that they weren't properly caring for Mrs. Morgan, that they were somehow making her condition worse.

"Men will eat anything," Fawn shot back.

"Now just you listen here, you little sawed-off, connivin' runt! I ain't takin' none of your shit—" Pearl sputtered, pushing the long sleeves of her blouse back, but Fawn cut her off as effectively as if she had thrown a quick jab of her own.

"I'm not listening to your foul words when it's clear as the nose on your face that Mrs. Morgan has been neglected. Just look at these dirty sheets and the way her hair hasn't been tidied. I'm certain that you haven't bothered to wash her even once," she said in a voice far louder than was necessary, her eyes flashing toward Eli. "She needs to be in town where she can receive the care she needs."

"Doc says she can't be moved," Hank objected.

"What right you got to walk in this here house and start makin' demands on us?" Pearl barked, obviously upset at having her toes stepped upon, her eyes glaring holes in Fawn. "Last time I heard, Mrs. Morgan had a son and a brother here to look after her welfare."

"I've more right than you to be here!" Fawn shot back.

Pearl snorted in response, which served only to agitate Fawn more.

"I've known the Morgan family for nearly as long as I have lived and they are from far finer stock than you," Fawn declared, her words both slanderous and sharp. "To think that Mrs. Morgan has to depend on the likes of you makes me sick. Why, if things go on the way they have, she's liable to end up as bad off as poor Abe!"

At Fawn's words, Hallie saw Mrs. Morgan wince as if she had been poked in her bad hip with one of the ranch's branding irons. The look lasted no more than a couple blinks of her eyes, but in that time Hallie could see a sadness far deeper than she would have expected, a regret that her eldest son could be held up as an example of poor living.

"Now, don't you two get in a catfight," Hank said, still hoping to make peace.

"She's gettin' as good of care as she would be gettin'

in town," Pearl snarled as if the man she'd begun to have feelings for hadn't uttered a word. "We're followin' doctor's orders. He said that she was not to leave that bed."

"I'll not leave her here at your mercy," Fawn retorted defiantly. "Before I'd do that, I'll come here every day and take care of her myself!" Fawn's face was that of a petulant child who always expected she would get just what she wanted. At her words, every face in the room showed disapproval, and for a moment, even Mrs. Morgan's.

"Suit yourself!" Pearl's voice was as strong and loud as Fawn's.

"That ain't the sort of journey a woman should make by herself day after day," Hank explained, sweat suddenly beading his brow. "I don't know if I'd be able to sleep at night knowin' you was gonna come out here alone."

"Then I'll make Seth come along with me."

"Seth?" Mrs. Morgan asked, a curiosity tingeing her voice. "Seth McCarty?"

Fawn nodded, her blond curls bouncing.

"Who in the hell is Seth McCarty?" Pearl asked.

For a brief moment, Fawn was silent, her eyes darting to the darkened space beyond Hallie's shoulder, the place where she believed Eli to still be standing. In that longing look, Hallie saw as clearly as if she were being told that Fawn's feelings for Eli had never waned, had never weakened with time, but had grown into something like an obsession. In those few seconds, she saw plainly that

Fawn was determined to have Eli Morgan and was using his mother's accident to wiggle her way into the house.

"Seth is my future husband," she explained, but Hallie could hear the lack of conviction in her voice. "Since I will soon be his wife, he'll be more than willing to do what I ask."

"Will he now?" At the sound of Eli's voice, Hallie turned as he took a step into the doorway. What she saw surprised her; where earlier his face had been a mask of grumpiness mixed with pain, it now was transformed into one of interest and determination. "Seems to me that Seth isn't going to take too kindly to you coming to the ranch, what with the way he reacted in town."

At that, all heads turned back to Fawn. She stammered for an answer, her eyes playing across the room, her jaw clenching and unclenching. All at once, it was as if she were both angry and hurt by Eli's words. Hallie's mind whirled. *What was Eli talking about? When had he run into Fawn in town without her?* Patiently, she waited to hear what Eli would have to say next.

But before she could turn to glance at him, there was an excited whoop that echoed all the way down the hallway. Mere seconds later, Abe shouldered past his brother to stand in the doorway, a smile across his face from one heavily bearded cheek to the other. He was so excited that he shook.

"She's awake!" he exclaimed.

At last, Mary was awake!

*   *   *

The room in which Mary lay was, in nearly every respect, no different from the one that Hallie had just left: small and cramped, with sparse furnishings that offered little in the way of comfort and a heat that threatened to over-power. But even with these similarities, Hallie was struck by the differences: smiles instead of frowns, genuine warmth instead of bitterness, hope instead of resigned despair. When she and Pearl burst in, gladness beat on the doors of their hearts for the first time in what seemed like forever.

"Is she really awake?" Hallie asked.

"It sounds too good to be true, gosh darn it!" Pearl added.

Mary Sinclair lay in the same bed in which they had placed her a week earlier. On that day, they'd refused to give in to the fear that she would be forever taken from them, denied a chance, a true chance at life. Now, with one weary arm raised to her temple, Hallie found herself having trouble believing that all their prayers had been answered.

"Mary!" she exclaimed, kneeling down beside the small bed. "Oh, Mary! I can't believe you're finally awake! I just can't believe you've come back to us!"

"Look at us, Mary girl!" Pearl prodded from her place at Hallie's side.

Slowly, Mary's head did as Pearl bade and turned to the side, her dark-circled eyes resting upon both their faces. She blinked once, twice, and finally a third time before they seemed to focus. What was written in her gaze sent a shiver racing headlong down Hallie's spine; instead of the joy and relief that she had expected, there was only fear.

"No . . . no . . . no!" Mary screeched suddenly, her raw throat not allowing her to voice the true measure of her fright. "Stay—stay away from me! He'll kill you."

"Don't fret, Mary," Pearl tried to calm her.

"You don't have to worry about all that," Hallie added, but she could see that Mary was beyond where her words could reach her. Even as she extended a hand, hopeful that she could calm her with her touch, Mary skittered away, her pencil-thin arms pushing fretfully on the bed.

"What's she talkin' about?" Hank asked. "Who's gonna kill you?"

"It ain't nothin'," Pearl offered hastily.

A sea of emotion rose and fell within Hallie's breast. Instantly, she knew that while life had continued to go on for her and Pearl, poor Mary had remained trapped in that horrid moment in which she had entered the swollen river. While a week had passed for all of them, Mary had awakened to the same fears, the same worries that had left her mute and paralyzed in the back of their wagon. *For her, Chester was still only a step behind.*

"It's all right, Mary," Pearl pressed. "You're safe now!"

"We're with people who'll help us," Hallie added.

"No . . . no!" Mary croaked, her voice harsh from disuse. Her eyes shot wildly about her, as if she were a small animal being stalked by a deadly predator. She shrank into the bed and pulled the scant coverings up to her chin, burrowing deeply into a nest of fear. "We'll never be safe! Chester will never stop until he finds me! Never, never, never!"

"Who is she talking about? Who's Chester?"

Hallie once again turned to the sound of Eli's voice to find him standing inside the door, his face awash with puzzlement. A sickening feeling spread over her at the sight of him. After all that she had done to keep the sordid details of their encounter with Chester at Whiskey Bend a secret, it would all have to come out now.

"He'll kill us!" Mary whispered. "He'll kill us all!"

"What's she going on about?" Eli demanded, his gaze shifting from Mary's horrified face back to Hallie's. "Who the hell is this Chester fella? Why does he want you? Why would he want to kill you?"

Each of Eli's brusque questions struck Hallie with the same force that they would have had they been real physical blows, each one more powerful than the last. Under such a barrage she became mute, even though she knew that each passing second of silence made her seem all the more guilty, of hiding something ugly.

"He's . . . just a man back in Whiskey Bend," Hallie stammered, her voice sounding as unconvincing to her own ears as she was certain it sounded to his. "She's— she's just been ill . . . and is still confused, that's all."

"Seems more than that to me," he said, his gaze narrowing on her face.

"No, Chester! No!" Mary shouted.

Suddenly, out from behind Eli stepped Abe, his face showing both worry and genuine concern. His eyes never left Mary as she writhed in her small bed. The tender way in which he looked at her mesmerized Hallie; at that moment, he had never seemed more presidential. When he stepped closer to where she lay, all eyes in the room were on him.

"Hush now, my darling Mary," he said to her, his voice little more than a whisper but still full of a deep strength. "You no longer have anything to fear. There's nothing here that will do you harm. You've just been having bad dreams and are confused, nothing more."

"Stay . . . away from me!" Mary shouted, more afraid than ever.

"You've been asleep for a very long while," he pressed on, bending carefully down onto one knee right at the edge of her bed, his hands held out before him. "We've all been watching over you, waiting for you to come back to us, back to those of us who love you."

"Just—just . . . I don't—don't know what . . ."

As she watched Abe reach out to Mary with his voice, Hallie felt a warm flow of hope rush through her. Even though she knew that Abe's feelings toward her friend were misguided, that he was wrong to believe her to be his dead wife, Mary Todd Lincoln, Hallie hoped that he might be able to reach her, that he might be able to calm her by offering his love and affection.

"I'm here, my love," Abe said and reached out his hand.

On hearing his words, Mary's hand shot out and slapped Abe hard across the face. The crack of her hand against his skin rang loudly through the room.

"Mary!" Pearl shouted, the word exploding from her.

But Mary's fragile body, still bone weak from her ordeal, gave out before the sound of Pearl's voice had faded. She collapsed into a heap, her confused head dropping onto the bed, all of the fight having left her. Slowly, the pain that had been written across her face disappeared. Without a word, Abe rose from where he knelt and covered her unconscious body with the sheet, smoothing her dark hair from her face when he had finished.

"I'm so sorry, Mr. President," Hallie offered him.

"I am not hurt," he answered stoically. "I may not be the youth who roamed the wild woods of my childhood Illinois, but I am not yet so frail as to be mortally pierced by the slap of a fevered woman."

"The poor thing thought ya was somebody else," Hank said.

"She weren't in her right mind," Pearl added.

"No, she was not," he agreed with a faint nod of his dark head. "My poor Mary is still not recovered from all that she has had to endure. All that we can do is continue with what has been done already . . . and wait."

As she watched Abe standing beside Mary's bed, his shoulders seemed to slump further, his chin near his chest. She couldn't help but wonder if, when Mary's hand had struck him, for an instant he was no longer Abraham Lincoln, president of the United States, but Abe Morgan, cattle rancher born and raised outside of Bison City, Colorado.

Could he have imagined how frightening he must have looked to the newly conscious woman he believed to be his wife? Could he have realized that she would have feared him as she feared Chester?

Hallie had no answers for those difficult questions. She turned to find Eli staring intently at her, his eyes boring holes into her as they silently asked the same questions over and over again. Without a doubt, Hallie knew that she would have to tell him the truth, the whole messy truth, sooner rather than later. The way that he was looking at her made it abundantly clear that he would accept nothing less.

Chapter Twenty-three

HALLIE STOOD IN the open door to the barn and breathed deeply. Outside, the sky had turned a rich, deep bluish-purple as the sun settled into its nightly resting spot beneath the horizon. Stars spotted the cloud-bruised night sky, and a soft wind rustled the leaves on the trees. It all seemed the perfect, peaceful end to a day that had been nothing of the sort.

"It's too bad my day wasn't as beautiful," Hallie muttered to herself.

Fawn's early-morning arrival at the Morgan ranch had been the beginning of her misery. The way in which the arrogant woman had spoken, her voice both condescending and sickeningly sweet, had set Hallie's teeth on edge. It was so staged, so fake, as if she were an actress onstage attempting to lure an audience into believing her act. *And the way she had spoken to Eli, the way that she had grabbed him by the arm . . .*

It had been an even greater indignity to have to listen to Mrs. Morgan agree with the litany of Fawn's many charges against them. In trying to care for the injured woman, she and Pearl had done all that they could to make her more comfortable: cooking the meals; doing the cleaning and washing; and, worst of all, listening to her never-ending complaints. To realize that it had all been regarded as worthless had been hard to bear.

After her brief awakening, Mary had once again slipped back into the murky depths of sleep. In those few short minutes when she was awake and back among her friends, she was gripped by a fear so real that it had made her act hysterically. When she spoke Chester's name, Hallie gasped with surprise. The interest that Eli showed over the matter only made things worse. Mary had retreated into unconsciousness, but the damage she left behind was greater than that of the storm that injured her in the first place.

When Mary had settled back into her deep sleep, and Fawn left for the day with the unwanted promise that she would return early the next morning to care for Mrs. Morgan, Hallie hoped that she and Eli would have a chance to talk. She wanted to tell him about Chester, about their desperate flight from Whiskey Bend, and even about her feelings for him. But when she'd finally approached him after supper, he'd given her a scowl and stalked away without a word.

Now, as she looked to the sky and marveled at its beauty, she wondered if it was too late to undo the damage done, if he would ever speak to her again. Then, from the growing darkness before her she heard his voice.

"Tell me the truth."

Eli walked toward the big barn in the murky twilight, rocks crunching beneath his boots. Even though the onrushing night held with it the promise of cooler air, a fevered heat boiled in his breast. The throbbing pain of his arm merged with his anger, a reminder of more trouble to come.

The whole day had been one messy confrontation after another—from Fawn showing up at their door to his mother's biting comments and constant complaints and finally the awakening of Hallie's friend. Eli felt as if the world were pressing down on him, eager to put him in the earth beside his brother and father.

Who in the hell is this Chester, anyway?

When the name had first burst from Mary's chapped lips, he felt as if a snake was coiled around him and beginning to squeeze. In spite of Hallie's feeble protestations, he knew that she was deathly afraid of the man. Mary's eyes darted about the room in fear when she uttered his name. He couldn't help but wonder if this Chester was the one responsible for what happened in the cemetery.

Was he even now watching the ranch, waiting for the moment to strike them down, each and every one of them?

I feel betrayed! After all that he and his family had done for the women, after the time he spent at Hallie's side, and especially after the passionate kiss that they shared, he couldn't believe that she wasn't what she pretended to be. Didn't she trust him enough to let him help her if she was in trouble?

"Goddamn it," he swore.

Finally, as his anger began to get the best of him, he decided to come to the barn and give her a piece of his mind. *No matter how evasive she is, no matter how much she tries to stonewall, I will insist on an answer! I'll make her tell me why they all left Whiskey Bend and who the hell this Chester person is!*

Eli stopped in his tracks before the open door to the barn. There, in the glow of the lanterns, stood Hallie. In the encroaching darkness of early night, she hadn't seen him, allowing him to stand and observe her. He was struck by her simple beauty, recalling how much he enjoyed the sound of her voice and gloried in the warmth that filled him every time she was near. As if his anger were the flame of a candle, it flickered, nearly went out, but clung to life, albeit not as hot as before. Still, as much as he wished the moment to stretch on forever, he knew that there were things he simply *had* to know.

"Tell me the truth," he said.

The suddenness of Eli's voice speaking from the darkness startled Hallie and a tremor of fear raced through her, but she refused to answer, staring intently into the night until she was sure it was he who spoke. Even then, he could see tenseness in her.

It was a long while before Hallie chose to reply and then the words finally came as little more than a whisper. "I wanted to tell you long ago," she began, "but every time I tried, I just couldn't bring myself to do it."

"Then tell me now," he urged her.

"I just . . . I just . . . ," Hallie trailed off.

Eli crossed from the blackness of dusk into the meager light of the barn. He came to her, still tense with the irritation he'd felt earlier, his back stiff and rigid; but with every step, the anger left him until he stood before her, the only desire in his heart to take her into his arms, hold her close, and reassure her that everything would be all right. She wouldn't return his gaze, so he took her hands in his and gently squeezed them.

"Look at me," he said.

Hallie refused, gently shaking her auburn hair.

"Look me in the eyes, Hallie," he said again, his voice stern.

This time, she did as he said, and he found her green eyes wet with tears that threatened to overflow. At that moment the last of his anger vanished as if it were a puff of smoke, leaving in its place nothing but a concern that pulled at his gut.

"Tell me," he said, his voice now gentle with worry.

And so she did. She told him how she and Pearl had witnessed Chester beating Mary in the streets of Whiskey Bend; how they had hatched a plan to ferry their friend away from a life of misery; how in doing so Pearl had shot the evil man in the leg; and how they had raced quickly away from there into the unknown west; and, finally, why Mary had run into the swollen Cummings River. She even told him what had occurred at the mercantile in Bison City, her voice cracking with emotion as she recounted the man's threats. When she had finished, she sighed with relief that the burden of her secrets had been lifted from her.

"And you expect Chester to come here?" he asked when she had finished.

"It's just as Mary said," Hallie answered as the tears she'd so valiantly held back finally broke free and tumbled down her cheeks. "He will do everything he can to find us and make us pay for taking Mary away from him. He'll kill us if he gets the chance!"

"Then we just can't let him have that chance."

"But how?" she said, sobs racking her small body. "He'll come for—"

Eli shushed her by placing his fingers gently against her lips. Just the touch of his skin against hers sent bursts of heat racing through him.

"Believe in me, Hallie," he soothed her. "I'll not let him

hurt you or Pearl or Mary. I and every man on this ranch will do all we can to protect you."

"But Chester will—" Hallie began again.

This time he hushed her by placing his lips against hers in a deep kiss.

When Eli's lips found hers, Hallie felt as if all her problems simply ceased to be, freeing her to revel in the passion and emotion that flooded through her body. But before the warmth could completely envelop her, she pushed against Eli's broad chest, breaking the kiss and bringing a worried look to his eyes.

"Why did you do that?" he asked quietly.

"What happened to your arm? What happened in town?" Hallie began, finally asking the questions that had been consuming her thoughts for days. *If I told him the secrets I kept hidden, he could do the same!* "You came back from the cemetery bleeding and I want to know what happened. After all we've been through together, after all that I've told you, the least that you can do is be honest with me and let me share your troubles as I have allowed you to share mine."

Slowly, Eli nodded. And he, in turn, told his story. He told her of all the emotions that he'd felt as he'd climbed the hill on the outskirts of town, of how he'd knelt before the pair of tombstones and given voice to things that had previously been unspoken, of the first gunshot and the burning in his arm, and of how he had escaped, into the woods and then to Bison City.

"Do you think this has something to do with Chester?" Hallie asked when he finished.

"I don't know," he admitted. "I suppose he could have followed us to town but why wouldn't he have tried to ambush me on the way? Why take the chance of being spotted in town? Besides, there's a feeling in my gut that this has to do with Caleb's death. Whoever followed me to the cemetery was likely the same bastard who killed my brother. He—"

This time, it was Hallie's lips that brushed his. The sudden urge to put her arms around him, to kiss him and comfort him, to give in to the passion than she'd delayed, had become a siren call that she could no longer refuse to answer. Eli was momentarily surprised, but in only seconds his passion rose to meet hers, and he held her close as his lips tasted her sweetness.

As their kiss grew, refusing to end, Hallie knew that she had given her heart to this man, this cowboy who had saved her life. The fear of Chester and of the strange man who had accosted her in the mercantile vanished in his arms. Now, having unburdened all the heavy secrets that had weighed upon her, to give unto him all of her, she felt free to give of herself, completely and unreservedly. *He can have me . . . all of me!*

"Sweet Hallie! My sweet, sweet Hallie!"

Without another word, Eli swept her up in his powerful arms, ignoring the pain of his wound, and began to carry her toward the rear of the barn. With every step he took, the passion in her heart grew; it was as if the sun had decided against setting, to rise once again and blaze from the heavens.

"I'll keep you safe," he repeated to her as they went.

"I know."

He stopped before each of the lanterns that were spread about the barn and Hallie leaned down to blow them out, the darkness of night steadily encroaching with every flame extinguished. When the last lantern went out, the inky blackness was nearly complete, save for the soft glow afforded by the early moon. Still, Hallie felt no fright, no fear of what she could not see, instead finding love and solace in the glow of their passion.

With the sureness of a blind man used to finding his way about in the dark, Eli led her to the rear of the barn and the hay on which Hallie made her bed. Gently, he laid her down in the straw. When his lips found hers easily, she drank of him with the intensity of a parched woman dying of thirst.

"Oh, Eli!" she said breathlessly into his ear. The heat of his mouth had sent waves of pleasure crashing over her. Her skin tingled as if it were aflame, her heart beating in a frenzy.

Eli's fingers found her blouse and deftly undid the buttons. Then, in an instant, his rough, calloused hands roamed across the soft, pale flesh of her breasts, tracing a path one moment and giving a gentle squeeze the next.

Shooting stars raced across the blackness that covered Hallie's eyes.

Hungrily, yearning to feel his skin as he did hers, she tugged and yanked at his shirt, completely the opposite of his delicate undoing of her own clothing, desperate to feel him. He paused from his own explorations to help her, whipping his shirt off so suddenly that the nakedness of his chest rose above her, and she buried her fingers into the thick, dark hair that matted the muscle beneath.

As their passion built, words gave way to heavy, jagged breathing. Their hands seemed to have thoughts of their own; hers worked at the belt buckle of his trousers as his undid the clasp of her skirt.

When his fingers first brushed across the flower of her womanhood, she let out a gasp and bit down hard on her lower lip. In that first flush of excitement, Hallie knew that she wanted more, that she wanted him joined with her, inside her as a man with a woman.

Suddenly, her fingers found the hard, turgid flesh of his manhood and he gasped. Hallie explored every inch of him, surprised by how he could be both hard and soft to the touch. As she caressed him, his passion grew by leaps and bounds, his breath sucked in through clenched teeth, his body squirming beneath her touch. Without words, she knew that he wanted to be inside her as badly as she wanted him to be there.

"I'm yours, Eli," she moaned into his ear.

Rising above her on his powerful arms, Eli positioned

himself between her legs and, with a gentle but firm thrust, he entered her body. A sharp, sudden pain shot through Hallie but she stifled the cry before it could escape her lips and instead, buried her face into the crook of his neck.

"Are you . . . all right?" he asked breathlessly.

"I'm . . . perfect, my love!"

Her words gave him courage and he slowly began to move in and out of her, his thrusts gentle but becoming more fevered with each passing second. Heat washed over her in waves until she felt nearly suffocated. The pain of his initial entry soon began to pass and, with each bucking motion of his hips, she found herself rising to meet him, joining him in a symphony of moans, passion, and wet kisses.

As she lay in the straw beneath Eli, all the troubles that had been plaguing her ever since that fateful morning in Whiskey Bend seemed to fall away, gone forever in the face of the love she found. Even the fear she felt in the mercantile became a distant memory, little more than a nightmare forgotten at first light of day. All that she wanted was here in the now, her body joined with his, a feeling spreading across her belly that she wanted to last forever, to burn as bright as the hottest flame!

She had never known anything like the sensual enjoyment she was feeling now. She moved against him, clutching at his back while he pressed into her. She writhed upward and tensed, wanting to know and have every little bit of him. His weight pressed her into the soft hay, and her arms tightened about him as they rode out the storm.

On and on their passion built until finally Eli began to shudder, his skin quivering. Hallie's drive raced alongside his, reaching a crescendo that trapped her breath in her chest. Eli met her at the same point and, his body spent, collapsed on top of her as her arms wound around his broad back, refusing to let him go.

Even in the darkness, Hallie turned her eyes up to his in silent answer to an unspoken question. He kissed her, slowly and gently, sharing the moment of sweet tranquillity with her. Propping himself up on one elbow, he gazed down at her tenderly, though only the faintest outline of her body was visible, as she sighed in contentment. In the soft cocoon of the bed of hay, her doubts and fears had dissolved, gone in the face of this new and wondrous sensation. Reaching up, she took yet another kiss, a gift he was more than willing to give.

"Oh, Eli," she moaned when their lips finally parted. "My darling, Eli!"

"How I have wanted you!" he admitted.

"I feel like I am floating on air!"

Silently, he agreed with her. Taking her in his arms, he nestled with her into the soft hay amid the noises of the growing night, none louder than the pounding of their hearts.

Chapter Twenty-four

"I'll stand for no such thing!"

Seth McCarty punctuated his words by slamming his fist down on to the top of his office desk. The glass inkwell jumped from its mooring and spilled an arc of black drops on the blotter. For a moment, the sound of his blow echoed around the cramped interior of his office before a dull ache began to race up his arm.

"I don't really care what you won't stand for . . . I'm going!"

Fawn stood before his big desk in a pool of early morning sun that streamed through the eastern window. In that light, her blond curls glowed like spun gold. He would have found his fiancée beautiful were it not for the scowl spread across her face.

"It's not your place!" he insisted.

"Not my place to help care for an injured woman?"

"That's for Eli and his to provide!" he barked, forcing his words to carry an authority he knew they did not possess. "Even if you're not satisfied with the kind of care she's getting, even if you believe it to be your Christian duty to tend to her, it is not right for you to have to ride day and night to provide it. She is not your mother, for God's sake!"

"I don't care!"

Anger bubbled in Seth's stomach as if it were coffee burning on a stove. What irked him the most was knowing that she would never have even bothered to tell him that she was traveling to the Morgan ranch to care for Adele Morgan had he not asked her why she needed the buggy for a second day. Even then, he had to press her, to pry the truth from her. *Why can't she just leave well enough alone?*

But the rage that threatened to consume him was not meant for Fawn alone; *there was plenty left over for Eli Morgan.* Time and time again, that miserable cowboy had turned up in his life, attracting his betrothed's attentions and making Seth look the fool. Fawn's idiotic claim that her reason for rushing to Mrs. Morgan's side was her concern for the woman galled him; he'd have had to be an even *bigger* fool not to be aware that she hoped to attract Eli's attention. If Fawn had her way, she'd throw him over for Eli.

And that is something I cannot allow!

Damn Eli Morgan! Since they were young boys scrapping on the rough streets of Bison City, Eli had always foiled him. To this day, he could still feel the sting of embarrassment of being beaten behind the mercantile, his punishment for what he had done to Eli's weakling of a brother! *Much laughter and scorn was heaped upon me that day.* All the relief Seth had felt when Eli left for the army was now nothing, less than nothing, and that was why he could not allow Fawn's shameful deceptions to continue even one moment longer.

If only he'd managed to finish the bastard off when he'd had the chance! If only his bullets had found their mark in the fool's belly, bleeding him slowly to death directly atop where his equally foolish brother lay. The cemetery was the perfect chance, but he failed. If only he could have another chance. If only he could torment Eli as he had Caleb. If only—

That's it!

Taking a deep breath, Seth stared directly into Fawn's eyes and said, "If you insist on going out there regardless of how I feel about the matter, then there's only one thing I can do . . . I'm going with you!"

"But—but—but—" Fawn stammered.

"Quite frankly, it's the only way that I will feel good about the whole matter, my dear," he added, the lie coming as easily to his mouth as if it were the truth. "No self-respecting husband to be would let his intended travel alone in this day and age! Why, who knows what might happen to you if I were not along?"

"What about the bank's business?" she asked in a feeble attempt to keep him as far away as possible from her interaction with Eli Morgan. "Surely, such an important man as yourself can't afford to be absent for a whole day!"

"If something were to come up, your father would be more than able to deal with it. After all, he's the man who founded this institution," Seth said slyly. The truth of the matter was that Fawn's father had largely withdrawn from the bank's day-to-day business, leaving others to carry the load. Nowadays, he was more apt to find comfort in the bottom of a whiskey glass and the whore he sneaked up the back stairs than in a ledger filled with figures and finances. While Fawn was certainly aware of her father's recent failings, she would not admit them.

"I suppose you're right," she reluctantly agreed.

"Let me make a few preparations and then we can be on our way," Seth said, ending the discussion. "Together, we'll make certain that Mrs. Morgan is well cared for. Doesn't that idea appeal to you?"

Fawn could only nod.

Chester Remnick spat, swore, and swallowed a large gulp of whiskey from the bottle that rode in his saddle. From where he sat upon his gray mount, high atop a hill at the edge of the valley, the bright early-morning sun blazing behind him, Bison City sure didn't look like much. Without the sign at the train depot, it would be hard to tell it was any different from Whiskey Bend, Mansard, or any of the other shit-hole towns he'd passed through over the years.

But this place is indeed different.

Somewhere down there, among the people scurrying about like mindless ants, was *Mary*. A fresh pang of pain at his separation from her washed over him, but rather than trying to tamp it down, he reveled in it, ingesting its poison and letting it course through his veins. With it came the hatred, the fury at those two bitches for coming into his life and destroying it, stealing the only thing that had ever mattered!

"Goddamn whores are gonna pay," he muttered to himself.

From the moment he'd received the telegram telling him where he'd find his wayward love, he'd done nothing but imagine the horrible retribution he'd commit upon those who had stolen her from him. He'd ridden for countless miles on his horse, the wound in his leg throbbing and aching with nearly every step, but the thought of exacting his vengeance was a salve that soothed his ache, pushing him ever forward in his quest to regain what he had lost.

Now, as he looked down on the rat's nest that those tramps had hidden in, all his sacrifice, all the agony and embarrassment that he'd had to endure seemed well worth the cost. He'd hardly slept a wink in anticipation of the carnage he would soon cause.

While the telegram had told him *where* his quarry had hidden, it didn't give any specifics. As he silently watched, the great train rolled into the station belching black smoke and splitting the air with its shrill whistle. Moments later, more people were disgorged into the already teeming streets, a difficult situation for a man trying to find one of three faces in the midst of hundreds.

He'd have to do what he always did; keep his head low and both his eyes and ears open for any sign, any glimpse, or any rotten sniff of them. As to methods, he would have little choice; he couldn't travel door-to-door, asking for assistance as if he were in search of a lost puppy. Thankfully, he was not a vain man prone to dressing the dandy, showing off in the latest styles from Denver or San Francisco. In his nondescript clothes, he wouldn't attract attention but would blend in with all the other riffraff—smelling of booze, dirty, and not worth another glance. All he could do was fade into the background and wait until what he wanted happened to come his way.

Chester took another long, hard drag from the bottle, emptying the last dregs, saliva and all, before wiping his whiskered mouth with the back of a filthy hand. He hurled the bottle to the ground, where it shattered.

With a hard dig at his horse's ribs, he set off for Bison City, to regain the property that rightfully belonged to him and him alone, and for the purpose of extracting a little revenge while doing it.

Walking briskly beside Fawn as she strode along one of the busy boardwalks that lined both sides of Bison City's main street, Seth McCarty couldn't have suppressed his smile if his life had depended upon it. With every step, he could feel the revolver resting snug inside his vest, lying in wait for its more sinister duty: to rid him of his nemesis *once and for all*. Not even the insufferable summer heat that pressed down on him nor the sour expression that Fawn wore could put a crimp in his assurance.

"I'm beginning to think this is a splendid idea," he crowed.

Fawn refused to make a sound in answer, but her silence didn't offend Seth in the least. On the contrary, her refusal to respond made him all the more sure that what he was about to do was righteous.

I am going to kill Eli Morgan!

That son of a bitch threatened everything that he had worked for, everything that he had cultivated. His attempt at assassination had been just the opening salvo, and that it had failed was but a lone setback. He was destined to succeed in the end. All he had to do was seize the opportunity presented to him, grab the bull by the balls, and he'd be back with Fawn on his arm and her father's wealth in his pocket.

But his plan was not without difficulty. To travel to Eli's home, to set foot on the Morgan family ranch was dangerous to say the least. He would have to be insane not to think of the many repercussions. He'd have to make it look as if there had been a struggle, as if he had defended himself from Eli's attack, and then have to hope for the best. Still, as life-threatening a chance as he was taking, it would be worth it when Eli Morgan was finally dead and Fawn Billings was his.

"I still don't understand why Eli doesn't simply send for a nurse to care for his mother," Seth said, his intent only to raise Fawn's ire, "have someone live there at the ranch until she is well."

"That's the problem," Fawn answered curtly.

"What are you talking about?"

"The reason that we are going to the ranch is because of the incompetence of the women who are currently doing the job," she huffed.

"What women?" Seth asked. "Are you telling me that there are already women tending Mrs. Morgan?"

"There are three of them. Three women that Eli and his uncle managed to rescue from that horrendous storm we had a week or so back," Fawn explained, her lip curling into a sneer. "One of them traveled into town with Eli a couple of days ago. It was from her that I learned Mrs. Morgan had been injured."

As he listened intently, Seth realized that his plans had now been complicated. If there were more people staying at the ranch, there were more eyes that must be accounted for if he were to go through with his plans. Still, it was far too late for him to turn back now. Regardless of the added complications, he had to go forward . . . *he must.*

"Who are these women? Where did they come from?" he pressed, hoping to learn something, anything that might make his grim task easier.

"I don't know much about them except their names, but they all seem pretty low class," Fawn said. "The one that came to town with Eli was named Hallie . . . Hallie Wolcott."

Suddenly, a man who had been crossing before them on the boardwalk came to an abrupt halt, standing ramrod straight as if he had been shot. Unable to take a step to avoid the man, Seth shouldered into the stranger, the hard collision bringing with it the sickly sweet stench of sweat mixed with whiskey.

"Why in the hell don't you watch where you're going?" Seth barked, briskly wiping away the perceived stink and grime that he'd received by coming into contact with the man's shoulder. "What kind of darned fool just stops in the middle of the walk?"

"Watch who yer talkin' to."

For the briefest of moments, Seth saw the white-hot flame of rage flash in the man's eyes. A blade of fear lanced across his gut that he'd bitten off more than he could chew, that the man would quickly pull a knife or a gun and strike him down without a sound. But, as fast as the stranger's anger had flared, it disappeared, replaced by a smile through dirty crags of teeth.

"Beg your pardon, sir," the man recovered, the anger draining from his voice. "I'm new in these here parts and ain't quite sure where I'm at, let alone where I'm headed. If'n you could point me toward the nearest saloon, I'd be obliged."

A few passersby had turned to witness the possible violence on the busy boardwalk but now went away disappointed. While inwardly Seth felt a sense of relief, his voice wasn't willing to concede that fact.

"It's that way." He pointed. "Next time, watch where you're going!"

"Yes, sir," the filthy stranger answered before shuffling away.

"That man could have had a knife," Fawn commented when the man was out of earshot, voicing the concern that had gripped Seth only moments before. "You could have been hurt."

"Nonsense," he said casually. "Now then, let us be on our way."

The last fragments of fear vanished from Seth as he herded Fawn along the boardwalk and toward their wagon. Replacing them were visions of a bullet entering Eli's stomach, of Fawn weeping in his arms, and the name "McCarty Bank" on the lips of every man and woman in town.

*   *   *

Chester stopped to watch the well-dressed man and his woman walk away from him, completely unaware how lucky they both were not to have had their throats slit. Hatred had been the only thing capable of making him endure the man's tongue-lashing, hatred and a desire for revenge that grew brighter and hotter than the summer sun above.

He'd only been in town for an hour or so, meandering around among the men and women doing their shopping, selling their wares, and simply going about their lives. Everywhere he had gone, he'd kept his head down, his ears open, and one eye cocked for something, anything that could lead him to that which he desired.

And his patience had paid off.

At the mention of Hallie Wolcott's name, he had frozen. It had sounded as clear to his ears as a church bell and had commanded his attention, his knees locking, freezing him where he stood. It was then that the rich bastard had slammed into him, launching into a tirade and making a scene.

I've killed men for less, he'd thought.

But just when his tongue had begun to get the better of him, he'd managed to hold it, and recognized the pair for what they were: *a one-way ticket to Mary.* From there, it had been easy to bear the man's words, secure in the knowledge that they would lead him right where he wanted to go.

Waiting until he was certain the pair was far enough along not to notice him, Chester stepped from the boardwalk and began to follow them, weaving in and out of the throngs of people, a warmth spreading in his gut in anticipation of the fruits of his labors.

"I'm comin', bitches," he muttered to himself. "Chester is comin'."

Chapter Twenty-five

THE MORNING CHORES had been done, a hearty breakfast cooked with plates cleaned, and the laundry begun when Hallie stepped out onto the long porch for a bit of a breather. The sky was a crystal-clear blue with only the wispiest of clouds stretching across the far horizon. For once, the air was cooler, a spring day lost in the months of summer.

"Perfect," she said to herself, unable to stop smiling.

Memories of making love to Eli had meandered across her thoughts for all the morning, bringing with them a flood of emotions—happiness and a strong desire—which filled her with a joy she had never before known. When he had finally left her alone in the barn, she'd stayed awake for hours, unable and unwilling to let herself sleep, reveling in the feelings he had inspired in her. Her image of him was so strong, so real, that she would have sworn that she could have reached a hand to them and touched his whiskered cheek.

"Ain't you the happy one this mornin'."

Turning slowly, Hallie beamed brightly at Pearl as she joined her on the long porch, her friend sidling up to her, putting one hand around her waist, and giving her a knowing wink.

"I suppose you'd have to be blind not to notice."

"Even a blind man would feel the heat comin' off you like a fire!"

When Pearl had finally returned to their bedding in the barn, nearly an hour after Eli had left—time that Hallie knew had been given on purpose—they said nothing about what had happened. But Hallie was certain that her friend *knew* without being told; Pearl Parsons was not ignorant of the ways of love!

"He makes you happy, don't he?" Pearl asked.

"He does," Hallie admitted. "He certainly does."

"Then listen close to this old bird," Pearl began, her eyes dancing with the glint of experience. "You cling to that there feelin' like it's the only thing in this here world that's keepin' you afloat. You don't never let it go 'less you ain't got a choice, 'cause if you do, you might never find your way back to it, no matter how hard you try!"

Hallie nodded in agreement. Meeting Eli Morgan had forever changed her life; from that fateful night by the flooded river, it had been her heart that had become swollen, overflowing its banks, and nearly drowning her.

In his presence, all her worries blew away like so much smoke; thoughts of Chester, the strange man at the mercantile, and even her worries about what had befallen Eli in the cemetery faded in the face of their passion. It was a feeling that she never wanted to end.

"I won't let go," she said, "no matter what happens."

"That's the spirit!"

"But what about you, Pearl?" Hallie asked. "Haven't you found something worth holding on to?"

"I reckon I might've." Pearl grinned, her interest in Hank nearly as clear as the blue in the sky or the blush of her cheeks. "It ain't quite as certain as what's happenin' to you, but I ain't gonna be complainin' no time soon, neither!"

"Kissing him might be a good first step."

"Don't think I don't know it!"

The two women laughed heartily, sharing an intimacy of friendship and the hopes of better days yet to come. But both of them fell silent at the sight of dust rising in the distance, a wagon making its way through the still-shimmering heat, headed right for them.

"Do you suppose that's Fawn?" Hallie ventured.

"If'n it is, it ain't gonna be good."

With that, Hallie could only silently agree.

Eli tilted back his hat and wiped the beads of sweat from his forehead with the back of one dirty hand. Though the day was much cooler than those that had preceded it, he was still sweating, his shirt clinging to his skin. He and Hank had stuck close to the ranch house all morning, repairing some of the damaged fence posts that made up the corrals. The work was backbreaking enough without the added problem of his wounded arm. Still, he went about his day with a smile plastered across his sweaty face.

"You seem to be enjoyin' this a lot more than you should," Hank pointed out.

"It sure isn't because of *your* company."

Even as he teased his uncle, Eli was well aware of just *what* had lit up his mood the night before, lodging such joy in his heart that it carried into the next day. From the first moment that he tasted Hallie's kisses until the time he finally parted from her, it was as if he were part of a dream that he wanted never to end. *Hallie Wolcott has me under her spell.*

"It looks like your own bachelor days might be coming to an end," Eli said.

"Oh, it does, does it?"

"I would have thought that an old codger like you wouldn't have the slightest clue as to how to romance a lady," Eli continued, needling his uncle in good spirit. "But I guess even the oldest of dogs *can* learn himself a trick or two."

"I've forgotten more about courtin' ladies than you'll ever know." Hank chuckled warmly as he set another fence post into place. "I reckon you could say the same thing about Pearl, too. Between the two of us, I'm sure we'll know what to do when the time comes."

Hank stopped abruptly as he caught sight of something over his nephew's shoulder. Eli turned to follow the older man's gaze, shielding his eyes with his hand. There, in the distance, was a wagon hurrying toward the ranch.

"That'll be Fawn, I reckon," Hank observed.

Eli nodded. As much as he'd wished to disbelieve Fawn, he'd known that her intention to come to care for his mother had been serious and that, like clockwork, she'd show up the next day, butting her nose into business that was none of her concern. He'd also known that her motives weren't what she claimed them to be; it wouldn't have mattered who had been hurt or how badly, he'd have been willing to bet his life that the only reason she wanted to come all the way from Bison City was himself.

"She ain't gonna let go so easy now, is she?" Hank asked.

"Never was one to accept matters when they didn't go her way."

"That's as true as the Gospel."

When they were younger, Fawn's attempts to win his affections had been even more blatant, more brazen and open. Whenever he had refused her, even taken pains to explain to her that he simply didn't feel that way about her, she had always laughed, telling him that he just wasn't accepting what fate had in store for them, then tried even harder than before. He'd hoped that she would grow out of her obsession; but if anything, time had made her desire all the stronger, engagement to Seth McCarty be damned.

"Well, would you look at that." Hank nodded as the wagon neared.

"What?" Eli asked, blinded by the sun's glare.

"Looks like Fawn didn't come alone."

It was then that Eli noticed the man sitting beside Fawn in the wagon seat, his hands snapping the reins and turning the pair of horses toward the ranch house, then pulling back on them and bringing the team to a dusty halt.

The man driving the buggy was Seth.

Without a word, Eli began walking toward the new arrivals, his jaw set and his hands balled into fists. *This is trouble!* With all that had happened, the sight of Seth coming to the ranch sent his hackles rising. He could not bring himself to believe that the banker's appearance here was mere coincidence. Besides the blood rushing in his ears, the only sound he could hear was that of Hank struggling to keep up.

"There don't need to be no trouble, now," his uncle cautioned.

"There ain't gonna be unless he starts it."

"Keep a cool head, son."

They arrived at the buggy just as Seth was helping Fawn to the ground, her dainty hand held in his, and a large wicker basket hanging from the crook of her other arm. As soon as she saw Eli approach, her eyes lit up as if they were Fourth of July fireworks.

"Eli!" she exclaimed. "I'm so glad you came to greet us."

"You really don't need to come all the way out here," he said in answer, his voice as flat and emotionless as he could manage. "Hallie and Pearl are certainly more than capable of caring for my mother."

"Oh, don't be silly. I told you that it would be my Christian duty to care for Mrs. Morgan and those are words I mean to live by. Besides," she said, hoisting the basket for all to see, "I've prepared a wonderful lunch for her, far better than the meals she was receiving."

"Much obliged," Eli thanked her.

"At least you didn't come alone this time." Hank nodded in Seth's direction. "That's a mighty fine gesture for you to bring her all the way out here. I told her yesterday I didn't feel quite right about her comin' by herself."

"It was the least that I could do," the banker answered. "I must admit that I shared your concern for her safety. A woman as beautiful as Fawn might very well attract the attention of more unsavory elements. Even though I had to leave the bank for a day, it was a price well worth paying to be by her side."

As Seth spoke, Eli watched the man's face closely, looking for something, any sign that might betray him, which might give away some secret. As his last words faded into the wind, he watched as Seth's eyes darted quickly toward him and then flickered away. The glance had not been long, but what Eli had seen had been illuminating; his eyes hadn't searched Eli's face, but had found his arm, the same arm that had been pierced by a bullet!

In that brief moment, a sickening suspicion wormed its way into Eli's gut. The thought that it was Seth who fired upon him at the cemetery, who meant to kill him at the very spot that his brother and father lay, had drifted around in his mind, trying to find solid ground upon which to stand. He resisted that thought, refusing to believe that Seth could truly be capable of such an act, but he was unable to completely shoo it away. But that brief glance, the look that could have been that of a gunman checking upon the wound that he himself had inflicted, sent Eli's mind into a raging turmoil. *Was it Seth who tried to kill me? Is he here to complete the task? For how long has he carried his murderous intent? Is it possible that Seth McCarty had something to do with Caleb's murder?*

"Might I check to see how Mrs. Morgan is faring today?" Fawn asked.

"That'd be fine," Hank answered.

"I hope she's better."

When his uncle led Fawn and Seth up the stairs and into the ranch house, Eli did not follow, staying behind as indecision raged in his breast. *How I want to act!* It took all the restraint he could muster not to rush after them, grab Seth by the throat, and wring the truth, no matter what it might be, from him, consequences be damned!

But he couldn't act until he was certain, until he had successfully determined that his suspicions were valid. He thought of Hallie, of how she would want him to act honorably, and that is what he would do. He would bide his time, get Seth alone, and then he would finally learn what happened to him at the cemetery and maybe even find out what happened in one of Bison City's dark alleyways, four years past.

"Patience," he whispered to himself. "The time will come."

As dusk began to fall upon the ranch, and deep reds and purples spread across the far sky, Hallie could still hear Fawn's voice from behind the closed door of Adele Morgan's room. She'd been in there for hours, since shortly before lunchtime, and the two women's cackling had long since become a source of annoyance. Fawn had only exited the room twice, both times for only very brief moments, and she had fixed Hallie with a severe frown on each occasion.

"I'm beginnin' to wonder if she's ever gonna leave," Pearl mused.

"If it were up to her, I doubt she would leave."

"And what about that fella that come with her? What's his story?"

Hallie had been wondering about that very thing

from the moment she had first laid eyes upon the man. He was clearly cut from the same cloth as his betrothed, arrogant and self-assured. But where Fawn was bubbly and talkative, her mouth and hands always moving, her fiancé was cold and reserved. The only words she'd heard him speak had been a greeting to Mrs. Morgan. Since that time, he'd stayed near the front windows, his eyes roaming.

"I don't think he'd tell us even if we asked," Hallie replied.

"To hell with him." Pearl shrugged. "I'm more worried about Mary."

They stood in the doorway of their friend's room, much as they had been doing for a week, watching Mary sleep, Abe having resumed his quiet vigil beside her bed. If she had not known better, Hallie would have assumed that, indeed, nothing had changed, but the pall of Mary's brief reawakening hung heavy over the air as if it were a funeral shroud, blackening their thoughts and mood. If Mary *did* awaken again, Hallie feared that there would be nothing more than the same chaos as before.

"Do you suppose she'll just keep sleeping?" Hallie asked.

"After spendin' all that time hopin' she'd wake herself up, I can't help but thinkin' it'd be better if'n she did sleep a spell longer." Pearl shrugged again. Nodding toward Abe, she added, "I still can't bring myself to believe how she acted toward him when she came to, what with the slappin' and all. My heart really broke for that there fella."

"Mine too," Hallie admitted. "It nearly brought tears to my eyes."

"Same for this here hard old broad."

If she were to close her eyes and listen, Hallie was certain that she could still hear the sound of Mary's slap echoing around the small room. It was as if she herself had been the one who had received the frail woman's blow. She marveled at how Abe could just ignore what had happened and resume his duty, caring for Mary.

"You reckon the day'll ever come where she ain't afraid of Chester?"

Hallie thought over Pearl's question for a moment. "I don't know if that day will ever come for any of us," she explained. "To know that that monster is out there somewhere, looking around every rock and behind every corner means we won't ever be safe . . . not really."

"He ain't gonna find us, Hallie," Pearl said. "He ain't."

Hallie didn't have the heart to tell her friend that he already had; the strange man who accosted her in the mercantile made that much plain. But she had yet to tell Pearl about the man for fear of upsetting her. The only other person who knew what happened was Eli.

"I hope not," she said weakly.

"Even if that dumb bastard managed to find us, we ain't alone no more. We got Eli and Hank standin' by us, protectin' each one of us as best they can. Chester ain't gonna be able to just have his way."

"I suppose you're right."

"I know I am."

Hallie threw her arms around Pearl, holding her dear friend tight and expressing her joy at knowing the older woman would never give up, would never surrender herself to fear, and would fight for their safety. Turning from the window, she failed to notice the man who peered into Mary's room, his face bewhiskered and worn, a face that would have brought a scream to her lips.

Seth stood on the long porch smoking a thin cigar. He took a deep drag, blowing the smoke out into a billowing cloud that swiftly dispersed in the evening wind. As much as he wished to calm his nerves, he was still filled with anxiety and the strong desire to accomplish what he had come to do.

All day Seth had paced about the house, forced to listen as Fawn rambled on and on with that old buzzard Adele Morgan, wishing to the heavens above that she would just be quiet for once. He'd nodded when spoken to, said a word here and there, and had waited for his moment to arrive. But the time to deliver the final blow had not come. He had to make sure that he and Eli were alone in order to make it all look like he was simply defending himself, but every time he spied his rival, he was always in his uncle's company. Now, as the sun began to set, his time was running out.

"Goddamn it all," he muttered under his breath.

Already, he could hear the sound of Fawn's grief-racked sobs and cries in his ear. She would be distraught at the loss of her beloved Eli, weeping tears that she surely would not shed if it were *he* who had been murdered. But time would heal the wound and, with the passage of weeks and then months, Eli Morgan would be naught but a memory. He'd be forgotten, relegated to childhood dreams.

The smile that had begun to spread across Seth's face froze, his eyes narrowing in the last gloomy light of the day, his heart pounding fiercely in his chest. He would have sworn that the gun inside of his vest twitched at the sight of Eli, finally alone, entering the large barn beyond the corrals.

My time of vengeance has finally come!

Chapter Twenty-six

Eli heard the cocking of a gun, followed curtly by, "Turn around slowly."

For an instant, Eli was incapable of moving; his breath caught raggedly in his chest and his heart thundered loudly. He had come to the barn alone in the hope that this moment would occur, that he would find out if his many suspicions held any grains of truth. Now, with the fading of Seth's voice, Eli knew that some of his questions had been answered.

He stood before the barn's long workbench that was scarred and nicked from untold years of use. He'd been replacing each of the tools that he and Hank had used to repair the fence posts, his oil lamp sending flickering ghosts of light dancing across the dark walls. He had been about to replace the last of the instruments, a long-clawed hammer, when he'd first heard the faint creak of the barn's side door, a noise that was as clear to him as the deafening crack of the pistol that had wounded him.

"Do it or I'll shoot you where you stand," the voice further ordered.

Without turning, even before hearing the man speak, Eli was certain who stood behind him. As his hand tightened around the rough wooden handle of the hammer, he *knew* exactly who commanded him—*Seth McCarty*!

"It was you in the cemetery," Eli growled, more statement than question.

"Yes," came the answer, simple yet certain.

Slowly Eli turned around. Seth stood framed in the sinking sun's light. A faint glint shone off the coal-black pistol clutched tightly in his right hand, the snub barrel pointed directly at Eli's belly. With his smartly cut clothes, slicked hair, and the corners of his mouth turned up in a faint smile, Seth looked villainous, cut from a far different cloth from that of the man he meant to kill.

"I always knew you were a goddamn coward," Eli declared.

"A coward is the man who will not do everything that he can to rid himself of his problems," Seth answered coldly, his eyes little more than slits, his words both clipped and precise. "I will do absolutely anything that I have to in order to be rid of mine."

"I'm not your problem, Seth," Eli argued, trying to make him see reason.

"I beg to differ." The banker scowled, the pistol rising

in his hand until it was pointed directly at Eli's skull. "You were always the one standing in the way of what I want. Even when we were boys, you had to stick your nose where it did not belong. It's no different now. If it weren't for you, if you hadn't come back to Bison City, Fawn and I could have been happy together. She would still have eyes for me alone."

"Fawn's feelings for me aren't returned. They never have been."

"It makes no difference."

"It should."

The laughter that sang from Seth's lips was cold enough to send a shiver racing down Eli's spine. "All that matters is that the love she feels for you threatens the plans that I have painstakingly put in place. Until you are gone, Fawn will go on chasing after you, rushing out to this godforsaken ranch to care for your mother, all in the slim hope that she will catch your eye."

As he listened to Seth speak, Eli recognized that there was no reaching the man. Seth had tried to kill him once and had accompanied Fawn to the ranch in order to finish the job. He was simply waiting for the right moment.

"You'll never get away with this," Eli warned. "The men working here will hear the shot and come running." His mind raced for some plan of action, trying to keep Seth talking long enough to figure out what he needed to do to stay alive. "You can't expect to just shoot me in cold blood and walk on out of here safe and sound."

"If I were to step from this barn much as you see me now, you would be right in your thinking," Seth explained, his self-assuredness taunting Eli. "That is why, after you lie on the ground cold and dead, I will take this pistol and shoot myself in the arm. To any who might inquire, the law included, I would simply have been defending myself."

"No one will believe you."

"Won't they?" Seth scoffed. "I have spent the last several years ingratiating myself with the good people of Bison City; I am the face of their bank and a most respected member of society, whereas you are no one. With our past hatred for each other, will a single person believe that it was *I* who meant to murder *you*?"

"Just like you murdered Caleb?" Eli asked, the desire to know the truth of what had happened to his brother even greater than his fear at facing his own impending death. *If I am to perish here, I will join my brother and father knowing the truth!*

A look of confusion crossed the banker's face as quickly as a summer breeze. Eli couldn't find meaning in it before it was gone as quickly as it had come. "Can you imagine what it was like for him that night, knowing that he was about to die? What do you suppose *his* last thought was?" Seth sneered, the thought of Caleb bleeding out his last, alone and afraid in the black of night, obviously entertaining him.

"You bastard . . ."

"Quite right."

Over Seth's shoulder, the sun had finally given up the ghost, darkness falling over all; the only light now came from the oil lamp. The flickering flame sent dark shadows rolling across the gunman's face, his intentions looking as dark as they truly were.

Even though Eli was taut with rage, he kept a tight hold on his wits. His hand squeezed down on the hammer's handle with such ferocity that his fingers grew as white as bone. Still, he forced himself to draw a deep breath. If he were to survive, he would need to be calm and act only when the right moment presented itself, not a second before.

"I won't give up without a fight," he said defiantly.

"I wouldn't expect anything else."

Before Seth could utter another word, Eli rolled hard to his side, reared back and threw the hammer with all his might. The suddenness of his movement startled Seth and the gun bucked in his hand, firing its lead bullet, which slammed into the workbench in a shower of splinters. The sound of the shot echoed around the barn, sharp and deafening.

The hammer crashed into Seth's gun hand, the metal head smashing into fragile bone. The smoking weapon fell in a clatter to the earthen floor, followed by a shout of intense pain bursting from the banker's lips in surprise and shock.

"Son of a bitch!" Eli roared as he leaped to the man, his fist cocked to punch.

I meant what I said—I won't give up without a fight!

"Ohh," the moan escaped Mary's lips as little more than a plaintive whisper.

Inside the small room, the sound of the woman's whimpering melded with that of the soft wind drifting in through the open window. Outside, the inky darkness had once again descended upon the ranch, matching the mood of all those within.

Pearl stood with her arms crossed severely across her ample bosom, her brow knitted in worry. There seemed little else she could do, few others with whom she could speak. Hallie had just left to find Eli and even the sounds of Mrs. Morgan and Fawn's conversation had faded. She was not alone; Abe sat beside Mary's bed, his vigil uninterrupted, even after the slap he had received the day before. Just like her, he seemed to be in it for the long haul.

"This ain't like it was before, is it?" Pearl asked him.

"She does not appear to be as restful as before," Abe agreed from his chair at the bedside. "I believe that my beloved Mary is suffering from some sort of nightmare, some worries that do not let her rest as she should."

"It's hard to have had her back, only to lose her again."

"Yes, it is." He sighed deeply. "Many tears and prayers

went into watching over her sleep, but we must keep confident that she will once again return to us. To do any less would be a grave mistake."

"I reckon you're right," Pearl agreed.

For a few moments, silence reigned in the small room, interrupted only by the wind and the lowing of the cattle in the pens beyond the ranch house. Finally, Abe breached the profound quiet, his voice hesitant and soft.

"Who . . . who is this Chester that Mary spoke of?" he asked.

Pearl's heart fell at his question. Abe had put up a good front in the face of Mary's hysterics, but he had not been immune to them. Rather, they had festered at his mind until he could no longer keep from giving them voice. She reminded herself that while Mary Sinclair was *not* the woman he believed her to be, that did not mean that his feelings for her weren't real and that he could not be hurt in return.

"Chester ain't nobody worth thinkin' about, you hear," she soothed. "Even if he might be in her head, poisonin' her dreams and muddyin' up the waters, he ain't a gonna be doin' us no harm, so don't go wastin' none of your time wonderin' about him."

Abe seemed to reflect upon what she had said, nodding and rubbing his heavy beard. "I suppose there is some measure of truth in what you're saying," he said. "If it is truly worth worrying about, then I will do so only after Mary has once again returned to us and we have an opportunity to speak about it together. Until then, I will pay it no mind."

"That's a right smart way of thinkin' about it," Pearl agreed.

Even as she encouraged Abe not to give Chester a thought, she found it much easier to offer advice than to put it into practice. It was hard not to wonder if Hallie was right—that regardless of where they ran to or what lives they tried to live, Chester would always be lurking around every corner, ready to ensnare them, making fear their constant companion. When they had first left Whiskey Bend, she'd thought that they left Chester Remnick behind as well, but they could not stop worrying about his following them. Not for the first time, Pearl wished she had shot him dead.

"If it is acceptable to you," Abe said, rising from the chair with a stiff creak, "I believe I might get a bite to eat and a breath of fresh air. I hope it will not be much of an imposition upon you."

"Not at all." Pearl smiled.

"Thank you kindly."

Once Abe had gone, she settled into his chair and dipped a strip of cloth into the washbowl that sat beside the bed and used it to cool Mary's fevered brow.

"Oh, Mary," she said, her voice cracking, "what a mess we done made."

When she heard the low creak of a floorboard, Pearl assumed that Abe was returning for a forgotten item or to ask if there was anything she might want from the kitchen. But when she turned, her welcome for him turned to icy dread.

Coming in through the open window was Chester!

He was much as she remembered him; thin, his wiry frame still quite muscular, wild unwashed hair, clothing more than the worse for wear. But it was his eyes that sent fear racing through her. They were tight and piercing, like those of a wolf with the scent of blood in its nose, patient but determined as it stalked its prey, ready to sink in its fangs.

As he settled onto the floor, she noticed the long knife he held, its steel blade cold and glinting in the lantern light. Equally cold was the thin smile that spread across his cracked lips.

"I found you, bitch," he boasted.

Raw fear convulsed Pearl's body, making her limbs twitch and her stomach lurch. Her jaw seemed to work on rusty hinges, opening and closing of its own accord with only the oddest, most unintelligible sounds coming out. A terror-laden scream remained stuck in her throat, building up in intensity as if it were floodwaters behind an unyielding dam.

"Ches—Chest—"

Before she could finish her nightmare's name, he was already across the room, the back of his fist flashing across her face, cracking against her mouth and sending stars flying across the blackness of her eyes. Instantly, coppery blood filled Pearl's mouth. She toppled from her chair and fell to the floor. The room spun even as she lay still. Somehow, she managed to keep one eye open, unable to look away from the horror before her.

Chester stood beside the bed, his eyes riveted on Mary's sleeping body. In a matter of seconds, Pearl had been forgotten by him. The object of his rampaging desire, the reason for which he had endured so much pain, was finally before him, and he drank in her image.

"My sweet Mary," he muttered.

With a gentle touch, Chester wiped his hand across Mary's brow as she slept fitfully, undoubtedly running from him in her dreams. He was her horror brought to life, a nightmare that drew breath, threatening her at her most vulnerable. When he pushed a strand of hair from her cheek, she shivered, as if she were somehow aware of how precariously her life hung in the balance.

"Your darlin' Chester is back," he said proudly.

Then, with the suddenness of a rifle's crack, his demeanor changed from day to night, his eyes going flat and hard. Pearl watched as his gaze shifted to where she lay on the floor, struggling to maintain her grip on a consciousness that grew more slippery with every passing second. In her waning lucidity, she wondered if he was suddenly thinking of that fateful day when she put a rifle slug in his leg.

"You bitch," he hissed and Pearl knew that he was.

When he knelt beside her, wincing from the effort of

moving his injured leg, he held the knife before her eyes, turning it this way and that so she could see every inch of the blade. If she hadn't already been paralyzed by fear, Pearl knew that the sight of the weapon in Chester's hand would have done the trick.

"Now we'll see who has the upper hand," he said as Pearl's world went black.

Chapter Twenty-seven

HALLIE STOOD ON the long porch and took a deep breath. On the distant horizon, the golden setting sun clung to the low clouds. Life at the Morgan ranch had begun to settle, calming itself for slumber and the promise of yet another day. Even with all that had happened with Mary, Hallie's heart still held bright hope for tomorrow, although she wasn't ready to sleep just yet. The night that lay before her seemed to be a peaceful one, full of nothing but stars, gentle breezes, and, she hoped, Eli's tender kisses.

"And maybe more," she whispered to herself.

She had been apart from Eli for much of the busy day, caring for Mary and helping Pearl with the housework, all the while keeping an eye and ear out for Fawn as she pranced in and out of Mrs. Morgan's room. As much as the young woman's presence galled her, Hallie did her best not to pay Fawn any mind. She had had only a few glimpses here and there of Eli, all of which were sprinkled with smiles and blushes, the memories of the night before shared without a word.

She'd never felt like this before.

Although she still lived with the fear that Chester would somehow track them to the ranch, and was troubled by what had happened to Eli in the cemetery, she felt a sense of belonging, a feeling of hearth and home that she had not experienced since leaving her parents' home in Ohio. *With Eli Morgan, I am beginning to know love.* She wanted to share her night at his side. Stepping down from the porch, the hard ground crunching beneath her booted feet, she set off in search of him. She first headed for the barn, hoping that just maybe he had the same idea and was waiting for *her*, thoughts of their night together exciting him as much as it did her.

Suddenly, a sharp crack split the silence, freezing Hallie where she stood. With horror, she realized that what she had heard was a gunshot. *It came from inside the barn, from where I expected to find Eli! The last time I heard such a sound was . . . when Pearl put a bullet in Chester's leg!*

"Eli!" she screamed, her voice cracking as she began to run.

Eli's clenched fist slammed hard into Seth's rib cage, lifting the man's body from the dirt floor. Beads of sweat fell from his brow like rain. At the point of contact, Eli could feel heat roaring through his muscles as Seth's midsection seemed to give way, the air driven forcefully from his lungs. The banker staggered, wobbling backward on unsure legs, his eyes wide with fear.

"You goddamn bastard," Eli roared.

He fell upon Seth, flinging a left hand that smashed into Seth's jaw, sending his head spinning to the side and blood pouring from a split lip. Eli threw another blow, then another, then even more, each landing, each hurting. The barn was soon filled with the odor of sweat and blood, the sounds of flesh striking flesh, the grunts of pain and exertion. The gun and hammer were abandoned somewhere underfoot.

Eli's strength seemed to be endless, fueled by a fiery rage that threatened to devour him. Year after year of frustration, the gaping loss of his dear brother, and all that had occurred while he was in the army blackened a part of his heart forever. Now he was punishing the man who had begun the madness, who had brought misery to all those around him; now he would exact a terrible vengeance for all that had been taken from him. *If I have to, I will tear Seth McCarty limb from limb!*

Even as Eli threw another punch, this one lancing forward and smashing into Seth's nose, flattening it and sending a shower of blood down the front of his shirt, he could not bring himself to enjoy the pain he was inflicting. It was a chore, a duty that must be done, not a pleasure. Without the gun that had given him a backbone, Seth McCarty was what he had always been: a conniving coward. Now defenseless, the fight was easily beaten out of him.

It was finally another punch to his gut that brought Seth down, dropping him to his knees in a cloud of dust, his eyes lowered, his hands raised above him in surrender, begging for an end to his punishment.

"No . . . no more," he panted, his mouth a crimson soup of blood and spit.

"You had this coming, you son of a bitch," Eli snarled.

"Don't—don't hit me . . . again."

Towering over Seth's broken and bleeding body, Eli felt no triumph. Even if Seth were to go to jail for what he had done, his hopes at the bank and with Fawn utterly destroyed, none of that would bring back what he had taken away; Caleb was dead.

Leaning down, Eli grabbed the beaten man by his now-filthy shirt and began to lift him back to his feet, muscles straining, the banker's limp body offering no resistance. But suddenly, as if he were a wounded animal biding its time, patiently waiting for the hunter to come near enough to lash out violently, Seth's hands shot forward and grabbed Eli's right arm, directly on the spot the bullet had entered his flesh.

"I hurt you before and I'll do it again," Seth cried through darkened, bloodstained teeth, a broad evil smile spreading across cracked lips, his eyes wild as he began to squeeze with all his might.

"Aaarrrrgghh!" Eli screamed as the pain coursed up and down his arm. The agony was so great that his vision swam, stars shooting every which way. It was as if he had been shot all over again, a white-hot poker painfully burning his flesh.

He tried to get away, to push Seth from him and relieve the agony that nearly overwhelmed him, but the other man held steady, refusing to let up for a second, maniacally laughing.

"You are going to suffer, you bastard," Seth cackled.

Eli's strength rushed from him. Darkness and stars continued to vie against each other at the edges of his vision. Nausea roiled in his gut as his legs trembled, finally buckling and sending him hard to his knees on the barn floor. It was then that Seth released him, sending a bony fist of his own crashing into Eli's jaw, driving him flat.

"You're not so tough now, are you?"

Before Eli could do anything to defend himself, Seth began to rain kicks upon him, thudding blows that knocked against Eli's ribs and arms.

"You'll not have Fawn!" he shouted. "Never, never, never, never!"

Eli was about to give up, to surrender to the inky blackness that was broken only by another sharp pang of pain, to stop fighting and accept the release the darkness was offering, when a scream split the air in the barn.

"Leave him be!"

As he lay on his side, one cheek pressed into the dirt floor, Eli recoiled with horror at the sound of the voice. Venturing a look through the slits his eyes had become, horror passed over him even greater than the pain of Seth's attack.

Standing in the barn's open door was Hallie!

She stood with her hands clenched tightly to her heaving chest and her green eyes blazing with anger.

"Don't you dare lay another hand on him," she yelled, her voice cracking.

Seth looked over his shoulder at the newcomer, an expression on his face not of concern or anger but rather of glee, a glint of mischief in his eyes. "Welcome, welcome!" he exclaimed. "I must admit that you're certainly a sight for sore eyes!"

"Don't . . . don't you . . . touch . . . ," Eli muttered.

"Don't I what?" Seth asked as he looked down at Eli's crumpled body, spittle hanging from his split lips. "Don't you see that this is perfect? Now, before I finish you off, you can watch as I take her from you just as you took Fawn from me!"

His eyes filled with horror, Eli watched as Seth began to step toward where Hallie stood frozen in place from shock and fear. *He means to have his way with her, and then kill her!* If he did not stop Seth, if he allowed him to get his hands on Hallie, Seth would be taking yet another person he loved away from him forever! *And that I will not allow!*

"No, you won't," Eli snarled.

Kicking out one boot, he clipped Seth in the back of the leg and unbalanced the man long enough for him to strike. As if he were a wildcat springing from atop a boulder in the mountains, talons raised to rend flesh from bone, Eli leaped on Seth, his anger giving him strength. Even though his arm still throbbed in agony, he began to throw punches with wild abandon, his body straddling the startled banker.

"You will not touch her!" Eli bellowed.

Blow after blow crashed into Seth's face, blasting past his raised hands as if they weren't there. Never in his life had Eli been so angry, so full of the desire to do harm. Soon, all sound faded away; he couldn't hear his own ragged breathing, his fists as they wetly slammed into Seth's blood-soaked face, or Hallie's screams for him to stop. But then, as the beaten man's hands fell to his side and his face lolled limply, all of the fight drained from Eli's body in an instant.

I've done what I set out to do . . .

"Stop hitting him, Eli! Please, stop!"

Hallie watched in horror as Eli's fists continued to slam into the man's face. No matter what she said, no matter how hard she yelled, he was beyond her, completely intent upon destroying the man who had threatened her only seconds earlier. The man was clearly beaten, his body falling limp, no longer a threat to anyone, yet still Eli pressed on, the dull thud of flesh upon flesh echoing inside the barn.

But then, as swiftly as Eli's rage had begun, it was over. Seth's broken body lay beneath the rugged cowboy, but the fight had clearly left him. When he finally rose to his feet and staggered away, his shoulders and arms slumped, there was pain on his face.

"Oh, Eli!" she cried as she ran to him, passing Seth without a glance, and throwing her arms around her cowboy's waist.

"Be careful, honey." He winced. "I'm not in very good shape right now."

Now that she was up close to him, she could see just how badly Eli had been beaten; the corner of his mouth was already swollen and an angry red, his lip was bloodied and cracked, and a knot of a bruise marked his cheek. *He looks as if he has been dragged behind a train!* Even though he was the victor, his body showed the violence of his struggle, with wounds that would take a long time to heal. Tears flooded her eyes seeing him in such a state.

"You're hurt!" she cried.

"I suppose it *is* as bad as it looks," he admitted.

With her face pressed tightly to his chest, she sobbed as Eli tried to comfort her, rubbing his bruised and bleeding hand through her hair, and whispering soothing words into her ear, but it did little good. Even though the danger had passed, she still felt that neither of them was truly safe, even in the security of each other's arms.

"We have to get you to a doctor," she insisted.

"He hurt me, but I've had worse," he tried to reassure her. "Hell, if you had ever been on the receiving end of a mule's kick, you'd know that what I just got doesn't amount to much."

As Hallie tried to accept his levity about what had happened, she found that she could not; too many questions continued to whirl around in her thoughts. She picked one and gave it voice. "Why did—did he try to kill you?"

"He's the son of a bitch who killed my brother and he came here to kill me because of Fawn," he told her, his voice still tinged with anger over all the havoc that Seth McCarty had wreaked upon his family.

Hallie gasped at the revelation. Pushing away from Eli's chest, she stared into his face through tear-filled eyes, unable to believe what she had heard. "He's the one? But why—why would he do such a thing?"

"He's always hated me, Hallie."

"But enough to come here and kill you?" she pressed. "Enough to kill your brother?"

As if lightning had struck the roof of the barn, an explosive crack hammered Hallie's ears, making her cringe and burrow back into Eli's chest. The rugged cowboy also jumped, pulling her closer to him, the muscles in his arms taut. Her first assumption was that it was Seth, rising from his feet to take aim upon them, to finish what he had set out to do, but he still lay where Eli had left him, although something about him was . . . different.

Two more cracks rang out and Hallie watched with disbelief as Seth's prone body jumped in a bizarre dance, his limbs twitching as if controlled by a puppeteer, followed by rivers of dark blood pouring from three open wounds on his chest. Repulsed and horrified, she quickly looked away, turning back toward the open barn doors, her eyes settling upon a sight that made her own blood run cold and her breath catch.

There, in the deepening gloom of night, stood Fawn, a gun in her hand!

Chapter Twenty-eight

Hank strolled to the back door of the ranch house with a spring in his step and joy in his heart. The deepening colors of the night, the low call of coyotes far out in the distant hills, and the summer heat that still hung in the air did nothing to dampen his mood. *I am on my way to see Pearl!*

He'd been a bachelor his entire life, satisfied to spend his days married to the ranch, working the land and the cattle without the encumbrance of a wife, all his nephews the children of his heart. *Until I met Pearl Parsons, I never knew what I was missing!* But now, having spent a week enjoying her fiery words and quick smile, he felt a longing that was as foreign to him as it was desirable.

"Time to go a courtin'," he muttered.

Bounding up the steps, in the door, and across the kitchen, he heard a distant crack, what must have been the beginnings of a storm on the horizon, but paid it little mind. He expected to find Pearl at Mary's side, her vigil over her friend seemingly never ending, and he headed down the hallway to the injured woman's room.

He stepped through the doorway with a smile on his face as broad as the Big Dipper was in the starry sky, and said, "And how are you folk holdin' up this evenin—" but the last word caught in his throat.

Inside the room was chaos, each sight vying to gain his attention. Pearl lay in a heap, her eyes turned to him in horror, dark blood coloring one corner of her mouth. Her mouth opened and shut as if on a hinge, but no sound came out, though none was needed for Hank to understand that she was in pain. Mary still slept fitfully in her bed, a sight that he had become used to, but it was the man that stood over her that he ultimately fixed upon.

The stranger looked as rough as a ragged nail, his filthy clothes hanging limply from his thin frame, his eyes small and feral underneath a mop of straggly hair knotted with grime. The man's arms were tense as if he were a wild predator preparing to strike. In one fist he brandished a knife, its long blade glinting brightly in the lamplight.

"What the hell's goin' on?" Hank asked incredulously.

Without even a hint of hesitation, the strange man shot across the small space that divided them, the knife's tip pointed at the cowboy's belly. In the scant second that

Hank had to protect himself, he would have sworn that he saw the beginnings of a smile cross the man's lips.

"*Uhnn,*" Hank grunted as his hands grabbed at the man's wrists.

Quick as a wildcat, the man attacked Hank, assaulting all his senses. Close up, the smell of his unwashed body was as repulsive as a dead, bloated cow. Air hissed through his yellow teeth. But it was the man's fury that caused the older man to step backward, an overwhelming relentlessness that knew no bounds, that wouldn't end until one of them was dead.

Darting quickly to one side, Hank spun the knife blade away from his flesh and drove his elbow into the stranger's jaw in the hope that he could gain a measure of distance from him, a chance to even the field. But even as the crack of bone against bone filled his ears, the man was back at him, grinning through a smile that began to fill with blood.

"That ain't gonna be enough, old man," he snarled.

He slashed out with the knife, his wrist cutting a tight arc through the stale air of the room, and a burning sensation instantly spread across Hank's chest. His hand reflexively found the spot, his shirt cleanly torn asunder, the flesh beneath it parted, a trickle of blood running down his chest. Hank grimaced as the younger man's smile grew.

With a grim certainty that soured his stomach, Hank *knew* that there was no hope that he could best the stranger. To face him here and now was to risk losing his own life, but he would not allow himself even to entertain the possibility of running away. To leave now would be to consign both Pearl and Mary to a fate worse than he could imagine. He must try to hold the man off long enough for Eli or some other help to arrive.

When the stranger came back for more, the knife cutting this way and that, Hank defended himself as best as he could, but soon he began to wear out, and it was then that the knife found him. Its point became buried deep into the meat of his shoulder, like a red-hot poker branding his flesh. Still, he would not give the man the satisfaction of hearing him scream; he fell to the ground in silence.

"Pe-Pearl," he muttered.

The last thing he heard before he surrendered to the blackness that hovered over him was Pearl's scream.

Sound exploded from Pearl's lungs when the man she'd begun to love fell to the floor. While Hank had struggled with Chester, the knife cutting and slashing across the divide between them, she had been unable to make a sound, unable to breathe, unable even to think clearly! But when the blade pierced Hank's shoulder and he collapsed to the floor, with blood pouring from the cut, all that she had held in was released in a rush.

"Oh, Hank," she sobbed, her throat raw and strained.

For a moment, Chester stood, leering above the fallen

man, his victim's blood dripping from the knife. Pearl feared that he was about to bend down and finish his work, but his intentions were elsewhere. His head slowly turned to the bed and his true reason for coming to the ranch and ruining her life . . . *he turned to Mary!*

"Don't—don't you touch her—," Pearl warned.

"Shut up, bitch!" he snarled.

Stars and darkness still swam behind Pearl's eyes from the blow that Chester had struck her. Struggling with all her might, she tried to rise from the floor, to stand up and stop him from what she was certain he was about to do, but she was far too weak and her rubbery legs once again collapsed beneath her. There was nothing she could do but watch.

With effort, she pulled her eyes from Chester to where Mary lay on the bed. It was then that her breath once again caught in her throat; she could not know whether it had been because of all of the fighting or her own shrill scream, but Mary had begun to stir, her hands lazily drifting from the bed, her eyes rapidly blinking as she tried to focus.

Chester had also noticed that she had begun to awaken. His emaciated body hunched, he slunk closer to the bed.

"That's it, darlin'," he encouraged her. "Come on back to your Chester."

"Don't wake up," Pearl warned, her voice only a whisper.

Slowly Mary's eyes fluttered open, a moment more of disorientation quickly followed by a focus upon what stood before her. Pearl could only watch as the nightmare that had plagued her friend for many long months prior to that fateful morning when they had left Whiskey Bend came back in an instant. Just as she had when she had wakened the first time and seen Abe, Mary once again was gripped by a terror that threatened to consume her.

"No . . . no!" she moaned, her dry voice cracking like kindling in a fire.

"I done found you, just like I said I would," Chester announced triumphantly.

At the sound of Chester's voice, Mary jumped as if her skin had been hit by lightning, twitching and flinching as if in pain. Her mouth swung limply, open and shut with only a low moan issuing forth. She tried to push herself away on her palms, but the weakness that had inhabited her body during her illness proved too great to overcome and she stayed in place as the man who had constantly abused her drew ever closer.

"Don't you lay a hand on her," Pearl protested weakly.

Chester sneered but didn't reply.

"I'll kill you if you do!"

As if that one exchange—Chester's finding humor in the horror that filled both the women—were simply one indignity too much, Mary finally broke, drawing breath and letting forth a bloodcurdling scream. Never in her life had Pearl heard such a sound; it was, she supposed, not unlike that of a small animal dying in the jaws of a large predator, full of a fear that sent shivers racing across her skin and up her spine.

"Hush up that racket!" Chester barked in annoyance.

"Don't—don't touch me!" Mary screeched further.

"I'll slap your goddamn mouth if ya don't quit that yellin'!"

In his tone and words, Pearl could see that Chester had already had enough of Mary's protests and screams. He grabbed her roughly by the wrist, her thin bones looking like sticks clasped in his grubby mitts, and yanked her toward him, trying to pull her to her feet.

"She's not well enough for that!" Pearl cried.

"I ain't come all this shittin' way to hear any complaints," he snapped, more at Mary than the woman who had spirited his beloved from him in the first place. "She's a comin' home to Whiskey Bend if'n I got to lash her to the horse and drag her the whole way!"

"I won't—won't go with you!" Mary protested. "I won't!"

"Shut up!"

"I don't want to go back with you! I don't—"

As if it were the forked tongue of a coiled rattlesnake, ready to strike as it lay in the desert sand, Chester's hand lashed out and snapped hard across Mary's pale face, sending her crashing down onto the mattress. The sound of the blow echoed around the room like a gunshot. To

Pearl, witnessing her defenseless friend being struck, it was as if she *herself* had taken the blow. Hopelessness filled her. In the face of Chester's fury, she knew that there was nothing that she could do, no defense that she could muster that would keep him from doing exactly what he wanted. If he wished to kill them, there was nothing that she could do to stop him. If he wished to spirit Mary away, to take her back to the life she had endured with him, there was also nothing that could be done.

"What's going on in there?" Mrs. Morgan's voice floated from her room.

No flame of hope lit in Pearl's heart at the sound of the older woman's voice. Even if Adele had been as fit as a fiddle, instead of being injured and bedridden, it would have been folly to expect her to do anything to stop Chester's impending rampage. With Hank having been bested, and Hallie and Eli out of sight, she and Mary were alone, alone to face the monster who had haunted their days and nights.

"Don't give me no shit and get outta that bed," Chester ordered Mary.

"I . . . I won't . . . ," she whispered hoarsely, still feeling the sting of his blow.

"If ya think I ain't gonna give ya another smack, ya best think again," he barked, once more grasping her by the wrist and making her wince in pain.

"Take your hands off my wife this instant!"

Every head in the room turned to the sound of the authoritative voice to find Abe standing in the doorway, his gaze blazing holes in Chester, his fists clenched tightly. Never in her life had Pearl, her heart pounding, been so happy to see anyone.

"Your what?" Chester asked, puzzled and confused.

"I'll not have you harming a hair on her head, sir!"

As Chester gazed at the sight of the strange man before him, his eyes blinked as he tried to come to grips with whether the figure before him was real or a figment of his imagination. A wry smile spread across his face, his lips curled over filthy, chipped teeth, as he let loose a snort of laughter.

"Who in the hell're ya supposed to be?"

"This is your last warning, sir," Abe said, ignoring Chester's question, as he took a step into the room, his eyes never leaving his foe. "I'll not be asking you again!"

With that warning, Chester finally saw Abe for what he was, an immediate danger. He let go of Mary's arm with a twist and turned to face the strangely bearded man, knife in hand. The murderous intent that had filled his eyes when he buried the blade in Hank's shoulder returned with a vengeance. He tensed as he prepared to attack.

"Don't worry, my dear," Abe soothed Mary, the woman he believed to be his bride, the woman whose slap he seemed to have already forgotten. "He'll not harm you."

Mary didn't reply, her eyes wide with fright.

"Be careful!" Pearl warned, fearful that Abe would meet the fate of his uncle.

"He is the one who should be concerned!"

"Goddamn crazy bastard," Chester spat.

The two men slowly circled each other in the small room, each holding the other frozen in his gaze. Chester occasionally swiped out with his knife striking nothing but air as Abe kept his fists close to his chest.

"I'm gonna carve ya up," the filthy man sneered.

Without wasting a word in answer, Abe's right hand shot forward and smashed into Chester's nose with a crack, sending a rivulet of blood spraying down onto his mouth and chin.

"Son of a bitch!" Chester barked in pain.

Before the sting of his first punch could subside, Abe waded back at his foe, throwing a couple of more sharp punches, each landing in quick succession. Not once did he boast about what he was doing, the pain that he was inflicting, his face a stoic mask that betrayed no emotion. One blow followed another as Chester's defenses faded, blood and bruises taking their place.

"Goddamn it!"

Blindly, Chester swung the knife just as Abe was coming in to hit him again, and an arc of blood spurted from a deep cut on Abe's forearm. Jumping back quickly, he gave it no more than a cursory glance before returning to confront the armed man.

"That's just the first cut," Chester said with a smirk. "There'll be more!"

Pearl couldn't *believe* what she was seeing. Never in

her wildest imagination would she have believed that Abraham Morgan would have been able to fight, to hold his own with a man like Chester Remnick. But even though he had drawn first blood, she knew that it was only a matter of time before Chester found him again with his knife.

"His leg!" she suddenly exclaimed, the memory of putting a bullet in Chester on that fateful morning springing to mind as if it were a brilliant sunrise, dazzling and bright. "Hit him in his left leg!"

Without any hesitation, Abe followed Pearl's direction and kicked into Chester's left leg, striking him flush on the point in which she had felled him.

"*Aaarrgghh!*" he howled in pain, collapsing onto his back.

Abe fell upon the man, pummeling him in the face while trying to control the still-dangerous knife that wavered in one hand. Pearl could do nothing but hold her breath as the struggle continued, losing track of the knife's blade in one moment, seeing it in the next before once again having it vanish from sight. Suddenly, a sickeningly wet sound reached Pearl's ears, a sound that she knew came from a knife being buried into flesh.

"Oh no!" she cried.

The seconds crawled by as if they were hours as the two men's bodies stayed clasped together as one, neither man moving an inch, uncertainty filling Pearl's heart as to who had struck the killing blow. Then slowly, the answer was revealed; Abe rose upward, a thick sheen of lifeblood coating his shirt as Chester remained on the floor beneath him, the knife's hilt protruding ominously from his belly.

Without hesitation, Abe turned to where Mary lay on the bed, her small hands clutched tightly together, her eyes wide and staring. Throughout the two men's struggle, she remained frozen and silent, a witness to a fight that was for her honor if not for her hand.

As Abe moved closer to her, Pearl worried that it would be the same as before, that Mary would be as fearful of Abe as she had been of Chester, that the only thing poor Abe would receive for his efforts would be cries of horror, tears, and another slap on his face.

"You're safe now, my Mary," Abe soothed. "You need not be afraid."

Tears once again began to fill the young woman's eyes, until they cascaded down her white cheeks, spilling onto her blouse and blanket below. But in that moment, Pearl could see something strange, something different from the first time Abe had spoken her name. Before Mary knelt a man who had fought to protect her, who didn't grab for her or demand that she do as he say, who was patient and kind. While Mary did not know what lay ahead, she knew that the horror she had lived through for far too long lay behind, and that it would never threaten her again.

Sobbing, she fell forward, right into Abe's waiting arms.

"It will all be fine," he soothed into her ear. "It's all over now."

Tears fell from Pearl's eyes. She knew that he spoke the truth.

Chapter Twenty-nine

Hallie's thoughts raced. As the sharp crack of the pistol's firing echoed in her ears and the tang of gunpowder hung in the air, she could not take her eyes away from Fawn, standing in the barn's open door, framed by the newly born night, no longer the woman that she had known.

"What—what happened?" she asked into Eli's chest.

He didn't answer, his eyes staring ever forward, his jaw set as if it were carved in stone as blood continued to trickle from the scrapes and cuts on his face.

No matter how hard she tried, Hallie could not believe her eyes. *Fawn had just shot and killed Seth, the man to whom she was engaged, the man she had professed to love!* No amount of hoping or wishing would ever return him to her. Even though Seth had meant to do her harm and had injured Eli, Hallie felt a sadness at his violent death.

"Eli . . . I'm frightened," she whispered.

"Hush now," he soothed. "Just stay close."

Fawn stared silently ahead, her eyes reflecting a detachment from the heinous crime she had committed, the gun still clenched in one hand, tendrils of smoke drifting from the barrel as it remained pointed at the ground. She seemed in a trance. She blinked once, then twice. Finally, she seemed to awaken and her gaze focused upon them. The look on her face was that of a child who had just committed a small, naughty act for which she feared she would be punished. But the gleam in her eye was one of amusement that said she was not sorry for what she had done. When she spoke, her voice was little more than a whisper.

"Why, Eli?" she said. "Just tell me why you don't like me anymore."

In his arms, Hallie could feel the cowboy startle at the question, as unsure of its meaning as she was. "I don't understand what you're saying, Fawn," he managed. "I don't—"

"You know damn good and well what I mean!" she suddenly screeched, her meek voice coming to life as she brought the gun up and pointed it directly at Eli's body. Hallie's breath caught in her chest, so certain that Fawn would pull the trigger and end the life of the man she loved. But no shot rang out.

"Why, Eli?" she asked again. "Why, after all I have done for you over the years, after all the attention that I have showered on you. Why have you chosen that worthless woman from nowhere over me?"

From the first moment that she met Fawn Billings, Hallie knew that the prissy banker's daughter was in love with Eli. Jealousy colored her words, her smile, and the very way in which she carried herself. It now appeared that there was no end to which she would not go to have what she desired.

Eli's words were measured. "Fawn," he began, his voice unwavering and as strong as the noonday sun, "while I'd be a liar if I were to say I haven't cared for you ever since we were kids, I've made it as plain as I could that I was not in love with you." He paused. "I thought that you returned Seth's affect—"

"Just shut up!" Fawn shouted, cutting him off in mid-word.

"No one wanted to hurt you, Fawn," Hallie ventured but fell silent when Fawn leveled the gun at her.

"Shut up!" Fawn yelled.

Hallie's eyes grew wide at the sight before her. Fawn looked nothing like the elegant, fashionable young lady that she first met in Bison City or even the shrill would-be nurse who appeared at the ranch house just one day earlier. Tears ran freely down her cheeks, melting trails through her face powder. Her hair, usually set in tight curls around her shoulders, hung in sweat-drenched strings. Hate had transformed her carefully groomed beauty into ugliness.

"Don't you say a word," she warned Hallie. "This doesn't concern you!"

"You're right, Fawn. Hallie doesn't have anything to do with this," Eli interjected. "This is between you and me."

Fawn shook her head violently. "She's ruined everything," she cried out. "If it weren't for her, you would have turned to me and discovered how much I love you and always have. It might have been me that you held in your arms and in your heart! You might have loved me!"

"It's not true, Fawn," Eli countered. "My heart had decided long ago, and there was nothing to be done to change it."

"No matter what I've done, no matter how hard I've tried, none of it made any difference," she kept on as if she hadn't heard a word he had spoken. "Everything I did failed! Even the last time I held this gun in my hand, even that didn't work! You still left!"

"Wha-what did you say?" Eli managed, his body suddenly shaking.

"The last time I held this gun in my hand," Fawn explained, "was the night that I killed your brother!"

As Fawn's words registered, Eli's knees grew weak, buckling under the weight of four years of pain that he had borne since that fateful night his brother had been stolen from him. His breath hissed through clenched teeth. His heart pounded and shook as if the earth itself were in upheaval. His eyes grew wet at the same moment that his blood began to rush through his veins and throb in his temples.

"You?" he asked, his voice trembling. "*You* killed Caleb?"

"It was a night very much like this one," Fawn began calmly, telling her story as if it were unconnected to sordid reality. "Still hot with the heat of the day, thousands of stars in the sky, crowds of people on the streets. I followed him leaving the saloon, gunshots and fireworks spilling all around me."

Each word that she spoke was like a dagger in Eli's heart, driven into the block of pain that sat heavy in his chest. Still, he could not bring himself to believe, could not wrap his thoughts around a truth he felt he had no choice but to reject.

"But I—I thought . . . ," he stumbled, searching blindly for the words that would force it to all make sense. "I thought that it was Seth. He followed me to the cemetery and tried to kill me . . ." He stopped, his voice trailing into the stale air of the barn.

"He did?" Fawn asked, as surprised by the new revelation as Eli had been at her own secret. "I wouldn't have thought that he had it in him to hatch such a harebrained scheme. I suppose that I underestimated his jealousy about the feelings he knew I have for you."

When Seth had first approached him in the barn, it was a confrontation that Eli hadn't shied from, had actually encouraged, all so that he could mete out the justice he knew Caleb could never gain for himself. He had thrown punch after punch, delivering a beating that could never return his brother to him but could allow him to move forward with his life, to leave some of his heartache behind. All that was wrong was suddenly right, and he couldn't so much as catch his breath.

Hallie suddenly sobbed in his arms, her voice cracking.

"Quiet now," he whispered, his words full of urgency and concern. A sickening fear gripped him at the thought that Fawn would now turn her festering vengeance upon the woman he loved, the woman who had captured his heart. For Hallie's safety, as well as his own sanity, he had questions that needed answers.

"But why?" he uttered, the one truth he needed, that he *must know*!

"Because I had to have you for my own and you were planning to go away to the army," she said simply, as matter-of-factly as if it were the most obvious explanation imaginable. "I just couldn't bear the thought of you out of my life, ruining all my hopes and dreams."

"What did Caleb have to do with that?" he asked, his anger rising.

"He had everything to do with it, silly." She chuckled.

"Tell me *why*!" Eli cried, no longer able to check his raging emotions.

Fawn looked coldly at him for a moment, unhappy at

the stern rebuke he'd given her, her face that of a child scorned. She then took a deep breath, her eyes softening, and said, "It was your fault. I killed Caleb because of you."

The force of her words was enough to tear the air from Eli's lungs, leaving him gasping. *What in the hell is she talking about?* His thoughts raced and rocked, unable to alight upon something that would make her words make sense, turmoil roiling in his gut.

"Why—why would you say such a thing?"

"Even though I had tried to convince you to stay, had begged you not to leave Bison City, you wouldn't listen," Fawn explained. "You were always so darn stubborn! There wasn't a blessed thing that I could do to change your mind, but it was then that I realized you might stay if you had suffered a loss, some tragedy that required you to stay at the ranch and, just maybe, drive you into my arms."

Hearing Fawn's explanation and understanding that it was insanity that lay behind it, Eli was overcome. *She killed Caleb, murdered my younger brother in cold blood in the hope that the tragedy would keep me rooted to home, to the ranch, and to her!* A bloodcurdling scream built in his lungs, but he could not let it loose, so intent was he on every word that Fawn spoke.

"It wasn't an easy thing for me to do," she further explained. "When I stood at the end of the alley, and watched him relieving himself in a drunken stupor, it took all my courage to finally confront him. I kept reminding myself why it had to be done and, when I finally pulled the trigger, I did so safe in the knowledge that it was for our love!"

While anger continued to stir in Eli's heart, hot tears began to fall down his cheeks, emotion no longer checked. *She killed Caleb!* Murderous intent swelled in his heart, his hands clenched as he fought the desire to wring Fawn's neck.

"Now she's going to kill us," Hallie whispered.

In that moment, Eli knew that she was right; Fawn was simply too far gone to let them live, to let her murderous secret become known. They were at her mercy, a mercy that could be snatched away at a moment's notice to leave them cold and dead beside Seth's corpse.

But what can I do?

None of the options which leaped to mind were appealing: to stand and do nothing was to court death, to dive for Seth's discarded gun was to bring the speeding bullet even faster. *But what other course is available?* If it were only *his* life that was in jeopardy, he might have chosen a more daring path, but with Hallie by his side, he had to be more cautious; if he were to lose her as well as Caleb, it would be more than he could bear.

Then the idea struck him, the one way in which he might be able to end the madness that had forever changed his life. He would have to swallow his revulsion and embrace a lie, but it might mean their lives, their love, their future together!

"It doesn't have to be this way," he began.

"It's too late," Fawn disagreed. "You've already made your choice!"

"But what if I've made a mistake," he said as he slowly disentangled himself from Hallie's arms, ever careful to keep her behind him and out of the line of fire. Hallie's face registered surprise and alarm, but he gave her a small nod that she seemed to understand. "What if I regret the choice that I've made and want to make it right?"

"What—what are you saying?"

"I'm saying that you've given me a great deal to consider here," he offered, smiling at Fawn as warmly as he could manage. Slowly, his heart beating wildly in his throat, he took a small step toward the armed woman, unsure and unsettled as to his safety. "If only I had known just how strong your feelings were for me all of these years, maybe . . ."

"Maybe you would have looked at me differently," Fawn finished.

"Maybe so." He took another step, then another.

"It can't be this way, can it?" she asked, her voice rife with confusion, her eyes darting about the barn looking for answers.

"It can be any way that you want it." Spreading his hands before his chest, smiling as if it were the most pleasant thought he could imagine, he moved steadily forward. "You and I, together, starting a life as husband and wife just the way you always wanted it to be, just like you dreamed."

He was only a few feet from Fawn, from the gun that threatened his life and Hallie's. He couldn't flinch, couldn't make any sudden movements lest he startle her into squeezing the trigger. The charade had to last but a moment longer . . .

"Will you have me, Fawn?" he asked.

She was taken aback by his question, blushing a most brilliant red, her lashes fluttering as quickly as her heart. This close, he could see the madness in her eyes.

"Do you mean it?" she asked hesitantly, her tears welling.

Swallowing his emotion and birthing a lie, he answered, "Yes."

"I will!" she shouted. "Oh, Eli! Of course I will!"

As joy overwhelmed her, Fawn dropped the pistol to the ground where it kicked up a cloud of dust. But before the dirt could settle, Eli swung his right fist like a hammer, striking Fawn's chin, snapping her head to the side, and sending her crashing to the ground, as immobile and unmoving as her weapon had been only a scant moment before.

Hallie ran to Eli, throwing her arms around his back and holding him with all her might. Even though she had known he was lying about his feelings for Fawn, enacting a ruse that would save their lives, it still pained her to hear him speak to Fawn the word she longed for him to say to her.

"It's over now," he told her quietly.

Through his words, she could feel the pain he had suffered since his return to town, wondering just who had snuffed out Caleb's life. Now that he knew, she hoped that he would find peace, but that was far away. Now the pain remained as raw and ugly as it had ever been.

"I'm so sorry," was all that she could manage to say.

Holding her hand in his for a moment before turning to face her and tip her chin upward so that he could gaze into her eyes. "You're safe now," he said. "That's all that matters."

He pulled her to him; once again she was in the safety of his arms, her face pressed to his broad chest. It was in these arms, with *this* man, that she felt her first stirrings of love, a love that she wanted to nurture and grow. What happened with Caleb, with Fawn, with Seth, and even with Chester was behind them. She had left Whiskey Bend to start a new life, to celebrate a new beginning and that was just what she intended to do.

Epilogue

Hallie stood on the long porch of the ranch house, a shawl wrapped tightly about her shoulders, a protection against the early spring morning air. The sun had just risen above the horizon. Already the last remaining winter snows were beginning to melt. It would be only a week or two before the first flowers peeked out of the thawed earth.

Hallie treasured moments such as these. She came out to see the beginnings of each day alone, reveling in the quiet. At this time of year, few birds dotted the high sky, usually only hawks and eagles searching for breakfast. The boughs of the neighboring elms and pines creaked in the slight wind, scant company but beautiful all the same.

"This is my home," she whispered, her breath a small cloud.

Just as the world around her was reawakening after the long winter months, so, too, were the inhabitants of the Morgan ranch. All that occurred in the scorching heat of the previous summer now seemed only a nightmare filled with unpleasant memories. They had survived and grown.

Pearl and Hank had decided to go forward together, marrying in a simple ceremony in Bison City, both of them dressed in their finery, although Hank's arm was in a sling, healing from the vicious wound he had received at Chester's hand. There had been much laughter and more than a few tears that day, at a party that had lasted until morning light. Both of them were a bit older, a bit rough around the edges, but Hallie was delighted that they had found each other. They were currently in Denver preparing to take the train across the mountains to California, to get away and celebrate their life as newlyweds. They would be back soon, Hank to work on the ranch, continuing the life that he had always led, Pearl to the settled existence of housewife, a life that she had always wanted but had been unable to find. They would be welcomed back with open arms.

As happy as she was for Pearl, there was a part of Hallie that was even more elated for Mary, for the life that she had finally found after all the tears and nightmares she had been forced to endure. From the moment that she collapsed into Abe's arms after that fateful night when Chester reappeared, a monster set upon returning her to a life of bondage, Mary's life was different. It had taken her a while to come to grips with the tall, bearded man's strangeness, but she responded to his gentle nature and he crept into her heart.

For his part, Abe remained the gentleman that he had always been, a bright smile at the ready for his beloved Mary. A week earlier, Eli had said that he had begun to see traces of the *old* Abraham Morgan shining through his brother's presidential exterior, and he wondered if, with the passing months, his malady might ease. Time would tell. In the meantime, Abe and Mary had each other. Theirs was a love that grew straight and pure, with new memories made daily to replace those that were best forgotten.

Another thing that Mary had going for her was the surprising affection of Adele Morgan. The older woman had slowly recovered from the injuries she sustained when she fell. Nowadays she used a cane, hobbling a bit here and there, but she was walking again. Even though her voice could still carry the authority of a whip, lashing out at those unfortunate enough to have incurred her wrath, she did not use such a tone when she spoke to Mary. Hallie imagined that Adele could see the change the young woman had wrought in her son, bringing him back from the darkness in which he had dwelled for so many years, and that she attributed the change to Mary's presence. Mary, in turn, seemed to be genuinely fond of Abe and Eli's mother.

The tension between Eli and his mother had also lessened considerably. They were not yet at the point where
they could sit down and have a private conversation, but
she now refrained from her constant badgering and cutting remarks. In regard to Hallie herself, Mrs. Morgan's icy
exterior had also shown signs of thaw; one week earlier,
the older woman had shared a recipe that had belonged
to her mother, a gesture that had been as surprising as it
had been warm and welcome.

Counteracting the matriarch's feelings for the rest of
the ranch's residents, Hank had laid down the law to his
sister before he and Pearl were married, telling her to
accept Pearl as his wife, or they would leave the ranch
and never come back. The threat worked, and the two
women now tolerated each other. It was a start.

Chester had been buried in a pauper's grave, a hole in
the Colorado earth, without even a marker to memorial-
ize the spot. In time, even the shanty he shared with Mary
back in Whiskey Bend would rot and collapse, blowing
in the wind and rain, until nothing would remain that
spoke of his life.

The matter was certainly not that simple when it came
to Fawn Billings and Seth McCarty. News of their scan-
dalous actions sent the people of Bison City talking, the
whispers and rumors soon outracing even the most heinous of their crimes and sins. Seth's death had set off a
crisis at the bank. Townspeople feared that he had committed the greater crime of stealing their hard-earned

savings instead of the somehow lesser offense of trying to murder Eli. He would have been proud to know, however, that his funeral brought mourners from as far away as Denver and Casper.

But it was Fawn's actions that truly set the town atwitter. Coming as she did from a prominent family, she set tongues wagging at the litany of accusations that had been brought against her. Her father, though sickly and mostly bedridden as a result of his daughter's acts, fought desperately to have her released, but it was Fawn herself who shooed away his efforts. When she faced a trial for her crimes, she openly admitted to each of her offenses, the murder of Caleb Morgan some five years earlier and that of Seth McCarty. She had not shed one tear, nor uttered one harsh word, and instead took her sentencing as stoically as if she had been carved from stone. If she were lucky, she would be released from prison before she was an old, decrepit woman.

Footsteps sounded loud on the wooden planks of the porch, but Hallie did not need to turn to know who was approaching her. The feet stopped behind her and strong, muscular arms embraced her. A steaming mug of black coffee was held out to her.

"You always know just what I need," she purred.

"It just so happens that I do," Eli agreed with a chuckle, the warmth of his body filling her as satisfyingly as the drink. "I figured I'd find you standing out here, freezing. Penny for your thoughts?"

In that moment, the only thought that Hallie had was of how meeting Eli Morgan on the banks of the swollen Cummings River had forever changed her life, how the pleasure she felt sharing his life, and his bed, was greater than any she had ever known.

After the horror of that fateful summer night, they were inseparable, two lives lived as one. They bent their backs to building a life on the ranch, working to increase the herd of cattle and erecting a small cozy cabin in the woods near the scarred old oak tree. Their days were filled with talk of the future and their nights filled with passion. Little more than a week after their ordeal in the barn, Eli proposed, as nervous as a boy asking for his first kiss and, despite his bruises, as handsome as any man she had ever seen. She accepted his offer with tears in her eyes, tears of unmitigated joy. They had slipped away and were married by the preacher in town.

"What if I said I was thinking of you?" she answered.

"I'd believe you." He nodded.

"You would?"

"Of course I would." He smiled down at her. "I'm darn near unforgettable."

As her lips found his, the spring morning was suddenly less chilly, and Hallie could do nothing but agree.

About the Author

DOROTHY GARLOCK is one of America's—and the world's—favorite novelists. Her work has appeared on national bestseller lists, including the *New York Times* extended list, and there are over fifteen million copies of her books in print translated into eighteen languages. She has won more than twenty writing awards, including five Silver Pen Awards from *Affaire de Coeur* and three Silver Certificate Awards, and in 1998 she was selected as a finalist for the National Writer's Club Best Long Historical Book Award.

After retiring as a news reporter and bookkeeper in 1978, she began her career as a novelist with the publication of *Love and Cherish*. She lives in Clear Lake, Iowa. You can visit her Web site at www.dorothygarlock.com.